Becoming Us

The Jade Series #7

Becoming Us

The Jade Series #7

By

Allie Everhart

Becoming Us

By Allie Everhart

Copyright © 2014 Allie Everhart

All rights reserved.

Published by Waltham Publishing, LLC

Cover Design by Sarah Hansen of Okay Creations

Photo by Toski Covey Photography

ISBN: 0988752492

ISBN-13: 9780988752498

Chapter 1

JADE

The man stands in front of me as I sit in the chair. We're in a small room in an abandoned building on the Camsburg campus. The man is tall, maybe 6'2, with dark hair that has flecks of gray in it. He looks handsome and sophisticated, wearing a black tailored suit. He has an average build, maybe a little on the thin side. His eyes are greenish-brown, his skin has a slight tan, and his face is just like his father's. I hadn't realized how similar they look. I've only seen a couple photos, but seeing him up close, he looks just like his dad, even more so than his brother did.

I meet his gaze, trying to remain calm even though my heart is pounding in my chest. "It's nice to finally meet you."

"You know who I am?" he asks.

"Yes."

But I don't know what he's doing here. Or what he plans to do to me. And I still don't know who Walt is, the other man in the room.

I keep my focus on the man in front of me. "You're William Sinclair."

He stands up straighter. "I suppose it makes sense you would know that, given your interest in my family. Perhaps you thought you'd come after *me* as well someday."

"Come after you? What are you—"

"It's not going to happen, Ms. *Taylor*." He emphasizes the last name, my maiden name. "This little scam you've got going ends now. Whatever you used to blackmail my father, and are currently using to control my mother, it ends now. I will NOT let you continue this!"

I jump up from the chair. "No, that's not—"

"SIT down!" He says it so loud and so forcefully that I freeze in place, afraid to move.

He waits for me to sit. I take a breath and slowly lower myself back into the chair. I'm about to tell him who I am but then he starts talking again.

"I must say, you definitely played the part well. The poor girl from Iowa, just trying to get a better life for herself. And you could've done it, Jade. I know all about your past. You were valedictorian of your high school. You had all A's at Moorhurst. You're obviously a smart girl. You could've succeeded in life and done quite well for yourself. But you didn't want to wait for that success, did you? You didn't want to put the effort in. You went to Moorhurst and saw all that wealth around you, and you wanted a piece of it. So you latched onto Garret." He shakes his head. "I would've thought Pearce Kensington would know better. But you somehow managed to fool both him and his son."

"I didn't fool anyone. You don't understand. If you'd just let me explain."

"You're right. You didn't fool them. You blackmailed them, just like you blackmailed my father."

This is not how I saw this playing out. I imagined meeting William some day, but not like this. Not with him yelling at me, accusing me of things I didn't do.

"I didn't blackmail anyone. I don't know why you think that, but I'm telling you, I didn't—"

"I found the documents, Jade. After my father died, I took over his finances and discovered that last spring, a very large sum of money was put into an account in your name. Fifty million dollars, to be exact. Then I did some more investigating and found you'd had five million of it transferred to a man in Iowa. The man who took you in after your mother died. I'm having him followed right now. And as soon as we have proof that he's in on this scam with you, he'll be arrested or dealt with some other way."

Now I'm pissed. William can say and think whatever he wants about me, but he can't involve Frank.

I bolt up from my chair. "You are NOT arresting Frank! He didn't do anything! You've got this all wrong!" I look back at Walt who is still blocking the door. "Can you leave, please? I need to talk to William alone."

Walt doesn't move, so I turn back to William. "I need to talk to you alone. I need to tell you something. Something hardly anyone knows."

"If you have something to say, just say it. But I'm telling you now I'm not going to believe your lies, Jade."

"It's not a lie. It's a secret. And it's the truth. I swear. But Walt shouldn't know this. It's better if he didn't."

"Walt's part of my private security team. He's worked for me for the past 12 years. There are no secrets between us."

I glance at Walt again. I don't know what his story is. Maybe he's part of the organization or maybe he's just a security guy. Either way, he can't know my secret. He can't know I'm a Sinclair. At this point, I'm not even sure I want to tell William, but if I don't, he'll do something to me and I don't want to find out what that something is.

"I can't say this with Walt in the room," I tell William. "If you want to tell him later, that's up to you. But right now, this needs to be just between you and me."

William looks back at Walt. "Wait outside in the hall. But remain by the door."

Walt does as instructed, closing the door behind him.

Remain by the door? What's William think I'm going to do? Pull a knife on him? I'm half his size and I don't have a weapon. *I'm* the one who's afraid of *him.* I don't know how he's going to react to this. What if he doesn't believe me? What if he still thinks I'm a criminal? What will he do to me?

My heart's racing again and I feel sick to my stomach. I wish Garret were here. He knows William. He could explain all this better than me, and William might actually believe him. And Garret could stop William from doing whatever he's planning to do to me.

William glares at me. "Go ahead."

I take a deep breath, then look directly at William and say, "I'm your niece. Royce Sinclair was my father. I didn't know until—"

4

"Stop right there!" He puts his hand up. "I am not listening to this. You may have managed to con some very smart, very important people, but you are NOT going to do it to me."

"I swear to you, I'm not lying. Royce was working on a political campaign 20 years ago and he came to Des Moines during the caucus. He was there for a speech and he asked my mom out for dinner."

William huffs as he crosses his arms over his chest. "Royce was married 20 years ago. He wouldn't ask a woman to dinner. You should really work on your story, Jade. At least try to make it believable."

"Would you just listen to me? I promise you, I'm not lying."

"Spoken like a true con artist. You've been doing this so long you believe your own lies."

"I'm not a con artist. I'm trying to tell you the truth. Royce wasn't the man you thought he was. He did something really bad to my mom and—"

"How dare you speak of my brother that way!" His arms drop to his sides and he takes a step closer, towering over me. "Royce was a husband. A father. He wasn't perfect, but he was a decent man. And I'm not going to stand here and listen to you make up lies about him and your mother in order to—"

"He raped her!" The anger I was trying to suppress suddenly explodes.

I didn't want to tell William this and I didn't think I ever would. I never thought I'd meet him. But here we are, face-to-face, and I can't take another second of this. I can't stand here and listen to him accuse me like this, making it sound like *I'm* the bad one. Like I did something wrong. And I hate the way he's sticking up for his brother, the man who committed a horrible crime against my mom. The man who destroyed her life, and mine. The man who killed my mom's parents. The man who tried to kill *me* and almost killed Garret.

William backs away, but I don't see his expression. I keep my eyes on the floor.

"He what?" I hear William's voice, but it's so faint, it's almost like he's saying it to himself.

"He raped her." I say it again, quieter this time. "Your brother raped my mom. She was my age and he asked her to go to dinner, but instead he took her to a cornfield and he—" My throat burns as I try to fight back the tears that are forming as I imagine the scene in my head. "He raped her. I don't know what else he did to her that night, but it was bad. Really bad, and she—" I stop to breathe, but now I'm crying so it's making it difficult. "He left her there to die. It was winter. It was freezing cold and he just left her on the side of the road."

William stands there, not saying anything.

I take a moment to catch my breath, the tears continuing to fall as I think about what happened that night. I've never had to tell that story to someone, at least not all of it, like I did just now. And saying it out loud wasn't easy. It still hurts when I think of Royce doing that to my mom. I can't even imagine how scared she was when he took her out to that cornfield. And how awful it was for her to wake up in

6

the hospital and have nobody believe her when she told them who did that to her. Only her parents believed her and then he killed them, leaving my mom with nobody. It's so horrible I try not to think about it.

I wipe my eyes and look up at William. "I didn't want you to find out this way. I didn't even want to tell you that. I'm sure you loved your brother and I didn't want you to have to remember him this way. That's why I told Grace I didn't want any of you to know about me. I told her I—"

"Jade!" The door swings open and Garret appears with Walt right behind him. Walt grabs his arm, but Garret shoves him back.

Garret sees me standing there, my cheeks still wet with tears. He races over and holds my face, his eyes doing a quick scan of me. "Jade, are you okay?"

I nod. "Yeah."

He pulls me into him, his arms in a protective lock around me.

"What the fuck is going on here?" He directs the question to Walt but then turns and notices William standing there. "What the hell? What are *you* doing here?"

"I was just…" William's voice trails off. He seems out of it, like his mind needs time to process this.

"I told him," I say to Garret. "I told him who I am and I told him what Royce did to my mom. But I don't think he believes me."

"Is that true?" Garret glares at William. "You really think she'd make up a story like that? You really believe your brother wasn't capable of that? Did you even know him?"

"Garret, stop." I motion to Walt.

"Get out!" Garret yells at Walt.

William nods at Walt, signaling him to leave.

Once he's gone, Garret continues, his eyes on William. "She's not lying. Your brother was a fucking rapist. And he left Jade's mom there, hoping she'd die." Garret holds me tighter. "Now you want to explain to me why you're here and what the hell you're doing with my wife?"

William wakes up from his daze. "How could this happen? How could I not know about it?"

Garret answers. "Because Royce paid people to keep their mouths shut. And if they didn't keep quiet, he killed them. He killed Jade's grandparents so they could never tell anyone the truth. He made it look like an accident."

William's eyes shift to the floor.

Garret huffs. "Yeah, I know it's what you do. You. My dad. My grandfather. I know they make you do shit and cover it up, but it's usually bad people, right?"

William doesn't answer. He doesn't even look at us.

"Whatever. I don't even want to know. The point is that Royce did this on his own. The organization had nothing to do with it. Royce hurt innocent people. He destroyed lives. He killed people."

William collapses down on the chair I was sitting in earlier. His shoulders slump and he rubs his temples with his hand. "Why didn't he…why didn't he kill her, too?" William looks at me. "He didn't, did he? He couldn't have. If he had, you wouldn't—"

"He drugged her," Garret says.

"Garret, he doesn't need to—"

"No, Jade. He needs to hear this. Royce gave Jade's mom some kind of hallucinogenic drug so everyone would think she's crazy. That way nobody would believe her if she ever told anyone what happened. The pills caused her to have addictions. She started drinking right after Jade was born and she became an alcoholic. She couldn't be a mother." Garret gently rubs my arm as he holds me against him. "She wasn't able to."

William is now staring at me and it's making me uncomfortable because I don't know what he's thinking. Does he still think I'm lying?

The room gets quiet again.

After what seems like a really long period of silence, William finally says, "You look like Sadie."

"Yeah. I've met her."

"So she knows?" William sounds surprised.

"No, she doesn't know."

"Jade went to a fundraiser at my house," Garret explains. "The fundraiser was for Royce. That's when Jade met him, but she didn't know who he was back then. Sadie was there that night and that's when Jade met her."

"But Victoria knows." He says it like it's a given.

"No," I say. "She doesn't know either. But I met Victoria the night I met Sadie."

"So who else knows about this besides my mother?"

"That's it. Just you, Grace, and Garret. Oh, and Pearce."

"My dad just found out." Garret blurts it out, like he's nervous or something. "Arlin told him. After Royce died."

From the worried look on Garret's face, I think I just spilled a huge secret. But why is it a secret that Pearce knew about me?

William nods. "I see. So when did my father learn about Jade?"

I answer. "After Royce died, Arlin found the police records from that night. They were in a file Royce had locked away in a safe. The file also had stuff in it about my mom and me. That's when Arlin learned I existed. Later he came to see me and we got to know each other."

"So my father didn't know what Royce had done until he found those police records?"

"He knew Royce had been with my mom, but Royce told him it was an affair, not a rape. And he didn't tell Arlin about the pregnancy, so he never knew about me. Until he found that file."

William lowers his head, shaking it side to side. He seems stressed or confused or both.

"Maybe I shouldn't have told you all that," I say. "I wasn't going to. In fact I wasn't sure if I'd ever meet you. But when you showed up here and started accusing me of all that stuff, I couldn't just sit here and not say anything."

"What do you mean he accused you?" Garret asks. "Accused you of what?"

"He thought I had a scam going. He thought I was trying to get your money and Grace's money."

"What the hell?" Garret says it to William, whose gaze is still on the floor. "Why would you accuse her of something like that? Jade's the last person in the world who would ever try to scam someone out of their money."

"Garret, it's fine," I say quietly to him. "It was just a misunderstanding."

"Where did you even get an idea like that? From that Walt guy?" He turns back to see Walt, but he's still in the hall. "What's the deal with that guy? Has he been following Jade around?"

"Yes." William looks up at Garret. "Walter works for me. He handles my private security. I asked him to gather information on Jade before we reported her to the authorities."

"Are you fucking kidding me? You were going to arrest Jade? Seriously?"

William clears his throat. "You have to understand that from my point of view, it didn't look good. As far as I knew, Jade had no connection to my family and yet fifty million dollars had been put into a trust fund for her. It didn't make sense. The only explanation would be if she were blackmailing my father. It's not like this doesn't happen in our world, Garret."

"Yeah, I know, but you could've done some more digging before you just decided she was a criminal."

"I did. And I found that my mother had also given Jade a credit card and was paying her bills. You have to admit that looks suspicious. And then there's the fact that your father allowed you to date, and then marry, a girl like Jade. The Pearce Kensington I know would never allow his son to even be friends with someone with her background. I assumed she was blackmailing him as well."

"And where do *I* fit in all of this?" Garret asks. "Was *I* being blackmailed?"

"Sadie told me Jade had something on you. Something you didn't want to go public and that's why you had to marry her."

Garret lets out an annoyed laugh as he shakes his head. "Sadie really said that?"

"Yes."

"And you believed her? You know almost everything Sadie says is a lie, right?"

"You used to be friends with her. You used to date her. I thought maybe you two were still close. Maybe you confided in her about Jade."

"Believe me, I didn't. And Sadie and I are not friends and haven't been for over a year. Everything Sadie told you was a complete lie."

"I see." He stands up from his chair. "Well, this is certainly not how I thought this would go today."

"It's not what I was expecting either." I smile a little.

"Do that again," he orders, his gaze fixed on my mouth.

"Do what?"

"Smile."

It would normally seem like a strange request but I know why he made it. I have the exact same smile as Royce.

I smile for William, a big smile this time.

A stunned expression appears on his face. "Did you know you have the same—"

"Smile," I answer for him. "Yes. I know."

"Jade." He extends his hand to me. "It was nice to meet you."

This is so weird. He acts like we're done here. So is this it? We just forget this ever happened and go back to our lives? Or what exactly do we do now?

Garret is still holding on to me but he lets me go so I can shake William's hand.

"It was nice meeting you, too." Actually, it wasn't nice. It was a horrible way to meet him, but I say it anyway.

"I don't mean to be abrupt but I need some time to absorb all this. And then maybe we could meet again." He reaches in his suit jacket and pulls out his business card. He gets a pen out as well and writes something on the back of the card, then hands it to me. "My cell phone number is on the back. I only give that number to family. Feel free to call me anytime."

I glance at the front of the card. It's from Sinclair Pharmaceuticals, the company that made the hallucinogenic drug that turned my mom into the person she became. I've always wondered who else got that drug. They wouldn't make it for just one person. So who else did they silence with those pills? And what other drugs do they make that are meant to harm people instead of help them?

On the card, under the company logo, it reads *William Sinclair, CEO*. As the head of the company, William knows exactly what goes on there, which means he knows they make drugs like the ones Royce gave my mom. It's another reason not to trust him. And yet I want to. I want him to be good. I want an uncle. I want more family.

"Are you going to tell Grace that we met?" I ask him. "Or do you want me to?"

"How often do you talk to her?"

"I try to call her every few days just to check in and make sure she's okay. I worry about her living alone. Plus, I know she's lonely without Arlin around."

He gives me a slight smile. "It's good that you call her. I'm sure she appreciates that. I don't call her nearly enough myself. Maybe once every couple weeks, if that."

"Really? What about Sadie and her sisters? Don't they call her?"

"No." He lets out a harsh laugh. "Those girls only call her when they want something their mother won't buy them. But Victoria buys them whatever they want, so no, they don't talk to their grandmother much."

"I didn't know that. Now I feel bad. I should be calling her every day. I didn't because I didn't want to bother her. She always seems busy but I guess she was just acting that way."

"It sounds like you two have gotten to know each other the past few months."

"I spent a lot of time with her and Arlin last spring when Garret was—"

"When I was acting like an ass in front of the entire world," Garret says, interrupting me. I forgot that William doesn't know what went on last spring and how Arlin orchestrated the bad publicity stunt that ended up saving Garret from the organization's plan for him.

"That was a difficult time for me," I say, playing along. "But Arlin and Grace helped me get through it. I got to know them both really well. I went to their house almost every weekend."

"Their house in the Hamptons?" he asks.

"Yes. We spent a lot of time on their sailboat and Arlin taught me—" My voice cracks and my eyes are all watery. Dammit. Every time I think of Arlin, this stupid crying starts. "He taught me how to sail. Sorry." I wipe my eyes. "I just miss Arlin a lot."

"I do, too." William pauses, then says, "You know, maybe we should get together sooner rather than later. I'm flying out first thing tomorrow morning but perhaps we could have dinner tonight."

"Yeah. Okay," I say, without giving it much thought. I feel Garret squeezing my hand and when I glance over at him, he's giving me a look like I shouldn't have agreed to dinner. Maybe he's right. I just met William and as much as I want him to be good, the truth is he could be bad like his brother. Grace said he's not, but what if she's wrong?

"I need to go back to my hotel and make some phone calls," William says. "When I'm done, I'll stop by your place and we can go."

"You know where we live?" Garret asks.

"Yes."

"Because you were spying on us." Garret says it in an angry tone.

William nods. "*I* wasn't, but Walter was."

15

"Did Walt take our garbage?" I ask William.

"I'm not sure. You'd have to ask him." William goes out in the hall and says something quietly to Walt. Then the two of them come back in the room.

"Did you take our garbage?" I ask Walt.

"Yes. Several times. I was looking for receipts, bills, that type of thing."

"Did you put it back after you looked through it?"

"I did. In fact, that time you saw the garbage can was empty, I had to hurry and replace the bags before you checked it again."

"That explains it." I look at Garret as I say it.

A few weeks ago the garbage can got knocked over by the wind and when I went to pick it up, nothing was inside. But Garret insisted there were two bags of garbage in there and when he went to check, they were there. I couldn't figure out how they just appeared like that.

William is standing by the door. "I have your number so I'll call before I stop over."

"No," Garret says. "Don't come to the house. We'll just meet you there."

He nods, then disappears into the hallway, with Walt right behind him.

I turn back to Garret. "So I guess that was my uncle."

Chapter 2

GARRET

William Sinclair is the absolute last person I expected to find in that room with Jade. I wasn't sure what I was expecting, but definitely not him.

"I can't believe that just happened," Jade says. "I'm not dreaming this, right?"

"No, it really happened. You just met your uncle. He's lucky I didn't beat his face in for luring you here like that. I searched every damn room in this building before I finally found you."

"How did you know to come find me?"

"I was talking to Sara and she said she'd noticed Walt only showed up at the coffee shop when you were there, like he'd been keeping track of your schedule or following you. I got worried and went to find you."

"But if you hadn't found me, you don't think William would've done something to me, right?" Jade has this sad look on her face and I know it's because she's so desperate for William to be good, and not bad like Royce. She wants to know more of her family and she was counting on William to be someone she could trust. She was hoping he'd accept her and eventually love her the way Grace does.

"Jade, I don't know William well enough to say what he's capable of. I've only talked to him a few times before today. But he's a member and that means—"

"I know," she says quietly, her eyes on the floor.

I want to tell Jade he's a good man, but I can't. I have no idea what he's like. My dad's known him for years but they're not close friends.

"Did William tell you anything else about Walt? I mean, before I got here, did he tell you anything?"

"He just said Walt's been working with him for the past 12 years. Why?"

"I think Walt's connected to the organization. If he works that closely with William, he'd have to be."

"I was thinking that, too."

Jade goes out in the hallway to check that they're gone, then comes back in the room. "Did it seem strange to you the way William just left like that? It's like he was in a hurry to get out of here."

"He just needs time to process what we told him."

I don't want to tell Jade this because she'd feel bad if she knew William thought she was a liar. But honestly, I don't think William believed her story about Royce, even after I showed up and confirmed it was true. He acted like he believed her, but I could see the doubt in his face. In his mind, he had Jade pegged as a criminal and now we told him his *brother* is the criminal. It's a lot to take in. It may take some time before he believes it.

When William said he had to make some phone calls, I'm guessing that means he's calling people to verify our story. It's what rich people do whenever someone claims to be a relative. This happens to my dad all the time. People claim to be his long-lost cousin or uncle or aunt. When you have a lot of money, you have to be careful.

But the only people William can call to check our story are Grace and my dad. They're the only ones who know the truth.

I get my phone out.

"Who are you calling?" Jade asks.

"My dad." I swipe through the phone and call his number.

"Why?"

"Because your uncle's going to call him in a few minutes."

"Why would he—"

"Hey, Dad." I walk over and shut the door.

"Garret, I'm busy. You need to make this quick."

"I think you'll want to make time for this."

"What is it?"

"You're never gonna believe this, but William Sinclair just showed up at our school."

"He knows about Jade?"

"He does now. He's had his security guy following her. He thought Jade was trying to pull some kind of scam to get money from his family."

"Did William speak with her?"

"Yeah, we both did. He took Jade to a room in one of the buildings here on campus and accused her of trying to con his family. I don't know the whole story. I got here late. But anyway, Jade told him who she was but I'm not sure he believes her."

"You're not?" I hear Jade behind me. I turn around and see the disappointment in her face.

"He believes you, Jade. He just needs to check out your story."

"Why would he think I lied?"

"He doesn't. It's hard to explain."

I don't know how to say this without hurting her feelings. This has nothing to do with her. It's just about the rich not being able to trust people.

My dad must've heard Jade talking because he says, "Put me on speaker, Garret."

I put the phone on speaker. "Go ahead."

"Jade, you have to understand that people such as William and myself are contacted by strangers claiming to be relatives all the time. William is just making sure you are who you say you are. I would do the exact same thing. It doesn't mean he thinks you're lying. It's just something we've been taught to do from a young age."

"He said I looked like Sadie. Why would he say that if he thought I wasn't related to him?"

My dad explains. "I'm sure he wants to believe you. It's just a different world for us. We have to keep our guard up. When William calls me, I will assure him that everything you said is true. And obviously Grace will as well. It's unfortunate that William didn't talk to her in the first place. How did William find out about you anyway?"

"He took over Arlin's finances and noticed that money had been transferred into an account for me last spring."

"What did you tell him about Royce?"

"I told him what Royce did to my mom."

"Everything, or just part of the story?"

"I told him about the rape and then Garret told him how Royce drugged her and killed my grandparents."

"What else does he know?" my dad asks.

"What do you mean?" Jade stares at the phone, confused.

"Garret, how much does William know?"

My dad's referring to what happened at our house the day Royce was shot. William doesn't know Jade was there that day. Nobody knows that, except the people who were actually there; the clean-up crew, the doctors, my dad, and me. And Grace knows because Arlin told her.

"He doesn't know about that," I say to my dad.

"Are you sure? You said you walked in late."

Shit, that's right. I hope Jade didn't tell him.

"Jade, did you tell William anything about the day I was shot?"

"No. Why?" She looks even more confused.

"I'll let you tell her," my dad says. "Does William know about my involvement?"

"No." Garret glances at me. "I told him you didn't find out about Jade until after Royce was dead."

"I have to go. Someone's calling on the other line. It's probably William."

"When you talk to him, ask him about Walt, the guy he's had following Jade. I don't trust that guy."

"Garret, I need to answer William's call."

"Yeah, okay, bye."

Jade's looking at me. "Why are you so freaked out about your dad? Why is it a secret that your dad knew about me?"

"Let's talk about this at home." I go and open the door. "I don't like being in this room."

She grabs my arm. "Wait. Why can't William know I was at your house when you were shot? Are you saying William doesn't know what happened that day? But the organization covered it up. So what did they tell the members? What did your dad tell them?"

"Jade, we can't talk about this here." I give her a look that I'm not kidding around. Someone could be listening. Walt could've planted microphones in the room. Knowing that's a possibility, I shouldn't have been talking to my dad in here.

"Come on." I take Jade's hand and we walk across campus back to the car. She's quiet on the drive home and so am I. I don't want to talk about this in the car.

When we get back, I drop our backpacks on the floor and lead her to the couch to sit down.

"Nobody knows, Jade. Not William. Not any of them. If they knew Royce came to my house to kill you that day, they would've known you were connected to him somehow. They would've found out you were a Sinclair. And we couldn't have them knowing that."

"Why?" Before I can answer Jade says, "Because they'd do something bad to William. The organization makes you disclose all information and Royce didn't tell them about my mom or me. So if they found out, they'd have to punish him. And since Royce and Arlin are gone, they'd punish William."

"How did you know all that?"

"Arlin told me. At the time, I didn't put it together. But now I get it. I see why your dad couldn't tell the organization the truth about that day."

"It's not just William's safety my dad was worried about. It was *your* safety as well. My dad didn't want them knowing you'd witnessed what happened that day. The cleaning crew. The doctors. The cover-up in the media. If the organization found out you'd seen all that, they would've—" I stop before I say it.

"They would've what?"

I don't want to say it. I don't even like thinking about it. She sits back on the couch. "They would've killed me."

"Which is why I always tell you not to talk about the stuff you've seen, or any of the stuff I've told you that I probably shouldn't have."

She's staring down at her hands, which are fidgeting in her lap. "So what story did your dad give them?"

"He told them Royce came to the house that day and accused my dad of having an affair with Victoria, and that when my dad told him it wasn't true, Royce went crazy. He said Royce took his gun out and threatened to shoot me if my dad didn't admit he had the affair. So my dad said he went along with it and admitted to the affair, which made Royce so angry that he shot me to get back at my dad. And that's when my dad shot him."

"And your dad just came up with that?"

"Royce was always accusing men of sleeping with his wife. He was paranoid about it and everyone in the organization knew that. Plus Royce had been acting really strange in the weeks before it happened, I think because he was freaked out about you. He thought you knew about him and he thought you'd tell the media and ruin his chance for the presidency. Anyway, the story my dad told them was so believable that nobody questioned it. Then Arlin found that file about you and he went to talk to my dad and my dad told him what really happened."

"Why did he tell him the truth? He could've just lied."

"I don't know. Maybe Arlin didn't believe my dad's story. Maybe he threatened to have the organization look into Royce's death. If so, my dad would've had no choice but to tell Arlin the truth."

"But your dad doesn't want William knowing?"

"No." I wish she'd stop asking these questions because I know she won't like the answers.

"Why can't William know?"

"Because my dad doesn't know him that well."

"Your dad's been friends with the Sinclair family for years."

"Yes, but that doesn't mean anything. My dad knew Royce since college, but he never would've guessed he was the type of person who would do what he did to your mom. Or the type of person who would try to kill his own daughter."

"So your dad doesn't trust William. Is that why I wasn't supposed to tell William your dad knew about me? I wouldn't have told him that if I'd known it was such a big secret."

"It's not so much a secret that my dad knew you were Royce's daughter. It's the timing of when he found out that's a secret."

"Why? What's the timing have to do with it?"

"Because like you said, members must disclose all information, including information they have about other members. But if you find out something after the person is dead, you're not required to disclose it, although they would like you to. Anyway, if my dad didn't find out about you until after Royce died, he can't be punished."

"You think William would've told on your dad if he knew the truth?"

"Maybe. I don't know William well enough to say, and until I do, we need to be cautious around him. I don't want him knowing our secrets."

"What does William do for the organization? You said they get rid of people and cover it up. What else do they make the members do?"

"I'm not talking about this, Jade. I never should've said that. I was just angry and it came out. I don't want you knowing what goes on there. And I don't want you thinking about my dad that way. He doesn't want to do this stuff. And I'm sure William doesn't want to either."

I can't tell Jade what goes on at the organization. I don't even know half of it, but I *do* know they make their members kill anyone who knows too much. A reporter who keeps asking questions and searching for answers. Someone who saw or overheard something they shouldn't have. A person the organization hired to do their dirty work who threatened to expose them. They'll basically kill anyone they suspect might tell their secrets.

The members don't do the killing themselves. They hire people. When my dad says he'll get 'his people' working on it, he usually means the people he hires to take care of shit, meaning get rid of whoever's on the organization's hit list.

It's similar to the mafia, but the organization would kill you just for saying that. They think they're better than that. They think they're saving the world. The way they explained it to me last spring is that they put the right people in positions of power in order to keep the world from the chaos that would ensue if they let just anyone take over.

The chaos they're referring to is the loss of their own personal wealth and power. For instance, if the president was someone they didn't put there, someone they couldn't control, decisions might be made that would disrupt their perfect little world.

They don't care about everyone else. All they care about is preserving the life they're accustomed to. A life of incredible wealth and power. But they'd never admit that's what they're doing. They prefer to stick to their saving-the-world mantra. And some of them actually believe it. In fact, when I talked with some of the members last year, a few of them actually said that the world as we know it would end if they weren't controlling it.

"Garret, do you think William still won't believe me? Even after he talks to Grace and your dad?"

"It's hard to say. I don't know how close he was to his brother. Sometimes when someone's dead, it's easier to forgive what they've done or to pretend those things never happened."

"If that's true, then he'll hate me. William will hate me for saying those things about Royce."

"Which is why he can't know what really happened that day at my house. If he gets pissed at you for saying that stuff, or if he thinks you might tell your story to the press and ruin his brother's name, he might decide to come after you."

"Come after me? What do you mean?"

"Think about it, Jade. Think about what would happen if he told the other members you were at my house that day and witnessed all of that. William wouldn't have to tell them you were Royce's daughter. He could just say he found out you were at the house when Royce shot me."

"You're saying William would tell the members that so they'd kill me?"

"I hope not, but we don't know anything about this guy. What if he's not that different from Royce? We can't be too careful."

"Why wouldn't he just kill me himself?"

"Because Grace might find out and he wouldn't want her knowing he did that. It's better if someone else did it."

"That doesn't make sense. William isn't a killer. If he was, he would've killed me when he thought I was trying to steal his family's money."

"I agree, and that's why I don't think he'll do anything to you. But since we're not one hundred percent sure, we can't take any chances. So it's best if he doesn't know you were there that day."

Jade leans over and hugs my chest. "I don't feel very good. I thought I'd be happy when I finally met William, but I'm not. I'm not sure how I feel."

"I'm sorry, Jade." I put my arms around her. "This whole thing is just complicated."

Nothing's simple in families like mine and the Sinclairs. After seeing how hard it was just to date me, Jade knows this, but she doesn't realize how complex things can get when the organization is involved. People like my dad and William have to be careful in everything they do. There are consequences to every action and your friend can become your enemy overnight.

I don't think William's an enemy, but in our world, you can never be sure.

Chapter 3

JADE

*M*y stomach's in knots as I try to process what Garret just said. I don't want to believe William would try to hurt me or send bad people after me. He's my uncle, and in my head I've already imagined him being this warm, kind person, like his parents. Maybe it's naive of me to think of him that way, given that he's part of the organization, but Arlin was a member and *he* wasn't evil, at least not the side of him I saw. And Pearce isn't either. Like Garret said, the organization forces the members to do these things. It's not a choice.

Last spring, Grace told me a little about William. She made him sound like a good man. She said he wasn't at all like Royce, and Arlin said the same thing. But maybe William has a dark side his parents don't know about. Royce certainly did, and Grace and Arlin didn't find that out until it was too late.

Grace said William works all the time and is married but doesn't have kids. His wife doesn't work but she's involved in a lot of charities, which I've found is what most wealthy women do to fill their time, including Grace and Katherine.

Other than that, I don't know anything about William. But I *did* want to meet him someday. Having Grace in my life makes me want to meet more of my family. And since I don't have anyone left on my mom's side, I wanted to get to know my dad's side, even if it's just William.

I've thought about meeting Royce's kids, my half-sisters, but I think it's probably better if I don't. Sadie already doesn't like me and given what I've heard about her and her sisters, I don't think we'd get along. And I know I wouldn't get along with Victoria. She's just another version of Katherine.

My phone rings. It's still in my backpack. Garret reaches over and hands it to me. It's Grace.

"Hi, Grace."

Garret is looking at me like I shouldn't be talking to her. Does he think I can't trust Grace now? I'm not sure what he's thinking, but he's motioning me to put the phone on speaker, so I do.

"Jade, honey, are you okay?" Grace's voice is full of concern.

"Yes, I'm fine."

"I just spoke with William. He said he met you earlier."

"He was at my school. He just showed up there."

"I have to apologize for him. I had no idea he was spying on you like that. It didn't even occur to me that he would discover the trust fund. But I should've known when William was going through Arlin's financials that he would find out about it. I'm so sorry, Jade. William should've come to me before he even considered doing something like that."

"It's okay."

"No. It's not at all okay. And I told him that. He may be a grown man, but I'm still his mother and I scolded him for his actions."

I cover my mouth as I laugh. Leave it to Grace to make me laugh at a time like this. I love my grandma.

"You didn't need to do that, Grace."

"You're part of our family and he shouldn't treat you like you're not."

"I don't think he believes I'm family. I tried to explain everything to him but I think he was too shocked to accept it."

"He needs to get over it. You're his niece, and if he doesn't treat you as such, he'll have to deal with his mother."

I almost laugh again. I see Garret smiling.

"So what did William say to you?" I ask Grace.

"He asked me about Royce and your mother." She sighs. "I know it's difficult for William to hear those things about his brother and I know he'll need time to accept it, but I won't let him take his anger with Royce out on you. I explained to William how you had a very difficult childhood and how Royce was the reason for that. I also explained that when Arlin and I met you, we vowed to support you in any way we could and the trust fund was one way of doing that. Then I told him what a wonderful young woman you are and I encouraged him to get to know you, if you agree to it."

"I *do* want to get to know him." Garret's motioning me to let him talk. "Grace, do you mind if I put you on speaker? Garret wants to say something."

"Of course. Go ahead."

I pretend to, since she's already on speaker.

"Hi, Grace," Garret says.

"Hello, Garret. William said you were there as well today."

"Yes, and I assumed he'd call you to check our story. I told my dad that William might be calling him, too."

"He called Pearce right after he called me. He's very worried about your father."

"He is? Why?"

"He's concerned your father might tell the organization the truth about Royce, which as you know, would mean William would be punished. I told him your father wouldn't do that, at least I hope he wouldn't, especially given what Arlin did for you last spring."

"No, my dad would never do that. He doesn't want anyone getting hurt here. That's why I wanted to talk to you. My dad's worried William might put Jade in danger. If he found out she was at my house the day Royce—"

"I didn't tell him about that day. And I'm not going to. But even if he knew Jade was there, he wouldn't tell the members."

"Are you sure? I mean, I'm not trying to say anything bad about William but you can never be too careful."

"I know what you're thinking, Garret. And I understand your concerns. But Royce and William are not the same. Arlin and I both knew Royce had problems. We knew that for years. But William doesn't struggle with the issues his brother had. He's nothing like Royce. He would never harm Jade."

Garret doesn't respond. Neither do I. I'm not sure if I believe her.

"Jade, are you fearful of William?" Grace asks. "Be honest with me."

"Um, yeah, kind of. I don't *want* to be, but I don't know him well enough to say that I trust him."

"I understand. Would you feel better if I were there the next time you and William meet?"

"Yes. I think that would be good."

"I do, too. So that's what we'll do. You think about when you'd like to see him again and tell me what works in your schedule and William and I will fly out there together."

"Okay, but I'm supposed to have dinner with him tonight."

"Oh. He didn't mention that. Well, if you want to cancel the dinner, I can call him and explain what we decided."

"That's all right. I'll be fine. It's just dinner and Garret will be there."

"If William makes you feel uncomfortable in any way, or asks you questions you don't want to answer about Royce or anything else, just leave the restaurant. Don't worry about offending him. But I don't think that will happen. William is a good man. He's very much like his father." Her serious tone lightens. "And I know how much you loved Arlin."

"If he's like Arlin, then I definitely want to get to know him."

"Okay, honey. I'll let you go. If you want to talk about this some more, just give me a call."

"I will. Thanks, Grace."

After we hang up, I turn to Garret. "So what do you think? Do you think we can trust William?"

"I don't trust anyone in the organization, but I feel a little better about him after hearing what Grace said. I don't think he'll hurt you, but like I said, we can't be too careful. While you were talking to Grace, my dad texted me and said he talked to William and everything's good. My dad had to go to a meeting but we can call him later to find out what William said."

"I don't need to. You can talk to him later if you want. I think I'll call William. I want to get this dinner over with."

"Jade, if you don't want to go, we won't go."

"I want to go. I'm just nervous about it and waiting around here is making me even more nervous."

"We shouldn't go if you're nervous."

"I'll be fine." I call William's number.

He picks up right away. "Jade, I was just about to call you. Do you mind if we have an early dinner? I fly out at five in the morning tomorrow and I don't want to be out too late."

"Early is good. What time?"

"Does now work? I was thinking we could eat here at my hotel. They have a small restaurant and it's quiet so we can talk. I'm staying at the Dominican on Walnut Street. Do you know where that is?"

"Yes. Garret and I will head over there. See you soon."

"We're going to dinner," I tell Garret as I run to the bedroom. "I need to change quick."

After I change clothes, we go to the restaurant. It's nothing fancy but like William said, it's quiet. Only three other tables have customers. The rest of the place is empty, probably because it's only 5:30.

William is already there. He stands up as we approach the table, then waits for us to sit down before he does so himself.

"Thank you for coming," he says. "I thought you might change your mind after what happened earlier."

William seems different than he did an hour ago. He's more relaxed. But I'm not. My stomach is knotting up again and my palms are sweaty.

We sit there in awkward silence. It reminds me of when I first met Arlin and Grace for lunch and none of us knew what to say.

"So tell me about yourself, Jade." William says it in the same take-charge tone that Arlin used to use and it makes me smile a little.

"Do you mind going first? I'm kind of nervous."

He smiles. "Don't be nervous. I'm just trying to get to know you."

Garret holds my hand under the table, but keeps his eyes on William. "You should tell Jade about your wife. Jade's a runner. And your wife is as well. Isn't that right?"

"Yes. She runs marathons. She's running one next week, in fact."

I keep forgetting that Garret knows this guy. He knows the whole Sinclair family but he doesn't talk about them unless I ask.

"My wife's name is Meredith." William shows me a photo on his phone. "This is her."

The photo shows a tall thin woman with short, dark-brown hair and brown eyes. She's wearing a white sweater and jeans. It's a much more casual look than I expected for someone as wealthy as her. I can't imagine Victoria ever wearing jeans, and Katherine doesn't even own a pair. Meredith is smiling in the photo and it seems like a real smile, not a fake, Katherine smile.

"Has she always been a runner?" I ask William as he takes his phone back.

"No, she started running about 10 years ago. She also swims. She was a competitive swimmer back in college."

"Oh, yeah?" Garret's interest piques. "I didn't know that. What school?"

"Stanford. She was on the team all four years."

"Garret's a swimmer, too," I say.

"Yes, I know. I hear he's very good." William smiles at Garret. "Your father brags about you all the time."

"He does?" Garret's surprised. I am, too.

"He has for years. He's very proud of you, Garret."

"When does he have time to talk about me?"

"Sometimes after the meetings several of us go out for drinks. We don't do it as much anymore. Our schedules just keep getting busier and it's harder to make time to social-ize." William's phone vibrates on the table. He checks it, then turns it off. "It's people from work. The phone never stops ringing. If I don't turn it off, I can't get a break."

"So you run Sinclair Pharmaceuticals?" I ask him.

"I do. After college, I got my MBA at Harvard, then worked alongside my father and learned the business. I took it over when he retired. I use the term 'retire' loosely. He continued to work there, just not every day. My father was someone who had to be active. He couldn't just sit around and do nothing."

"Do you know how to sail?" The question is way off topic, but when he mentioned Arlin, the sailboat image popped in my head.

"I've known how to sail for as long as I can remember. My father taught both Royce and me when we were very young. I try to get out on the water when I can, but with my work schedule it's difficult."

"So you have a sailboat?" That sounded way too eager. I feel my face heating up.

"Yes." William smiles. "Would you like to go sailing sometime?"

"Um, maybe." I glance over at Garret. I know he doesn't want me agreeing to this until we figure out if we can trust William.

"Then let's plan on it," William says. "The weather's getting cold now but we'll plan on it next spring."

I don't agree to it but I don't need to. It's still months away and by then, he might change his mind. He's so busy with work, I can't imagine him taking time out of his schedule to take me sailing.

I place the cloth napkin on my lap. "Grace said you live in New York. Where exactly?"

"Scarsdale. It's just north of Manhattan. Westchester County."

I've never heard of the town, but I've heard of Westchester County and I know it's full of rich people.

"I didn't know you lived so close to your parents. I mean, to their house in the Hamptons."

"Yes, it's a short drive, but I don't get out there much. I'm rarely at my *own* home. I spend most of my time traveling for work or I stay in the city. The next time you're out east, let me know and you can come for a visit at the house. I'll rearrange my schedule to make sure I'm there. And you can meet Meredith. Do you get back to Connecticut much?"

"We were there in July," Garret says. "We haven't been back since. But we're going back there for Christmas."

"Your father's house isn't that far from us, probably an hour's drive. Perhaps you two could come visit us for the day. Or Meredith and I could go to Connecticut."

"We'll talk about it and let you know," I say, not ready to commit to anything yet.

The waiter comes over and asks for our order. Then William talks some more and I just listen.

After our food arrives, William says, "Are you ready to tell me about yourself, Jade?"

I was just about to bite into the pasta I ordered, but instead I set my fork down. "There's not much to say. I think you already know everything about me."

"What do you like to do for fun?"

"Um, I don't know."

Garret puts his arm around me. "We're still working on that. Jade's been a little consumed with her classes ever since we moved here. But we're trying to work some fun back into her schedule."

"I like to run," I tell William.

"But I don't let her go alone, so she hasn't been running much." Garret takes his arm back and picks up his knife and fork and cuts his steak. "There was a robbery next to where we live so I don't think it's safe for Jade to run by herself."

"Is that why you have the cameras everywhere?" William sets his wine glass down. "Walt showed me photos of your beach house. I saw the cameras."

"My dad had those installed. It wasn't because of the robbery. He just thought we needed some security."

"You should have him get some tech guys out there. Those digital security cameras were easily disabled. When Walter was doing surveillance around your place, he was able to disrupt the signal and blur the images."

"Shit, I wondered about that. I noticed the blurry images. I thought it was just the wind blowing the cameras around."

"If you'd like, I could have Walt stay here and keep an eye on things for you, especially if you think there might be more robberies in the area. Walt's background is in security. He's worked for me for years, investigating anyone around me who seems suspicious. He knows how the criminal mind works and he's good at getting people to talk and give up information. He could prove useful, especially if that robber has friends who might start lurking around your neighborhood."

"I don't think we need that," Garret says. "I'll talk to my dad and have him get someone to fix the cameras."

"Just think about it. Sometimes it's better to have someone actually watching the place rather than relying on cameras, which can be tampered with." He takes another sip of wine. "So Jade, have you made many friends here?"

"Not really. It's another thing I need to work on. I have a friend at the coffee shop I go to. And I talk to my friend, Harper, all the time. She goes to Moorhurst, so I don't see her anymore but we still talk. She's from Malibu. Her dad's a Hollywood director."

"What's his name?"

"Kiefer Douglas." I feel Garret nudge my foot under the table as I say it. He doesn't want me talking about Kiefer because of his connection to the organization. But I wasn't even thinking about that when I said it.

"We're finding it's hard to make friends when you're our age and married," Garret says, trying to steer the topic off of Harper's dad.

William's looking at me and I can't read his expression. It's either curiosity or concern or a mix of both. "So you're good friends with Kiefer's daughter?"

"Yeah, we're best friends. We lived next door to each other all summer and she was in my wedding. Do you know her dad?"

Garret nudges my foot under the table again.

"Yes, I know him quite well."

Garret pretends to pick his napkin off the floor. As he leans down to get it he whispers, "Don't ask."

"How's your dinner?" I ask William. It's obvious I'm trying to change the subject but I didn't know how to be subtle about it.

"It's very good."

Garret starts talking about his classes and the college and then I do the same. We stay on that topic through the rest of dinner.

When we're done eating, William looks at me and asks, "Would you like dessert?"

"No, thanks. I'm really full."

"Garret?"

"None for me either."

"Well, then, shall we call it a night? I'll take care of the check if you two want to head out."

Garret and I get up and go around the table to where William is now standing.

"Thank you for dinner." Garret shakes his hand.

I do the same. "Yes, thank you."

William hesitates, then steps up and puts his arms around me and hugs me.

"You're my niece," he says. "What am I doing shaking your hand?"

"Jade." I hear Garret whisper it next to me.

I notice I'm standing there with my arms at my sides. I reach around William and hug him back.

William's hug reminds me of Arlin's hugs. Is that weird? Maybe I'm just imagining it, but it really does feel like one of Arlin's hugs; strong, with his arms fully wrapped around me. And when I let go, William holds on a little longer, just like Arlin used to do.

When he finally releases me, William stands back and smiles at me. "I hope to see you again soon."

We leave the restaurant and as we're in the car driving home, Garret asks, "So what did you think?"

"I liked him. I thought he was nice."

"Yeah, I did, too. It's hard to believe he's Royce's brother. Grace is right. William and Royce are not at all alike."

"Garret, you're an expert on hugs, right?"

He laughs. "I don't know if I'm an expert. Why do you ask?"

"Can people have different hug styles? Like if you had your eyes closed and I hugged you, would you know it's me?"

"Definitely. I could pick your hug out anywhere."

"Do you think it's genetic? Like you're programmed to hug a certain way?"

He laughs again. "No, Jade. Hugging is learned. Usually your parents teach you, but in your case, you got me as a teacher. And not to be cocky, but I think I'm a damn good teacher. You were a mess when we started and now you're almost an expert."

"Yeah, you did a good job with me."

"These are very odd questions. Why are you asking about this?"

"No reason. I was just asking." I gaze out the side window, smiling as I think about William's hug. It *was* like Arlin's. I wasn't just imagining it. Arlin taught him that. It's part of him now. And I get the feeling William is like Arlin in a lot more ways than that.

Garret reaches over and holds my hand. "What are you thinking, Jade?"

"I was just thinking that..." I turn to him. "Sometimes you can tell a lot from a hug."

Chapter 4

GARRET

$\mathcal{I}$ wasn't sure how that dinner would go but it went better than I thought it would. I was predicting awkward silence, or worse, that William would want to just talk about his job. Guys like him tend to make their whole lives about work so it's all they have to talk about. Shit, the guy runs one of the world's largest pharmaceutical companies. He must spend every waking moment at the office. I'm sure he works even more than my dad. I know he does, because my dad's cut his hours significantly the past year. And thank God he did. He was headed for a heart attack if he kept working like that. William's probably headed for one as well. He looked tired and stressed.

When we get home, Jade calls Grace and tells her about the dinner. They don't talk long because it's late on the East Coast and Grace was getting ready to go to bed.

When Jade hangs up, she says, "William called Grace and told her our dinner went well."

"He already called her, huh?" I pull Jade in for a kiss. "See? You won him over."

"He didn't say that."

"He raced back to his room and called Grace to tell her how much he liked having dinner with you. Plus, he invited you to his house and wants you to go sailing with him. That means you won him over."

"That's not what—"

"Don't argue with me." I kiss her again, then smile at her. "I know these things."

"Oh, really? How do you know?"'

"The guy runs a massive international corporation. He works 24/7. So if he's willing to make time for you, that means he likes you."

"It means his mother's making him do it."

"Once again, you're wrong, Jade." I walk off toward the bedroom.

"Hey! I'm never wrong." She laughs as she says it.

I turn around and she's right behind me. "You're always wrong about this kind of stuff." I hug her, lifting her off the ground. She needs a good hug. It's been a rough day.

"What stuff?"

"People stuff. You always think people don't like you and you're always wrong." I walk in the bedroom, still holding her. "That's why it's good I'm here to set you straight." I put her down. "I need to go to the pool. I got yelled at today by my physical therapist for not being in the pool enough. So grab whatever you need and let's go."

"What? I'm not going."

"Yeah, you are. I'm not leaving you here alone."

"Why not?"

"Because I'm not. So let's go."

I don't want Jade sitting here all alone. If I leave her here, she'll think about William, overanalyzing every word that came out of his mouth and every expression that crossed his face. Then she'll be back to thinking he doesn't like her or she'll wonder what he does for the organization. I need to get her mind off all that, which is why she's going with me.

"You're being kind of bossy." She says it jokingly as she goes to a stack of books on the floor and picks up her calculus book.

I go over and take it from her. "No studying tonight."

"But I need to read chapter ten."

"You already read it. I saw you reading it earlier."

"Well, I need to re-read it."

I swear, the girl never takes a break. I thought my laziness would wear off on her by now but it hasn't at all.

"You can read it again tomorrow. Your brain needs to rest. Now get your swimsuit."

"You're making me swim, too?"

"We're going to the pool. That's usually what people do there." I smile at her.

"I'll bring my suit, but that doesn't mean I'm swimming." She takes her swimsuit from the dresser. "I'll decide when I get there."

"I just want you in the water." I grab my gym bag from the closet, then meet her at the door to the bedroom. "I never said you had to swim."

"Yeah you did."

"'I said, in general, people swim when they go to a pool. I didn't say *you* had to."

"Then why would I go in the water?"

I lean down and whisper in her ear, "We can find plenty of other things to do in the water."

She shivers as I lightly kiss the side of her neck. "Okay, I'll get in the water."

"I thought so." I grab her hand and head out the door.

I can always distract Jade with sex, although I don't plan to have sex in the pool since there's a good chance someone will walk in. But I can do plenty of other things to distract her and keep her mind off the earlier events of today.

We arrive at the pool at eight. Nobody's there, which isn't unusual for a Monday night. The gym is always empty as well. It was the same way at Moorhurst. People partied over the weekend and were too tired to work out on Monday nights.

"You get in first." Jade's standing at the edge of the pool in her black bikini, looking hot as hell. "Tell me if the water's cold."

I jump in, splashing water on the tile around her feet. "It always feels cold when you first get in. You'll get used to it." I hold my arms out to her. "Come on. Get in."

"Don't you want to do your laps first?"

"I'll do them later. Come on."

She steps closer and dips her toe in the water. "It's cold."

"It's not that cold. And once you're in here I promise I'll warm you up."

She smiles. That did the trick. I should've started with that.

She sits at the edge of the pool, dangling her feet in. "I have to get in gradually."

"It's all or nothing, Jade." I grab her around the waist and pull her in the water, submerging all but her head.

"Hey! I wasn't ready." She pretends to be annoyed, but she's laughing.

I hold her against me and she instantly wraps her legs around my waist. My face is wet and when I kiss her she feels the slickness of my lips and moans.

Jade loves the water. Shower. Pool. If water's involved, she's instantly turned on. What are the odds that the girl of my dreams also happens to love making out in the water? Could I get any luckier? Seriously, I have no idea what I did to deserve this. Maybe I was a saint in a prior life.

I slip my tongue in her mouth and back her up against the side of the pool. My hands are currently under her ass, but I move one of them to her breast, still teasing her mouth with my tongue.

She moans again and it echoes in the open room. I hope nobody walks in. It wouldn't embarrass *me* if we got caught, but Jade would be totally embarrassed. But right now, she's too into this to care. She might not even notice if someone walked in.

"Get me wet," she whispers.

I look at her, surprised. "I'm pretty sure I already did."

"No." Her cheeks turn pink. "That's not what I meant. I want you to dip me in the water. Get my face wet."

I pull her away from the wall and lower her into the water. When I bring her up, she leans her head back and pushes the water from her eyes.

She starts laughing. "I can't believe I said that. I wondered why you gave me that look."

"I've never heard you talk dirty like that, so yeah, I was a little shocked. But hey, feel free to do it again. It's not like I minded." I back her against the side of the pool and leave kisses along her chest, then up the side of her neck. "You wet enough?"

She smiles, her eyes closed. "Yes."

I wet my face, then put my lips to hers and gently kiss her a few times. She parts her lips and I take the kiss deeper as she pulls me closer, pressing herself into my swim trunks. She starts moving her hips, rubbing against me.

Damn, if she keeps this up, we might just do it in the pool. I know I said I wouldn't, but shit, there's a limit to my self-control and she's pushing that limit to the absolute max.

My hand's still under her ass but I move it down a little and slip my finger under her suit and keep going until she gasps.

"Garret," she whispers, her eyes still closed.

"Yes, Jade." I keep my lips on hers.

"We shouldn't do this here."

"You're right. We shouldn't." I shove my swim trunks down.

"We could get caught."

"We could." I yank the string loose on one side of her bikini, moving the fabric aside as I line myself up.

"But we're doing it anyway?" Her lips draw upward.

"We are." I'm already inside her when I say it. To hell with self control. This is way more fun. I don't know why

I was even fighting myself over this. I've wanted to do this with Jade since that first kiss we had in the pool. I'm glad we didn't do it then. It would've been too soon. But shit, I was really tempted that day. And now I've waited a year and here we are, in a pool with nobody around. So what the hell? It's about damn time.

We've barely started and Jade is already coming close. Just kissing her in the pool got her halfway there.

A wife who loves sex *and* doing it in the water? I'll say it again. I'm a lucky son of a bitch.

I'm almost there, too. Watching Jade get this turned on always gets me going. And then there's the fact that we're doing it in the water and she feels freaking amazing.

I've got my hands wrapped around her tight little ass, trying to go slow. I want to keep this going as long as possible, but from the way Jade's reacting I think it's going to be quick. And it is. Moments later, she holds onto my shoulders and lets out a really loud sound that echoes in the room. That's all it takes for me to finish up, then we both take a moment to catch our breath.

"That was so good." She relaxes her legs down around me.

I lower us into the water, then run my wet lips along her shoulder. "Just good?"

"It was better than good. I'm just too out of it to find the right adjective to describe it." Her dreamy sex haze fades and she looks at me, her face very serious. "But we still shouldn't have done it."

"No, we shouldn't have." I try to be serious.

"But we did." She grins like a little kid who just stole candy.

"Yes, we did." I kiss her.

"That was naughty of us."

"Very naughty." I kiss her again.

"I kind of like being naughty."

"Yeah, I could tell."

"Was I too loud?"

"You were kind of loud, but that's okay. I like loud."

She smiles at me. "I love you."

"I love you, too. You want to let me get some laps in now?" I yank my swim trunks up as she fixes her bikini.

"*Let* you? You're the one who lured me in here. It wasn't *my* fault."

The door to the pool swings open and Jade shoves away from me and swims into the other lane.

Keith, the swim coach, walks in. "I didn't think anyone was in here. Hey, Garret. Haven't seen you here much."

"The physical therapist said I need to start upping my time in the pool, so I'm doing the exercises he taught me."

"How's the shoulder feeling?"

"It's a lot better."

"Even if it's better, make sure you keep going to therapy."

"I will."

"Hi, Jade. I see you decided to go for a swim as well."

Jade's cheeks are bright red. "Yeah, I thought I'd do some laps." She takes off down the lane before Keith can say anything else to her.

50

"Garret, I'd like you to start coming to practice. Get to know the team. You don't need to be at every practice, but you could drop in once or twice a week."

"Sure. That'd be great."

"All right, then. I'll let you get back to swimming." He walks off. "Bye, Jade."

She waves at him as she swims. When she reaches the end of the lane, he's gone.

"That was so embarrassing!" She wipes the water from her face.

"Why? He didn't see anything."

"He would've if he'd walked in just a few minutes sooner!"

"But he didn't, so we're good."

"It doesn't bother you that your coach almost walked in on us?"

"No, it doesn't bother me at all." I pull her into me. "Are you saying you regret what we did?"

She grins. "No. It was great."

"You still need a better adjective." I let her go and hear her laughing as I swim down the lane.

We stay in the pool for an hour. Jade mostly sat at the edge with her feet in the water while I did my workout. I like having her here. Even if she doesn't swim, it's nice to just have her here with me at the pool.

We get out of the water and I hand her a towel to dry off, then grab one for myself. "Thanks for coming with me."

"You didn't give me a choice."

"Yeah, I guess I didn't. But you had a good time, right? Even after the sex?"

"Don't say that out loud! Someone will hear you."

I glance around. "There's nobody here, Jade."

She checks the door, then reaches up and kisses me. "Yes, I had a good time. I love watching you swim."

"I didn't do much swimming. Mostly just shoulder exercises."

"I still like being here with you." She wraps the towel around her waist. "I'll go change. Meet you in the hall outside the locker room?"

"Yeah, okay."

I finish changing before she does, and as I wait in the hall I check out the bulletin board that's hanging just outside the locker room. There's a sign asking for volunteers for a kids' swimming class and some flyers underneath it with more information. I take one of the flyers.

"That's a program we started a few years ago." Keith appears in the hallway. He must've seen me standing here from his office. "My church sponsors it. The college agreed to let us use the pool. They were hesitant at first because of the liability issues, but we got that figured out and now we've been doing the program for three years."

"What is it exactly?"

"It's free swim classes for kids whose parents can't afford swimming lessons. We just teach them the basics, mainly so they don't drown if they ever find themselves in the water. And if they get the basics down, we teach them a few strokes. You know how kids are. They're eager to learn."

"How old are the kids?"

"We get all ages. Mostly younger kids but sometimes we get some teens. Anyway, the program goes throughout the year, one Saturday a month. There's a class in a few weeks. If you're interested, let me know. We could really use more volunteers."

"I'd be happy to do it. Go ahead and sign me up."

"You don't have to decide right now. You can think about it."

Jade comes out of the locker room. "Hi, again," she says to Keith, her cheeks turning pink. He didn't even see anything and she's still blushing. She would've been so embarrassed if he'd walked in on us while we were doing it.

"Jade, I was just telling Garret about a program we have here at the school that teaches kids how to swim. He was thinking of volunteering."

"Oh, yeah? You should do that, Garret."

"Yeah, I told him I would. It's one Saturday a month."

"Would you like to volunteer as well?" Keith asks Jade.

"I'm not a very good swimmer. I don't think I could teach someone how to swim."

"We need volunteers to help with snacks and to supervise some of the younger girls in the locker room."

"Um, sure, I could do that."

"Great! Then I'll sign both of you up. If you have any questions, you know where to find me."

On the way to the car, I link hands with Jade. "You sure you want to volunteer?"

"Yeah, it sounds fun."

"You do know it involves kids, right?"

"Yes." She laughs. "I'm just handing out snacks. I think I can handle it."

"What ever happened to your babysitting gig? Are you still going to watch Caleb?"

A few weeks ago, Jade agreed to babysit for her friend, Sara, when she goes on job interviews. Sara's trying to find a job that pays better than the coffee shop because Caleb's dad won't give her child support and she really needs money.

"Sara has to get an interview first. She hasn't had much luck finding anything, but when she does, she still wants me to babysit Caleb. Oh, speaking of babies, did Harper say anything to you when she was here for my birthday?"

"About what?"

"Babies. She's obsessed with us having one."

I open the car door for Jade, then go around to the other side. Whenever the kid topic comes up, I never know what to say. It's such a sensitive topic that I just let Jade lead the conversation and try not to say too much.

I start the car but leave it in park. "Jade. Seatbelt."

She always forgets to put it on. She clicks it in place, then says, "Harper keeps telling me to hurry up and get pregnant so she can play with our baby this summer."

"It's already mid-October. It's getting kind of late for that."

"That's why Harper's been telling me this for weeks now. She's driving me crazy with all this baby talk."

"She's just joking."

"I don't think so. I think she's really counting on this."

"She knows how you feel about kids so you know she's not serious."

Jade's quiet the rest of the drive home. She goes and unlocks the front door as I grab my gym bag from the back seat.

When we get inside, she lies down on the couch and stares up at the ceiling. "Harper doesn't know."

"Doesn't know what?" I set my bag down and get a bottle of water from the fridge.

"She doesn't know about the kid thing. How I feel about it."

I go to the couch and Jade moves her legs so I can sit. "You guys never talked about this? You're best friends. You talk constantly."

"Yeah, but I didn't want to tell her this. It's private."

"Again. You're best friends. This seems like something you would talk about with your best friend."

"Well, I don't, okay? I don't want to tell her."

"Why not?"

"Because then I'll have to tell her about my mom and my childhood."

"You haven't talked about that, either? What exactly do you talk about with her?"

"You. Sean. Other stuff. She doesn't need to know about my past. And she doesn't need to know how I feel about being a mom. She'd never understand. She loves kids. She'll probably have five of them if she ever marries Sean."

"Are you afraid she'll judge you because you don't want kids? Is that why you won't tell her?"

"Maybe. I don't know. She just wouldn't understand." Jade climbs onto my lap. "Garret, don't say I don't want kids. Because I don't know yet, so I don't want you saying I don't want them. And I don't want you thinking that."

She lays her head on my shoulder.

I kiss her forehead. "I think you should reconsider telling Harper about this. She's your best friend. She's not going to judge you. And it might be good for you to talk to her."

"No. It's something I need to deal with myself."

Jade says that, but the thing is, she's not dealing with it. Like I said, it's a sensitive topic—so sensitive she won't even talk to *me* about it. But she *needs* to talk about it, if not with me, then with someone. Otherwise she'll never come to a decision about having kids.

Jade sits up. "I'm really tired. I'm going to bed."

"I'm going to stay up a little longer."

"Goodnight. Love you." She gives me a kiss. "Oh, and, um, thanks for the pool sex."

"No need to thank me, Jade," I say as she walks away. She always makes me laugh when she thanks me for sex. Like it was a chore or something.

I watch TV for an hour, then call my dad back.

"Hey, can you talk now?" I ask him.

"Yes. Let me just go in my office." I hear him walk in there and close the door.

"So what did William say when he called you?"

"He asked how long I've known that Jade was a Sinclair. I went with the story you told him and said I didn't find out until after Royce died. Then he asked if I knew anything about Jade's mother and I told him I knew nothing about her."

"What did he ask you about Jade?"

"Not much. I assured him Jade's not the type of person who would try to con someone out of their money. Grace told him that as well. I think William believes Jade's story now. He just needs time to accept it. He's still trying to understand how his brother was able to hide a secret like that all these years."

"Yeah, he was shocked when we told him. But he seemed more accepting of Jade when we saw him a few hours ago. Jade and I had dinner with him."

"Yes, he mentioned you were having dinner. How did it go?"

"It was fine. He seemed okay. Actually he seemed like a nice guy, but you know him better than I do."

"I've always liked William. We've gone out for drinks several times. But you know how it works. It's a thin line between friends and enemies and I don't want to risk him crossing that line. I don't want you trusting him any more than you'd trust any of the other members."

"Jade really wants to get to know him. He asked her to come out and visit him and Meredith at their house in New York."

"We need to get to know him better before she does that. I'll invite him to dinner, maybe have drinks with him after the next meeting. And although I'd prefer not to, I'll talk to your grandfather. Now that he's in this higher up posi-tion, he has access to all the information we have on our members. If William is hiding something, your grandfather will know."

"He won't help us if he knows this is for Jade."

"He has no idea Jade is a Sinclair. You know that."

"Yeah, I wasn't thinking. It's been a long day."

"Anyway, I'll just make up an excuse. I'll tell your grandfather I'm inquiring about William because I'm considering asking him to serve on the board. Your grandfather won't question that."

"Did you do any checking on that Walt guy?"

"Yes, he's one of us. Well, he's not a member, but he works for us. He's been doing contract work for years. Then William hired him for his own personal security needs and since then, Walt hasn't had time to take on additional projects."

It's just what I thought. Walt isn't as innocent as he looks. He may come across as a harmless old guy, but if he's done work for the organization, he's done his share of bad shit. 'Contract work' could be code for anything from covering up stuff to killing someone.

"William suggested Walt keep an eye on our place. He said the cameras aren't enough."

"Walt will not be acting as your security personnel. If you think you need that, I will find you someone else."

"I already told him I didn't want Walt sticking around. But William also said the cameras weren't working right. Walt was able to mess with the digital signal so when I viewed the images on my phone they were all blurry."

"I'll get it fixed right away. Oh, and I also asked William if he had anything to do with the burglar or that fake police officer. He said he had nothing to do with it, and from his response, I believe him."

"You really think he'd hire some guy to rob us? Why would he do that?"

"He assumed Jade was a criminal. I thought maybe he hired that man to go through your house and see if Jade had stolen anything from Grace."

"But the guy robbed the neighbors. If he was targeting *us*, he wouldn't have robbed someone else."

"It was just a theory. It still bothers me that I can't find that police report or that fake officer. I might have to ask your grandfather for help. He has more connections than I do. For now, just continue to be careful."

"I will. I'll talk to you later."

"Goodnight, Garret."

My dad's really freaking me out about this fake cop and that robbery. I've been trying to forget it. The cop hasn't been back and the robber's dead so I don't know why my dad's so concerned about this. I wonder if there's something he's not telling me.

Chapter 5

JADE

The next couple days I keep thinking about William, wondering if he's really the man I want him to be or if he's bad like his brother. I want to believe what Grace said about William being a good man, but part of me doesn't, knowing she had no clue what Royce was capable of until she found out what he did to my mom.

I've been calling Grace every day now that I know the rest of her family never calls. What is wrong with them? She's all alone and still grieving over Arlin. Can't they at least call her once a week just to check in? Anyway, I told Grace I needed some time before we get together with William. She didn't question me. She understands my hesitation.

I feel better knowing Walt's not following me around anymore. That guy creeped me out. Garret told me his dad confirmed that Walt's done work for the organization. And if he's worked for them, he's done bad things, even worse things than the members. Maybe that's why I'm having trouble trusting William. I don't know why he'd want someone like that working for him.

Now it's Thursday and I go to chemistry class feeling anxious because today we get our exams back. It was one of three major exams we have during the semester and we took it last Tuesday. I felt like I did okay on it, but you never know. The professor hands them out at the start of class. I smile when I see the 93 written in red ink at the top of my exam. Finally, my grades are where they should be. I'm so happy about it, I decide to reward myself with a smoothie after class.

When I get to the coffee shop, Sara's outside talking on her phone. I wave as I walk past her. I haven't seen her since last week.

I find a seat at one of the small round tables and scan the restaurant, making sure Walt's not there. I know he's gone but I check anyway, just in case.

"Hey." Sara sits down across from me. "I'm on break so I have a couple minutes. I haven't seen you for forever."

"Yeah, I know. How have you been?"

"Good. How was your birthday?"

"It was great. A bunch of people flew in from out of town and stayed all weekend. My best friend, Harper, was here with her boyfriend, Sean. I was totally surprised." Sara doesn't seem to be listening. She's staring at the wall behind me and hasn't blinked for a while. "Sara?"

Her eyes dart back to me. "Sorry. I spaced out for a minute."

"It's okay. Were you up with Caleb last night?"

"No, he slept the whole night."

"So you were just daydreaming?"

"No, well, maybe." She rests her forearms on the table and leans across it. "Remember when I had that interview for the secretary job at the architecture firm? It was that week I got sick so I missed the interview and someone else got the job."

"Yeah, I remember. What about it?"

"This guy who works there just called and asked me out." She smiles really wide. "Can you believe that? He asked me out!"

"Who is this guy?"

"His name is Alex. He's doing an internship there. He's 24. I met him when I dropped off the application. Actually, I met him in the parking lot. He was parked next to me and he was staring at my car so I asked him what he was doing and he said my tire looked flat. It wasn't. It just needed air. Anyway, we started talking and he rode the elevator up to the third floor with me and I found out he worked there. He gave me his card and told me to call if I needed help with the tire. I didn't need help, but I called him just to tell him thanks."

"Yeah, right. You called him so he'd have your number."

She smiles. "Maybe."

"What's he look like?"

"About 5'9, dark hair, dark eyes. He had that light layer of stubble on his face that's intentional, not like he forgot to shave. How do guys do that anyway? Do they have some special razor or something? Anyway, he was wearing glasses with thick black frames. I usually don't like glasses, but on him they looked good. They give him kind of a quirky, artsy look. He's really hot. And he was flirting with me. Me!" She pauses. "And then I ruined it."

"What do you mean?"

"He had on this great cologne." She sighs. "And I told him he smelled good."

"You did?"

"Yes!" She throws her hands in the air. "Who says that to a total stranger? Only crazy, sleep-deprived, undateable people like me."

"Sara, you may be sleep deprived, but you're not crazy or undateable. He just called and asked you out."

"It's probably a pity date. He felt sorry for the crazy girl who goes around sniffing people and commenting on their smell." She sighs again. "I can't believe I did that."

"What did he say after you told him he smelled good?"

"He laughed. And then he said thank you and that no one's ever told him that before. Of course no one's told him that before! Because only a crazy person would do that!"

"I tell Garret he smells good all the time."

"Yeah, but you're married to him. You can't say that to a guy you just met!"

"It's not a pity date, Sara. He likes you. Did you agree to go out with him?"

"Yes. He asked me to meet him here for coffee." She laughs. "He didn't know I work here. After I told him, he suggested a coffee shop across town, so that's what we're doing."

"When's your date? Do you need me to babysit?"

"It's tomorrow. I called my day care lady and she said she could watch Caleb for me."

Sara doesn't want me to watch Caleb? Was I that bad with him? I thought I did an okay job when she brought him over a few weeks ago. And Garret would be there to help.

"You don't want me to babysit?"

"You can't. You'll be gone."

"Where am I going?"

"Damn!" She covers her mouth with her hand. "I wasn't supposed to tell you that."

"Tell me what?"

"Ask Garret." She stands up. "I'm going to leave before I screw up even more. Do you want anything to drink?"

"Yeah, a strawberry smoothie. Now tell me where I'm going."

"The smoothie will be out in a minute." She runs off to the kitchen.

So Garret has something planned and it sounds like it's not in town. There aren't any classes tomorrow so we talked about driving up the coast and going to a different beach just to hang out. So maybe that's what he's planning.

Sara brings back the smoothie. She added whipped cream and sprinkles to the top and placed a candle in it. "It's your birthday gift. It's on me. Happy Birthday!"

"Sara, no, I'll pay you for it."

"I get them for half price and I can't afford to get you anything else. So just take it."

"Okay, thanks. I love the birthday topping."

"Maybe I should cancel the date." She checks that her boss isn't watching, then sits down again.

"Why would you cancel? You seem to like this guy."

"I do, but once he finds out about Caleb, it's over."

"You don't know that."

"He's 24. He doesn't want to date a girl with a kid." She gets her phone out. "I'm going to call him back and tell him it won't work."

I cover her phone with my hand. "No, don't. Just give him a chance. You never know what will happen."

"I *do* know. I'll tell him I have a baby and he'll run out of the coffee shop and never speak to me again."

"Why don't you test that theory by going out with him? Sometimes people can surprise you. Look at Garret and me. When I first met him, I couldn't believe he wanted to go out with someone like me. First of all, he's super hot and could have any girl he wants. Second, he's rich and I grew up on food stamps. And talk about embarrassing. You should've heard all the embarrassing things I said to him. When I get nervous my brain shuts down and really stupid things come out of my mouth. The point is that Garret's the last person in the world I ever thought would ask me out on a date. But he did, and now we're married."

"How did your first date go?"

"It was great, but we were friends before we went on our first real date. He tried to date me before that, but I kept telling him I just wanted to be friends. I didn't want to get involved with him because I was sure it'd never last." I raise my eyebrows. "Sound familiar?"

She smiles. "Okay. I'll go out with him. But I'm telling him about Caleb right away. I'm not going to wait."

"You don't need to tell him the second he sits down. Just relax and talk to him like you'd talk to a friend. Then bring up Caleb. But don't talk about Caleb the whole time. I know you can't help yourself because you love him to pieces but try to talk about other stuff, too."

"Now you're making me nervous. I don't think I can do this."

"Sara, it's just coffee. There's nothing to be nervous about."

"You're right. It's just coffee. I've never had a coffee date before. How long do they last?"

"As long as you want." I sip my smoothie.

She sighs as she stands up. "I don't think I'm ready for this."

"You're ready. He asked you out, which means he already likes you, so just go and talk to him. You always say you miss adult conversation."

"That's true. I have to get back to work. Enjoy the smoothie."

She walks back to the kitchen. Even though she's nervous, I can tell she's excited about this date. She couldn't stop smiling when she was talking about it. I hope it goes well.

I don't see Garret until later that afternoon when we meet up in front of the library to go home. I check him out as he approaches. Tall, muscular, tan, wearing sunglasses. Damn, he's hot. I don't know how I ever went out with him without being a nervous wreck like Sara is right now. I guess it's because I never thought Garret was that interested in me. It took months before I'd let myself believe that.

He comes up in front of me. "You're pretty hot. Are you a student here?"

I laugh, but play along. "Yeah, but I'm married so back off."

"Go out with me." He drops his backpack and wraps his arms around my waist. "I know I'm better than some old married guy."

"He's not old." I kiss his soft, warm lips. "And nobody's better than him."

"You just kissed a stranger, so your husband can't be that great."

"How long are you going to keep this going?"

"I don't know what you're talking about." He holds me closer, so our bodies are touching. People are walking past us and starting to stare. "How about you let me show you what you're missing?"

"I'm not missing anything. I'm perfectly happy."

"Happy's boring. You need more than happy. So what do you say?"

"Hmm. It's tempting. But I don't know."

"Let me help you make a decision." He leans down and gives me a hot, sexy kiss that should not be done in public and yet I can't pull away. It feels way too good.

"Get a room," some guy yells as he walks by.

Garret pulls back a little. "You heard the man. Let's get a room. My car's just down the street and there's a hotel not far from here."

I laugh. "Yeah, okay. Just don't tell my husband."

He picks up his backpack, puts his arm around my shoulder and starts walking to the car. "You seem to really like this husband of yours. You won't stop talking about him."

"I *do* like him. I like him a lot."

When we're in the car, Garret takes off in the opposite direction of home.

I turn the radio down. "Are we going somewhere?"

"We're getting a room, remember?"

"Yeah, that was a joke. Where are we *really* going? To the grocery store?"

He doesn't answer, but he's smiling. He's up to something. He keeps driving and I ask him again where we're going but he still won't tell me.

After 20 minutes, he turns onto a road that goes along the ocean. He stops at a large, all-white hotel. It looks very modern, almost like an art museum with a circular entrance lined with sculptures and topiaries in pots.

"What are we doing here?" I ask him.

"I got us a room, because apparently what we were doing earlier wasn't appropriate to do in public." He parks the car in front of the entrance. "Also, we wouldn't want your husband to find out. I like to be discreet." He hands the car keys to the valet as another valet opens my door.

"Welcome," the valet says. "Enjoy your stay."

Garret goes around the car and meets up with me. His arm wraps around my middle as he leads me into the lobby. There's a big fountain in the center and a woman comes up and offers me cucumber water.

"No, thanks," I tell her, wondering if I'm dreaming this. One minute I'm in class, the next I'm at some fancy hotel. This must be the surprise Sara alluded to earlier. Garret must've booked us a room here for the long weekend.

"We're checking in," he says to the desk clerk. "Garret Kensington."

"Yes, we have you booked for one night in a suite. Is that correct?"

Garret smiles at me. "That's correct."

The desk clerk hands him the key. "Your luggage has already been brought up to your room. Enjoy your stay."

"Thank you." Garret leads me to the elevator, not saying a word as we ride up to the fourth floor. His arm is still around me but his hand drops down to my hip. It's just resting there but it's getting me all hot inside. I don't know how he does it, but he somehow manages to have this effect on me with just the smallest movements. Or maybe it's this role-playing thing he's doing. Who knows? All I know is I really want to get to the room.

As soon as we're inside he shuts the door, then forcefully pulls me into him and says, "Now where were we?"

"I think we were—"

His lips crash into mine before I can finish. His kiss is hot and urgent, and I kiss him back the same way while undoing his belt. He rips his t-shirt off, then his eyes meet mine in an intense gaze as he unbuttons my white cotton shirt. Luckily I wore my lacy push-up bra today instead of one of my boring cotton ones. And I have a skirt on, which is Garret's second favorite clothing item on me, the first being lingerie.

He shoves his pants and boxers off and walks me to the bed, his eyes on mine. I lie down and he slowly pushes my skirt up and slides my panties off.

I reach up and grab him, pulling him toward me. "Don't you at least want to know my name before we do this?"

He positions himself between my legs. "That'll just complicate things. I like to keep things simple."

"So this is just a one-time thing?" I run my hand through his hair as he leaves soft kisses along my collarbone.

"We're doing this a lot more than once tonight."

"I meant you and me. Will I see you after tomorrow?"

His cocky smile appears. "I'm guessing you'll be back for more." His lips meet up with mine as he thrusts inside me, my skirt and bra still on. He likes it that way. He'll take them off later when we do this again. Or maybe not. I forgot. I just met this guy. I don't know what he likes. But I know what *I* like and he's doing all those things now, sending my body on a sensory overload. We haven't had sex since doing it in the pool so I was more than ready for it.

Minutes later, we're sweating and breathing heavy, our bodies collapsed on the bed. I open my eyes and notice the windows are wide open, the cool ocean breeze blowing the sheer white curtains back. People probably heard me. I wasn't exactly quiet. I never used to make sounds during sex. I was too embarrassed. But then I got over it and now sometimes I can be a little loud.

As we lie there, I take a moment to glance around the room. It has dark espresso-colored furniture and there's a white upholstered chair in the corner. We're lying on a king-size bed with a white comforter. There were bright orange throw pillows on the bed but we tossed them on the floor. I can only see a glimpse of the bathroom but it looks like it has dark cabinets and a white marble vanity. It's a very modern, upscale room.

"Hey." Garret sits up on his side and kisses my cheek. "I love you."

I smile. "We just met. It's a little early to say that, isn't it?"

"You're my wife. And I wanted to say it."

"So we're done role-playing?"

"That was just to get you in bed. Now you're my wife again. Although the handsome stranger might reappear later tonight."

"I think I'd rather have my husband."

"That can be arranged."

"Thanks for the surprise trip."

"The past few weeks have been kind of rough so I thought it'd be good to get away. Plus, we don't have classes tomorrow so we might as well start the weekend now."

"This hotel is great. How'd you find out about this?"

"I just searched online for hotels. I thought you might like this one."

"I do. I love it. But why are we only staying one night?"

"Because we're going to the harvest festival tomorrow."

For some reason hearing him say that sounded funny and I laugh. "What's the harvest festival?"

"Sara told me about it. It's like an hour from here. She said people come from all over to go to it. There's a carnival, bands, food stands. There's even a pie eating contest."

"It sounds like the Iowa State Fair."

"Then you'll love it. It'll remind you of home."

"Actually, I never went to the fair. It cost too much."

"Well, now you can go to this one and you don't have to worry about what it costs. I'll buy you whatever you want. Corn dogs. Snow cones. Funnel cakes."

"Can we go on the carnival rides?" I say it in that excited tone I get that sounds like a kid.

He smiles and gives me a kiss. "We can go on as many carnival rides as you want. I'll even get you one of those wristbands that give you unlimited rides."

"This is going to be so much fun. When are we going?"

"We'll leave after breakfast tomorrow." He's staring at me. I'm sure I'm grinning like an idiot. "I didn't think you'd be so excited about this. But it's good. I wasn't sure if you'd want to go."

"Are you kidding? Rides and junk food. I love both of those things. And I bet they'll have pumpkins."

"Yeah, they have a pumpkin patch with a corn maze."

"Seriously? Can we get a pumpkin?"

"You can get more than one if you want."

I kiss him. "You have the absolute best surprises."

"I do?"

"Yes. And you're the absolute best husband."

"Then maybe you shouldn't have been fooling around with that other guy."

"I'm done with him."

"You sure about that? Because you seemed to really like what he did to you earlier."

"I guess he'll have to do it again so I can decide."

The handsome stranger does it again. And then we go to dinner at a restaurant that's just down the street. We asked the concierge where to eat and he suggested a fancy restaurant downtown, but then we drove past this barbecue place and the smoked meat smelled so good we ended up eating there instead. It was better than some fancy restaurant. We ate outside and had ribs and coleslaw and homemade cornbread.

It's good Garret planned this trip. He knows this thing with William has been consuming my thoughts and he knows I'm feeling lost after dropping those classes and changing my major back to undecided. If I were home right now, I'd be thinking about all that. But now I'm not. Sometimes you just need some time away to clear your head, which is why Garret took me here.

He always does stuff like this. He goes and surprises me with something like this trip and I'm reminded just how lucky I am to have him.

Chapter 6

GARRET

I planned this trip because Jade and I needed to get away and do something. And although last night was great, I wanted to do more than just spend all our time at a hotel. So when Sara mentioned the fair, I figured what the hell. Maybe it's not the greatest idea but at least it's something. Little did I know Jade would get so excited about it. I forget that she didn't do this stuff as a kid.

"What am I wearing today?" Jade's sorting through the suitcase.

We ordered room service for breakfast, then showered, and now we're getting ready to leave.

"Jeans and a t-shirt. And I think I threw a sweatshirt in there."

She laughs as she pulls out a tiny red shirt. "You packed the tightest t-shirt I own. It makes my boobs look huge."

I shrug. "That's what you get when you make me pack your suitcase. I pick what I like."

"I didn't *make* you pack it. If you would've told me about this, I would've packed it myself." She takes the jeans out. "Why this pair?"

"They make your ass look good."

74

"My other jeans don't do that?"

"Some do, some don't. Plus, you haven't gained back the weight you lost when you had the flu so most of your jeans don't fit right. But those do."

"I didn't know you paid so much attention to my clothes." She wiggles into the jeans, then slips the shirt on.

I stand back and look her up and down. "See? I did good. Spin around."

She rolls her eyes, but turns around. "So? How's the view?"

"It makes me want to grab your ass, so we better get out of here before I do, because you know where that will lead."

I take my wallet and keys off the bedside table while Jade zips up the suitcase. Then we head to the car. It's a perfect fall day; a little cool but sunny with no wind.

As soon as we drive off, Jade gets her phone out.

"Who are you calling?"

"My little sister." She smiles as she swipes her phone screen. "Your dad said they have teacher conferences today so Lilly doesn't have school." She listens, then ends the call. "She doesn't have her cell phone on. I'll just call the house number."

"If you do that, you know who's going to answer, right?"

"Yeah. But I can't avoid her forever."

Jade hasn't talked to Katherine since last spring. Whenever we call the house, I'm always the one who gets the pleasure of talking to Katherine, or more like fighting with her.

"Put it on speaker," I tell Jade.

I hear the phone ringing, then Katherine picks up. "Hello?"

"Hi, Katherine. It's Jade."

"Jade, what a surprise." Katherine uses a tone that sounds like the witch who pretends to be nice as she offers you the poison apple. "Are you enjoying California?"

"Yes, I love it."

"How are your classes going?"

"Fine." Jade shakes her head. She knows this small talk is just Katherine's stall tactic to keep us from talking to Lilly.

"I was just out in Malibu last week at your little friend's house."

Jade rolls her eyes at the condescending comment. "You mean Harper?"

"Yes. I stayed there a few days. Kelly and I are co-chairs for a fundraising event in LA later this month."

"Okay, well, anyway, I was calling to talk to Lilly. Is she around?"

"It's a shame you don't come see us more often. You're my daughter-in-law and yet we've spent no time bonding. We should really plan some girl time." She says it all fake-nice but it's clear she's being sarcastic.

Enough of this shit. "Katherine, put Lilly on the phone."

"Garret, I didn't realize you were there. And how is my son doing?"

"I'm not your son. Would you put Lilly on the phone, please?"

"She's in her room reading a book she was assigned to read for school. I can't disturb her."

"Katherine, I don't have time for this. Just put her on the phone."

"I told you, she cannot be disturbed." Her tone switches back to the evil bitch Katherine I know so well. I knew she couldn't keep that fake nice thing going for much longer.

"Do I need to call my dad? It's a work day. He won't be happy if I interrupt him in the middle of a meeting to tell him his wife won't let me talk to my sister."

"He won't answer your call during a meeting."

"Then I'll text him. My father and I have become quite close the past few months and he responds to all of my messages."

She sighs. "How long are you planning to talk to her?"

"You're not setting a time limit, Katherine."

She finally agrees and goes upstairs to Lilly's room.

"Garret?" Lilly's voice fills the car.

"Yeah, it's me. How's it going?"

"I miss you." She says it every freaking time we talk. I thought she wouldn't miss me so much when she started school, but she still does.

"I miss you, too. So I hear you're reading a book."

"What book?"

"Your mom said you were reading a book for school."

"No, I was braiding Maggie's hair."

Maggie is the name Lilly gave to the doll we gave her for her birthday.

So Katherine lied. What a shock.

"Lilly, Jade wants to talk to you."

"Hi, Jade."

The two of them talk for the rest of the 45-minute drive. Jade loves talking to Lilly, but they never talk for this long. I'm sure Jade dragged it out just to piss off Katherine. Another reason I love Jade.

She ends the call as I park the car. The fair is packed and it's only 10 a.m. I had to park a half mile from the entrance.

"You ready?" I stand there with her door held open as she puts her phone away.

"Why was Katherine being so weird?" Jade gets out of the car and takes my hand as we walk to the ticket booth.

"It's Katherine. Do you really need to ask? She's a psycho bitch. And a liar."

"Why was she putting on that fake nice act?"

"Who the hell knows? I don't give a shit. I'm not going to waste energy trying to figure out Katherine's motives."

"I didn't know she was such close friends with Harper's mom."

"She's not. They're just on a committee together."

"But she stayed at their house, like they're good friends."

"Jade, that house was like a hotel. There were so many rooms, Katherine could stay there without them even noticing. Besides, Kelly probably just offered to let her stay there to be nice, not expecting Katherine to take her up on the offer." I squeeze Jade's hand. "We're here to have fun, which means no talking about Katherine. Got it?"

"Got it." She steps in front of me. "Can we go on the rides first?"

"I thought we'd walk around first, but okay, we can go on the rides."

"And we're still getting those wristband things?" She's just as excited about this as Lilly would be. It's so damn cute.

"Yes, we'll each get a wristband." I stop as she walks ahead of me. "Hey."

"What?" She turns back and smiles and I get that warm feeling in my chest that I get every time she smiles.

"Get back here a minute."

I wait until she's right in front of me, then take her face in my hands and kiss her. "I love you."

"I love you, too." She's still smiling. "Was that it?"

I laugh. "Yeah, that's it. I just wanted to say it, you know, in case we die on one of those carny rides."

"That's not gonna happen." She yanks on my hand. "Come on. We don't have much time."

"It's only 10 in the morning. They're open until midnight, Jade."

"Yeah, but we've got a lot to do before then."

She wasn't kidding. The rest of the morning she drags me on all the rides, then we eat our way through the food stands. After that, we walk through the exhibit hall, which has stuff for sale, like fall crafty stuff. Then we tromp through the pumpkin patch that's next to the fair and Jade picks out two pumpkins.

We drop them off at the car, then it's back to the midway for more rides. I don't mind going on rides but one time each is enough for me. Not for Jade. She wants to go on them as many times as possible. She said the last and only time she was on rides was in fourth grade when her class went on a field trip to some amusement park in Des Moines.

Now that I know how much she loves rides, I'll have to take her to Universal or Six Flags or one of the other big theme parks so she can go on some real rides. I can't do it now because I'm still too well known from that reality show, but in another year or two I'll take her.

For dinner we get corn dogs, then stroll down the midway. It's dark now and everything's lit up.

Jade eyes all the cheap prizes dangling from the game booths. "Do you think you could win me something?"

"I *know* I could. What do you want?"

"Are you serious? You could really win me something?"

"Yes." I point to one of the booths. "You want that giraffe?"

It's a huge stuffed giraffe. I hope she doesn't want it because it's really ugly.

"No, I don't want the giraffe." She scopes out the other booths. "How about that?" She points to a brown bear wearing a red bow tie.

Jade doesn't seem like the teddy bear type. She seems like someone who wouldn't like stuffed animals of any kind, but she always surprises me. "You really want the bear?"

"Yeah. It's cute."

"Okay." I go up to the booth. It's the ring-toss game. You toss rings and try to hook them around the neck of the bottles. It's a tricky game because the bottles are so close together but I have a strategy for this one.

I buy three rings for a dollar. I toss the first ring and miss, but the next one I toss lands on the bottle.

Jade kisses me. "Garret, you won!"

"Yeah, I'm not done yet. I've got one more ring." I hook it again, then say to the carny guy, "She wants the bear."

He hands me the medium-sized bear, which is what you get for two wins.

"Thank you!" Jade takes the bear and kisses me. "You're really good at that."

"I'm good at most of these games. I practiced a lot when I was a kid."

"You practiced playing carnival games?"

"In seventh grade I wanted to impress this girl by winning her stuff at the carnival. Before I asked her out, I wanted to make sure I could actually win. My dad gave me a hundred dollars and I spent the whole day there, practicing all the games along the midway. By the end of the day I got good enough to win some stuff."

"So was she impressed?"

"She never went out with me. After all that, she said no."

"How could she say no to you?"

"Back in seventh grade, I wasn't the tall, muscular, handsome man you see before you." I smile. "I was about 5'7 and hadn't developed all these manly muscles. I had to rely on my charm and carnival game skills to woo girls, although my carnival game skills didn't do me much good."

"Well, they do now. Winning me this bear means you're getting lucky tonight. And if you win me that pink heart, you'll get *really* lucky." She's pointing at a booth that has pink stuffed hearts. They have red ones, too.

"Pink heart, coming right up."

To win it, you have to knock down bowling pins with a baseball. I've played this game a million times. I swear the pins are weighted so they don't fall down, but if you hit them at just the right angle, they'll knock over.

I give the guy enough money for six balls even though I'll probably only need three. I throw the first ball straight on and the pins just wobble. I did it on purpose. I want to build some tension here. It's more fun. I can tell Jade thinks I can't do it and she really wants that heart. I throw the next one the same way and the pins wobble again.

"I don't know, Jade. This is harder than it looks."

Her shoulders droop in disappointment. "It's okay. At least I got the bear."

I hate seeing her disappointed. It's time to break out my carny game skills. I take another ball and line it up at just the perfect angle, then throw it hard but with control. The pins come crashing down. All three of them at once.

"You won!" She hugs me.

"Actually, *you* won. Pick your prize."

"I'll take the pink one," she says to the carnival guy.

He uses a long pole to take it down off the wall, then hands it to Jade.

"I'll just finish throwing the rest of these." I throw the fourth ball and knock all the pins down.

"You won again!" Jade yells. "How did you do that?"

The carnival guy looks at me, annoyed. He grabs his pole again.

"I played a lot of baseball in high school," I say, loud enough for the guy to hear.

Jade picks a red heart this time, and as the guy's getting it down, I throw another ball and knock the pins over.

The guy sighs and turns to Jade. "Three wins means you can trade the small ones in for a bigger prize." He reaches under the counter and pulls out a pink stuffed heart that's twice as big as the one she already has.

"Hmm. I don't know. I like them both. What do you think, Garret?"

"Let me finish up here." I throw the last ball and win again.

The guy's onto me. He gives me a dirty look, but he sees how excited Jade is and says, "Since he just won again, you can have the big heart and one of the small ones."

"Okay, I'll take the pink ones, please."

He gives her the hearts and we walk over to the ferris wheel.

"You were amazing!" She hugs me while trying to hold on to her winnings.

"You should thank 13-year-old Garret. That was all him."

She laughs. "I'm thanking both of you, but I'm taking 20-year-old Garret home with me. He gets an extra-special thank you."

"You want to ride the ferris wheel again?"

"Yes. I love going at night when it's all lit up."

We wait in line for 10 minutes, then get in the cart and wait some more as each cart's loaded. This is why I've never liked the ferris wheel. You wait longer than you actually ride the thing. But Jade likes it, so I've gone on it five times today.

Once everyone's loaded in carts, we go around a few times and then the unloading begins. We're at the very top. Jade leans her head on my shoulder and within a minute she's asleep, her hand intertwined with mine, hugging her stuffed hearts and bear against her chest. She looks so cute I have to get a photo. I use my free hand to grab my phone and get a shot of Jade, then one of the two of us. I put my phone away as the ferris wheel moves us down a little.

Jade wakes up. "Was I sleeping?"

"Yeah." I kiss her forehead. "We'll go home after this. It's been a long day."

She yawns and lays her head on my shoulder again. It's only 10:15, but we have an hour drive back and Jade's worn out.

I look down at the crowd of people. My eye catches an older man in a dark green jacket standing by one of the food stands. I caught him staring at me, but as soon as I saw him, he turned and started walking the other way. Now he's on the phone and headed toward the exit.

I only got a quick glance at his face but he kind of looked like that fake police officer that came to our house. I need to follow that guy. I need to find out if it's him. If it is, I'm going to make him tell me why the hell he showed up at my door impersonating an officer.

I get my phone out again to take a photo of him but just as I'm doing that, the ferris wheel moves and I can't see him anymore. Since he was heading for the exit, I'm guessing he left. I'll never make it through this crowd fast enough to reach him. But that had to be him. Why else would he be watching me and then just leave like that when he realized I'd seen him?

Then again, maybe it wasn't him. Ever since I found out that guy wasn't a real cop, I've been looking for him. I thought I saw him one other time, too, but when I caught up with the guy, it wasn't him. So maybe I'm seeing what I want to see instead of what's really there.

We finally get off the ferris wheel and there's a huge line of people waiting to get on it. The midway's jam-packed with high school kids. I wonder if they all came from Friday night football games. Seems like something I would've done at that age. I was always looking for shit to do after the games so I wouldn't have to go home.

Jade and I make our way through the crowds. It's really loud now with the music playing and kids screaming. But through the noise I hear some girl yell, "Katie, look! I think that's Garret Kensington!"

I turn my head to see who said it, and hear another girl say, "Oh my God, it is! It's totally him!"

Jade's so out of it, she didn't even hear them. "Jade, we gotta get out of here."

"What?" She rubs her eyes.

"These girls recognize me. We have to get out of here. Fast."

She looks around. "What girls?"

"It doesn't matter. Just walk fast. Head to the parking lot."

"Garret!" Several girls yell it at once and a swarm of them come racing toward me.

"Shit!" I keep hold of Jade's hand and walk faster.

Two blond girls in cheerleader outfits step in front of me. "Can we get a picture with you?"

"No, I'm in a hurry." I go around them but more girls block my path.

"What are you doing in California?" It's another cheerleader, wearing the same uniform as the two blond girls. I got the whole damn squad after me. "Don't you live in Connecticut?"

I don't answer her. I push Jade in front of me, keeping hold of her so we don't get separated. She hasn't said a word. This whole thing's probably freaking her out. The crowd around us has grown as people try to figure out what's going on.

"Why aren't you with Ava?" some girl yells. "I heard you were back together with her."

Seriously? Where do they get this shit? I haven't looked at the tabloids or those celebrity websites for months so I have no idea if they're still talking about me. But obviously somebody's spreading rumors about me.

I spot an opening in the crowd and steer Jade toward it. She sees it, too, and walks even faster. The gate is just up ahead and once you go past it you can't get back in, so I know the girls won't go past that spot.

"Garret, wait!" one of the cheerleaders says.

The girls continue to yell stuff at me as they chase after us.

"Who's that girl you're with?"

"Garret, marry me!"

"Does Ava know you're with that girl?"

"Can I get your autograph?"

The questions keep coming, but as predicted, the girls stop following us once we reach the gate, their voices fading as we get closer to the car.

"I didn't think we'd ever get out of there," Jade says. "Where did they all come from?"

"Some high school around here. They probably just left a football game."

"I guess this is why we never go anywhere. People still know you."

"They always knew me. It's the curse of being a Kensington. That reality show just made it worse."

As we walk through the parking lot, I search for that guy but there's nobody around. It probably wasn't the fake cop. I couldn't see him that well from the ferris wheel.

We get in the car and as I drive off, Jade sets her giant stuffed heart against the side window and lays her head on it. "Garret?"

"Yeah?"

"I'm really sleepy. I know I said you'd get lucky tonight for winning me all this stuff, but could it be tomorrow night instead? Or tomorrow morning?"

"You don't owe me anything." I reach over and hold her hand. "I liked winning that stuff for you. Too bad you weren't around when I was in seventh grade."

I don't think she heard me. She's already asleep and she sleeps the whole way back.

Once we're home and in bed, she says, "Thanks for a perfect day."

"You're welcome. Goodnight, Jade."

A perfect day. It's funny. To most people, hanging out at a crowded carnival would not be the perfect day. And to most guys, Jade would not be the perfect girl. But to me she is. Even with all the issues she still struggles with, and even though she frustrates the hell out of me sometimes, she's still perfect. At least to me.

Chapter 7

JADE

I wake up to bright sunshine and check the clock. "Garret, wake up." He's on his side with his back to me. I tug on his arm. "Garret, we need to get up. We have to be at lunch in an hour."

He rolls on his back. "What lunch?"

"The lunch we're having with Brook and Dylan. I planned it last Monday when I called her, remember?"

He yawns. "Yeah, I remember. What time is it?"

"Eleven, but we're meeting them at 12."

"How'd we sleep so late?" He stretches his arms out, then turns on his side and wraps them around me.

"I don't know. I guess that fair really wore us out." I kiss him. "I still can't believe you won me all that stuff."

"If I'd known you wanted a stuffed bear that bad, I would've just bought you one. A better one."

"But this one's special because you won it for me."

"Jade, that bear is probably covered in dirt and germs and who knows what else? The shit you get at carnivals is disgusting. You should really wash that stuff. Or just throw it out."

"I'm not throwing it out. I'm saving it. That's the first time you ever won me something. I'm going to save it and put it on a shelf and remember the day you took me to the fair."

"How about you keep it in a box? I don't want that stuff on a shelf. And I really think you should wash it."

I laugh. "Okay, fine. I'll wash it. Because I'm definitely keeping it." I smile and run my hand down his chest. "And I didn't forget my promise. You're still getting lucky. Just not right now. Later."

He tugs me into him and kisses me. "Later, as in later today?"

"Yes. As soon as we get home from lunch."

"Then let's get this lunch over with." He lets me go and gets out of bed.

"I thought you *wanted* to go to lunch with them." I climb out of bed and follow him to the bathroom.

"I do. But I don't want it to last all afternoon. I have stuff to do."

I turn the shower on. "Like what?"

He pulls my tank top up and over my head. "Well, after I do *you*, I have some reading to get done for class."

"Yeah, I have some calc problems to do. So we'll eat lunch, have sex, then do homework." I step in the shower, leaving the glass door ajar.

He turns to the sink and picks up his razor.

"Aren't you coming in?"

"If I do, we'll be late for lunch."

I smile. "That's true."

On the way to lunch, I check my phone to make sure they didn't cancel. They didn't, and I start to feel anxious.

"I'm kind of nervous about meeting Brook," I say as I put my phone away.

"Why? She's friends with Harper."

"Yeah, but they're not close friends. It's not like they talk all the time. They just went to high school together. And Brook was a year ahead of her so they weren't even in the same classes."

Garret pulls into the restaurant. It's a sushi place. I don't like sushi, but I think I'm the only one who doesn't. Everyone else seems to love the stuff. I don't get it. I tried it once and it made me gag. Brook suggested the restaurant and said it was her favorite place in town so I didn't bother suggesting someplace else.

"Looking forward to the sushi?" Garret smiles as he holds the car door open for me.

"Yeah, you're funny." I take his hand as we walk toward the entrance.

"Hey." Garret's waving at someone in the parking lot. I look and see that it's Dylan. I've never met him, but I did a quick Internet search of both him and Brook so I'd know what they look like.

"You just get here?" Dylan walks up to Garret.

"Yeah, we thought we were late but I guess we're right on time."

Dylan puts his hand out toward me. "Hi, I'm Dylan."

He's good-looking, but Garret's way hotter. Dylan's about six feet tall, with dark eyes and really dark hair. His hair is almost black and the top is spiked up with hair product. He has a dark tan that makes his white teeth look even whiter. He's wearing a light green polo shirt, khaki pants, and loafers.

"Hi. I'm Jade." I shake his hand.

Just as he's about to say something, a tall brunette in a short yellow dress and wedge heels, holding a phone in her hand, walks up behind him. It's Brook, but I almost didn't recognize her. She had wavy, shoulder-length hair in the photo I saw online. But now she has long, straight hair, held back with a pair of giant sunglasses perched on top of her head. She's really pretty; deep-brown eyes, perfect skin, and long legs like a model. Her dark tan and bright white teeth match Dylan's, like maybe they went to the same dentist and tanning salon.

"Hi! You must be Jade." She comes over and hugs me. So she's like Harper in that respect. Harper hugs everyone.

Brook has to really lean down to hug me. I'm guessing she's at least 5'10, even taller with her heels. And her boobs are huge. They pressed against me when she hugged me and felt hard, like they might be fake.

"Nice to meet you." I have to look up. Otherwise I'm directly eye level with her boobs. "Sorry it took me so long to call you."

"Don't worry about it." She smiles, then looks at Garret. "And you're the famous Garret."

She shakes his hand. I'm glad she didn't hug him. I don't want those giant boobs rubbing against my husband's chest.

"I'm not exactly famous, but yes, I'm Garret."

"Are you kidding? At my old college, every girl on campus was obsessed with you. You must have girls following you around all the time."

Brook's really smiling at him, almost like she's flirting. I don't think she is. I think she's just one of those girls who's super friendly and outgoing, which sometimes comes off like flirting.

"I don't get recognized much here," Garret says.

"Don't the people at Camsburg know who you are? I don't know how they couldn't. That reality show was huge."

"I haven't had anyone come up to me and say anything about it, so I guess they didn't watch the show."

"I watched every episode. I loved that show!" She flips her hair back.

Flipping your hair is a flirting technique, isn't it? I read in a magazine that it was. And she's still smiling at him and staring at him. So maybe she *is* flirting with him. With Dylan standing right next to her. And me right next to Garret.

I try not to judge people right away, but they say first impressions are everything and so far, I'm not sure I like this girl.

Dylan takes Brook's hand. "We should get a table. We can talk inside."

The two of them walk ahead of us inside to the hostess stand. Brook's dress is really short and very tight. It shows off her perfect butt and those legs that seem to go on forever.

I glance over at Garret. He's not even looking at Brook. Instead he's looking at me, pulling me into him and kissing my cheek.

"You still nervous?" he whispers as Dylan talks to the hostess.

"No, I'm good."

"Right this way." The hostess motions the four of us to follow her. She takes us to a booth, then waits for us to sit down and hands us the menus. "Your waiter will be here shortly."

Brook's sitting across from Garret and I'm across from Dylan. Something seems off. When Garret and I used to go out with Sean and Harper, the guys would sit across from each other, leaving Harper and me face-to-face so we could talk.

"Maybe we should switch places," I say to Garret. "That way it's easier for you to talk to Dylan."

"Yeah, you're right." He steps out of the booth and we switch places. Dylan's turning off his phone and doesn't notice. Brook's also messing with her phone but her eyes dart up when Garret and I switch seats. She looks disappointed. So she wanted him to sit across from her? What did she think was going to happen? She'd play footsie with him under the table? He'd stare at her boobs all through lunch? Maybe I'm reading too much into it. She has a fiancé. She's not interested in Garret.

Once we're settled in our seats, Dylan asks Garret about a football game that's on TV later today.

Brook sets her phone down and says, "Do you come here much?"

"To this restaurant? No. We've never been here."

She opens her menu. "It's really good. Well, not as good as the places in LA but good for here."

"So does your family still live in Malibu?"

"Just my mom. My parents divorced years ago. My mom loves being single. Right now she's dating this guy she works with."

"She's an actress, right?" Harper told me Brook's mom was an actress but I'd never heard of her.

"Yeah, she's on Creston Hills. Do you watch it?"

Creston Hills is a daytime soap opera. I don't watch soap operas so I've never seen it other than when flipping through channels.

"No, I haven't seen it."

"My mom plays a woman who runs a perfume company. Her character sleeps around a lot so she gets a new guy to make out with almost every week."

"I think that would be weird."

She shrugs. "I wouldn't mind it. But I can't act. I tried when I was younger and I was horrible. So I decided to go into public relations. I want to be a publicist someday." She checks her phone. "So Harper said your major is chemistry."

"Yeah, it was but I—"

"Hold on." She puts her phone to her ear. "Ashley! I totally meant to call you the other day. How was Maui? Did the shoot go okay?"

I feel Garret's arm around my shoulder. He leans over. "You know what you want to order?"

"I haven't looked at the menu yet." I open it up. All I see is sushi.

"How about this?" He points to an entree that has beef strips and green beans sautéed in a sauce. "It's the only thing on the menu I thought you'd eat."

I smile at him. "You searched the menu trying to find something for me?"

"I did." He squeezes my shoulder.

"Thank you. That's very sweet."

"No problem." He kisses my cheek, then sits back in the booth, his arm still around me as he talks to Dylan.

I look over and see Brook watching us. She's still on the phone. She stops talking just long enough to give her sushi order to the waiter, then returns to her conversation. Dylan and Garret order sushi as well and I order the beef strips.

While Brook talks to Ashley, I try to join in Garret's conversation with Dylan but it's all about sports and they seem really into it so I just sit there and wait for Brook to finish her call. She finally does when our food arrives.

She stares at my plate. "You didn't order sushi?"

"I don't really like sushi."

"Who doesn't like sushi?" She pauses, like she realizes how rude that sounds, and says, "I mean, have you ever had it?"

"Yes, and I didn't care for it."

"Not everyone likes it," Dylan says. "My roommate in college hated it. He couldn't even look at it. So whenever he pissed me off, I brought sushi back to our room and ate it right in front of him." He laughs. "Brandon. I miss that guy. We had some good times."

"Brandon was an idiot," Brook says.

"Yeah, but he was fucking hilarious. Just the look on his face sometimes was enough to make me laugh."

"So when did you two meet?" She waves her hand at us, but directs the question to Garret. "You must've known Jade before you were dating Ava. You and Ava didn't break up until March, right?"

Brook is completely obsessed with that reality show, which wasn't even reality. Some actor who looked like Garret just pretended to be him. But maybe it wasn't just the TV show she liked. Maybe she liked the bad-boy Garret that was in the press all last spring. From the comments online, it seemed like a lot of girls liked that version of him.

"I'd rather not talk about Ava," Garret says.

"She seemed like kind of a bitch." Brook leans forward, angling herself toward Garret. "I could never figure out why you two were together."

Dylan nudges Brook. "He doesn't want to talk about his ex."

Brook ignores him. "There was so much drama on that show. My girlfriends and I loved it. In fact, a couple weeks ago, there was an all day marathon of it with the original episodes from high school followed by the new ones. I spent the whole day watching it."

Is she serious? Who would watch that stupid show in reruns? And why was the cable channel replaying it? Maybe that's why those girls were following Garret around at the fair. They'd probably just watched all the episodes. I didn't even consider the show would be replayed like that.

"Did you get paid much?" Dylan asks. "I always wondered how much those people on reality shows make."

"I didn't get paid." Garret takes a drink of his soda.

"Really?" Dylan laughs. "So you just wanted to be on TV, or what?"

Garret shifts a little in his seat. I can tell he's annoyed with Brook for bringing this up. "I didn't want to do the show. Ava dragged me into it."

"You know what you need, Garret?" Brook asks, but she doesn't wait for an answer. "You need a publicist. Someone who could show people the real Garret. The media made you out to be a villain last spring but I can tell you're not like that at all. I could make some calls and set you up with a PR agency in LA. I'll call my mom's agency. It's one of the best—"

"No." Garret cuts her off. "I don't want that. I'm trying to stay out of the media."

"Why? You had a huge fan base. You could use that to your advantage someday."

Dylan turns to her. "Like how?"

She shrugs. "I don't know. Maybe he could run for office."

I bump Garret's leg under the table. He needs to say something to get her off this topic.

"People vote for a familiar face and name," she says to Garret. "That's why celebrities always win elections. You could be governor someday. Or maybe be a senator. I could totally see you doing that."

"I'm not interested in politics," Garret says.

"Yeah, he hates politics," I say. "And politicians."

Brook's phone vibrates on the table and she picks it up. "Giselle! Oh my God. How *are* you? I haven't talked to you forever. Did you find a dress?"

Dylan rolls his eyes. "Brook's addicted to her phone. I've tried to get her to turn it off when we go out to eat, but having it off makes her so anxious it's better to just let her keep it on. She even sleeps with the thing." He mouths the words 'hang up' to her. She just smiles at him. He looks back at us, shaking his head. "Total addiction."

Thankfully, the phone interruption ends any more talk about Garret going into politics. I can't believe she said that. If she only knew the real story.

Brook remains on the phone as she eats her lunch. Garret notices and quits talking about sports so I can join in his conversation with Dylan. We talk about Camsburg and then Dylan tells us about the college he went to in LA.

Dylan seems like a really nice guy. I figured he would be given that he went out and got that stuff for me when I was sick. But even if he hadn't done that, I'd still think he's a nice person. Brook, on the other hand, isn't as nice as I thought she'd be. I didn't know what to expect, but I didn't think she'd ignore me all through lunch. She didn't even look in my direction. Instead, she either looked at her phone or stared at Garret.

After we leave the restaurant and are standing in the parking lot, Brook goes up to Garret and says, "Would you mind if I got your picture? My friend, Giselle, loves you and I told her I'd send her a photo."

"Um, no, I don't think so."

"Please. It won't take long." She hits the camera icon on her phone.

Garret glances at Dylan.

"She won't let you leave until you agree to it," Dylan says. "She's very persistent."

"Okay, fine." Garret stands next to me, his arm around my waist.

"Can I get one with just you and me?" Brook bites her bottom lip and tilts her head. Very flirtatious. No doubt about it that time.

Dylan doesn't even notice as he swipes through his phone.

Garret looks annoyed. "Sorry, but I really don't like my photo being taken so I'll have to pass."

"But why?" Brook uses this whiny tone that makes me want to slap her.

"I just don't." Garret takes my hand. "Jade and I need to go, but we'll talk to you guys later."

Dylan waves, but doesn't look up from his phone. "Yeah, see ya."

As we're walking to the car, I glance back and see Brook with her hand on her hip, pouting because she didn't get her way. She watches as Garret opens my door, and doesn't take her eyes off him until we drive away.

"I don't think I can be friends with her," I say to Garret.

"I don't *want* you to be friends with her. She's a bitch, and I don't say that about many people."

"You thought so, too? I thought it was just me. I thought I was being overly critical. I was trying to give her a chance but she wouldn't even talk to me."

"Yeah, what the fuck was that about? She talked on the phone the entire time. Did she even say anything to you?"

"A few things when we first sat down. And then her phone rang."

He shakes his head. "Fucking rude."

I didn't think Garret would react this way. I wasn't even sure he noticed what was going on over on my side of the table, at least not during the first half of the lunch when he was engrossed in sports talk with Dylan.

"You seem really mad about this."

"I *am* mad. Brook treated you like shit. She was a total selfish bitch." He brings my hand to his lips and kisses it. "Nobody treats my wife like that."

"I thought you'd tell me to give her another chance. You're all about giving people second chances."

"Yeah, well not her. Don't even talk to her anymore. If she calls, just ignore her."

"Wow. You really don't like her. I don't either. I can't believe she acted that way. And did you notice how she was flirting with you?"

"How could I not? She was so damn obvious about it. And she did it right in front of you and Dylan. Like she didn't even care. That's another reason she's a bitch."

"I don't think Dylan even noticed."

"Yeah, I know. I like the guy, but what the hell? How could he not see what was going on?"

"Maybe he just didn't want to say anything and embarrass her."

"Either that or Brook does this all the time, so now he's used to it."

"I'm glad you didn't let her take your picture."

"That whole photo thing pissed me off. And I'm pissed that Dylan didn't back me up when I told her no. And then she wants a photo of just her and me? I mean, seriously? Could she get any more obvious?"

"Yeah, that was bad. If her friend really wanted a photo of you, it could've been just you, not you and Brook."

"Her friend didn't need a damn photo. There are photos of me all over the Internet."

"Can you believe she said that stuff about you being a politician? When she said that, I thought maybe she knew something. I know she doesn't, but it still made me nervous."

"She was just making a dumb comment. But I didn't like her saying that shit about how I needed a publicist to fix my image. Like it's any of her damn business what people think of me."

"I know. She seems to really want people to know you're not like that anymore. If she starts telling people about you, she could ruin all the work we did last spring."

"She needs to keep her mouth shut and stay out of it. That's another reason to stay away from her. I don't want her knowing anything about me. Or us."

I sigh. "So there goes our chance at finding a new Harper and Sean."

"We'll find another couple. Maybe Sara will find someone to date and we can go out with them."

"She already did. I forgot to tell you. Some guy asked her out last week. Their first date was yesterday at a coffee shop.

He's 24 and an intern at an architecture firm. She was super excited. I hope the date went well."

"Does this guy know about Caleb?"

"No, but she was going to tell him on their date. She thinks he won't want to date her after she tells him, but I told her sometimes people surprise you. Like you, wanting to date someone like me."

"What do you mean? Because I had money and you didn't? You know I don't care about that shit."

"Yes, but most people do, so you surprised me. And maybe this guy will surprise Sara and be okay with the fact that she has a kid. What do you think?"

"It depends on the guy. If this guy's still in that stage of life where he wants to drink and party all the time, then no, he probably won't want to date someone with a kid."

"I don't think he's like that. At least Sara didn't make him sound like that."

"Then maybe it'll work out. If he's ready for a relationship and feels something for her, then he'll probably want to keep dating her. The problem is, he won't know how he feels about her until after he's been dating her for a while. And he's finding out about Caleb before he has a chance to get to know her. So he may not stick around. He may decide it's too much responsibility."

"But it's not *his* responsibility. It's hers."

"Guys always feel like it's their responsibility. Decent guys, at least. Losers don't give a shit. But if he's a decent guy, he'll want to take care of both Sara and Caleb and that's a big responsibility. This guy she went out with may not want to take that on, especially since he doesn't even know her."

This is why I like talking to Garret about stuff. It's good to get a guy's perspective. But given what he said, now I feel bad for getting Sara's hopes up.

Chapter 8

GARRET

*W*e're home now and Jade goes to the kitchen and gets a glass of water. "That really sucks."

"What sucks?" I meet her at the sink and take a swig of her water.

"That this guy may not give Sara a chance."

"Maybe he will. And if he doesn't, she'll find someone else. She just needs to find the right person. That's true for everyone."

"I know, but—"

"Jade." I place my hands on her shoulders. "She'll find someone. It may not be tomorrow or next week, but eventually she will. So don't worry about it."

"Maybe I should call her and see how it went."

"She takes Caleb to the park every Saturday afternoon."

"That's right. I forgot. I'll call her later."

I tilt her face up and lean down so that our lips are almost touching. "Wasn't there something else you were going to do after lunch?"

"I don't think so," she says, closing her eyes.

"Think harder." I kiss her, slowly, gently.

She smiles, her eyes still closed. "I'm starting to remember. Maybe if you did that again?"

I kiss her again, taking my time, my tongue doing the things I know she likes. My hands are around her face, my fingers buried in her hair. I pull away just enough to say, "You remember now?"

"Yeah." She gives me her sexy smile.

"Let's go." I take her hand.

"Wait. Can we stay here?"

"In the kitchen?"

"I want to kiss some more before we go to the bed. I really like your kisses and we always skip ahead to the other stuff so fast I don't get enough kissing in."

It's true, but only because the kissing gets us both so ready for what comes next that we can't help but keep going. But if she wants more kissing, we'll do more kissing.

I pick her up and set her on the kitchen counter. "You'll be more comfortable this way."

She smiles. "Thanks."

I take my shirt off, then place my hands on her knees and slowly push her legs apart. "I need to get closer. I can't kiss you with your legs in the way."

Just that simple move has got her breathing heavy. I have a feeling we're going to be flying past the kissing stage.

Did I mention she's wearing a skirt? Yeah, that's causing *me* to do some heavy breathing. I slide the fabric of her skirt all the way up her legs.

"I wouldn't want it to get torn, you know, when I'm kissing you." I keep my eyes on hers as I say it.

"No, we wouldn't want that."

Our gazes remained locked on each other as I step between her legs until I'm right up against her. I reach behind her neck, bringing her face to mine, planning to start with a soft, slow kiss. But instead she leans in and kisses me hard and fast as she undoes my belt, then my shorts, and shoves them, and my boxers, to the floor.

Yeah, so much for the kissing.

She scoots to the end of the counter, lifting up just enough for me to take her panties off, then hooks her arms around my neck. I thrust inside her and she starts grinding her hips into me.

Shit, she's really getting into this, even more than she normally does. Must've been seeing Brook flirting with me. Jade always gets like this when a girl flirts with me. She gets all territorial, the same way I do when some guy flirts with *her*.

I love it when she gets this way. I didn't like that bitch flirting with me, but hey, I'm all about turning a negative into a positive. And this is definitely positive.

Jade's got her hips moving so much I have to hold on to her so she doesn't fall off the counter. It's a freaking work-out, but I'm not complaining. I love trying something new and I had no idea I'd be getting this just for winning some carnival games. Thanks again, 13-year-old Garret. You had to wait seven years but your efforts paid off.

I can tell Jade's getting close so I grab her ass and thrust deeper inside her, then pull back and do it again. Jade digs her fingers into my back and moans my name. And there's the sound I love to hear. She gets louder as I keep going, her body tensing up, until moments later, she relaxes into me, her head collapsing on my shoulder, her legs still wrapped around me. I finish up, then bring her to the bedroom and lay her down and lie next to her.

We're both breathing hard and I'm soaked with sweat. I kiss her forehead. "I'm going to take a shower, okay?"

"Yeah." She smiles really wide, her eyes closed.

I laugh. "You happy?"

"Very. I think I'll just lie here a minute."

I glance down and notice her skin is slick with sweat. "You might want to shower, too."

"I will. In a minute."

After we shower, we do the next item on our agenda; studying. We take our books to the deck and study out there. Before Jade dropped those classes, she never would've done this. She wouldn't study outside and she wouldn't study with me. She had to be alone and inside and have complete silence. She said it was the only way she could concentrate. She was so stressed out during those first few weeks of the semester.

But now? She's finally relaxing, her grades are better, and she insists we study together instead of apart. It's a night and day difference.

"Hey." She's holding my hand and lying back in her chair with her feet resting on the table. We both have our textbooks out and have been studying for a couple hours. "What do you want for dinner?"

"I thought I'd grill some burgers. We have some hamburger in the fridge."

"That sounds good." She looks back at her book, then over at me again. "What time do you want to eat?"

I laugh. "Given your question, I'm guessing you want to eat right now."

"Maybe. I *am* kind of hungry."

"I'm hungry, too. I'll get the burgers started." I set my book on the table and get up.

Jade jumps up and hugs me. "I love you."

I wasn't expecting the hug, but it's nice. I hug her back. "I love you, too."

"Garret?" She looks up at me.

"What?"

"I love our life. I love just hanging out here at home with you, studying, or watching TV, or making dinner together. I know most people our age would say it's boring, but it's not to me. I love it. I love every second of it. I wouldn't change a thing."

"I wouldn't either." I hug her again and kiss the top of her head. I don't know what made her say that just now but it's good to hear. More than anything, I want Jade to be happy and it sounds like she is. And I am, too. I still worry about shit, like our safety and people like William dropping into our lives, but I'll always have to worry about that. That'll never change. But if you take those things out of the equation, I'm happier than I've ever been. Living with Jade, being married to her, going to school together. It's great.

Before I met Jade, I thought my college years would consist of drinking every night and having sex with random girls. I didn't think I'd have a girlfriend. I didn't want one.

And now I'm married and spending Saturday night grilling burgers with my wife. But like Jade said, I love our life. I wouldn't change a thing.

She reaches up and kisses me. "I'll get the burgers ready if you want to start the grill."

"Sounds good."

She goes inside and I walk around to the driveway. I have the grill by the garage. As I'm scraping the grates, my dad calls.

"Hey, Dad. Staying home tonight?"

"No, Katherine and I are leaving in a few minutes to attend a dinner party for Kent Gleason."

"Where's it at?"

"Your grandfather's house."

"No shit? He never hosts those things. He always makes you do it."

"In his new position, he's required to host this event. Plus, this isn't for just anyone. Kent could be our next president."

"Yeah, wouldn't that be a shock?" I say it sarcastically since we both know Gleason will win the election. The organization will make sure of it. "So who's watching Lilly? Or is she going with you?"

"She's going with us, but we can't have her at the party so Harper's going to watch her. She's meeting us here at the house in a few minutes and we'll all ride over together."

"I'm surprised Harper agreed to that on a Saturday night. Usually she's out with Sean."

"I believe he had to work. Anyway, Harper was thrilled when I called and asked her to babysit. And Lilly's excited to see her."

"So is that why you called? To tell me about Harper?"

"No, I was calling because I spoke with your grandfather about William. He said there was nothing to be concerned about. Of course, he was talking in the context of my offering William the board seat, but given how much my father values Kensington Chemical, he'd never allow William to even be considered for the board unless his record was clear."

"But now you have to offer him the position."

"I'd planned to anyway. William will be a good addition to the board."

"Then you're saying I don't need to worry. Jade can go visit him?"

"You'd be going as well?"

"Well, yeah, of course."

"Then I wouldn't worry. But I would stay away from Walt. I can't say for sure what he's done but—"

"Yeah, I got it." I interrupt him when I see Jade coming toward me with the burgers.

"Here they are." She hands them to me.

I give her the phone. "It's my dad. Say hi while I put the burgers on."

"Hi, Pearce."

Jade listens, then starts laughing at whatever he's saying. Those two get along better than I ever thought they would. I thought my dad would tolerate Jade, at best, but now he loves her like a daughter.

"I need to wash my hands," I tell Jade as I head inside. She nods.

When I come back out, she tells my dad goodbye and hands me the phone.

"Did you tell her all my childhood secrets?" I ask him.

"No, I'm saving those for Christmas."

"Great." I laugh. "I'll talk to you later. Tell Grandmother I said hi. And say hi to Grandfather for me, too."

"I will." My dad's tone changes. It's quiet, almost sad. It means my grandparents still have no interest in having a relationship with me. "Goodbye, Garret."

"Bye." I hang up and finish cooking the burgers.

Jade and I eat dinner outside, then watch a couple movies before going to bed.

Around 2:30 in the morning I wake up and Jade's not there. I woke up earlier and heard her get up to go to the bathroom but I don't know if she ever came back. I fell asleep before she did. And now she's in there again, or maybe she never left. Shit, I hope she doesn't have the flu again.

The bathroom door is closed but I see light coming from underneath it. So she must be in there, but I don't hear anything. No water running. No toilet flushing. Nothing.

I get out of bed and stand by the bathroom door. "Jade? Are you okay?"

She doesn't answer but I hear her making some kind of noise. I'm not sure what.

"Jade, can I come in?" I lightly knock on the door a few times. She still doesn't answer. Something's wrong. "I'm coming in, okay?"

I slowly open the door and see her sitting on the bathroom floor, leaning against the wall, hugging her knees to her chest, her head bent down. She's quietly crying and from the pile of crumpled up tissues on the floor, I'm guessing she's been crying for a while. Physically, she seems to be okay. She's not vomiting. She doesn't appear to be sick.

"Jade." I sit down next to her and stroke her hair. "What's wrong?"

She shakes her head, raising it enough for me to see her red, tear-filled eyes. "I can't."

"You can't what?"

"I can't do this."

"Do what?"

She drops her head to her knees and cries, her shoulders shaking.

I put my arm around her. "Jade, what can't you do? I don't understand. Is this about your classes?"

There's no answer. Just more tears.

"You can't take a test? You're not ready for it? Is that what you mean?"

"It's not…" She takes a breath. "It's not about school."

"Then what's wrong? Tell me, Jade."

"I can't."

"Why not? You can tell me anything. You know that."

"Because if I tell you, it might be real." She sniffles. "And it can't be real."

"What can't be real?" This is so frustrating. It's like the old Jade from last year. The one who was so hard to read. The one who tried to hide everything from me so I was left constantly guessing what it was she needed and hoping I got it right.

"Just talk to me, Jade. Tell me what's wrong."

The only answer I get are more tears. I hug her into my side and she lays her head on my shoulder. I notice something sitting next to her on the floor. I reach over and pick it up. It's a small calendar with last Tuesday circled in red marker.

"What's this?" I hold it in front of her.

"Don't look at that!" She snatches it from me and tosses it across the bathroom floor.

"Jade, why do you have a calendar in the bathroom?"

She says nothing as she sits back against the wall again, hugging her knees.

I'm so confused. I have no freaking clue what's going on here. Was that date she circled some kind of anniversary? It's not the day her mom died. It's not the day her grandparents died. It's not any kind of anniversary for Jade and me. So what the hell's the significance of that day?

I move in front of her. "What happened last Tuesday?"

"I told you I can't talk about it. Not right now. Just go to bed."

"I'm not going anywhere until you tell me what's going on. Now tell me what happened last Tuesday."

"Nothing! Don't you get it?"

"No, I don't. I don't understand."

"It's always the same," she says, her voice shaky. "It's like clockwork. Every 28 days. It never changes. It hasn't since I was 13."

I'm really tired, but the 28-day thing sticks in my head. What's 28 days? And she said it's always the same. What's always the same and 28 days?

Her period.

She's late.

Her period was supposed to be last Tuesday and now it's Sunday. Normally I don't even think about this. Jade just takes care of it. She doesn't talk about her period or cramps or PMS. I don't even think she gets PMS. If she does, she doesn't talk about it and it's not like she gets all cranky before her period, the way some girls do. If it weren't for the fact that we don't have sex on those days, I wouldn't even know she was having her period.

She's late. She's never late.

Holy shit. No wonder she's freaking out.

She's sitting cross-legged now, her head bent down, tears dripping on the floor.

I take both her hands and gently hold them. "Jade. It's just a few days. You'll probably get it today or tomorrow."

"No. You don't understand. It's never late. Not even a day."

"So maybe your body's changing. Or maybe this month, you're just a little off. That happens, right?"

"Not when you're on the pill. The pills make it regular and for me it's every 28 days."

I guess I knew that, but I was trying to find a reason for her being late. A reason that would change the outcome.

"So what are you saying?"

It's such a stupid question and I regret even asking it, but before I can say anything else, Jade finally lifts her head and looks at me.

"I'm pregnant." As soon as she says it, her eyes tear up and the crying continues.

I take her into my arms. "You don't know that, Jade."

"Yes, I do. There's no other explanation."

"You're on the pill. It's almost a hundred percent effective."

"Yeah, 'almost' is the key word. It's not a hundred percent. Just ask Sara. She got pregnant on the pill. She said she never missed a day and she still got pregnant."

Jade never told me that. Sara really got pregnant on the pill? So I guess it *does* happen.

"I didn't take it every day." Jade says it so quietly I could barely make out the words.

"You didn't take your pill every day?"

"When I had the flu, I forgot to take it. I was so sick I didn't even think about it."

Shit. I didn't think about it either. Not that I would. I'm so used to her taking over the pregnancy prevention part of our relationship that I didn't think to remind her to take it when she was sick. Not that it would've mattered. She would've thrown it up anyway.

"We should've been using condoms." She's staring at the floor. "We should've been using them all last month. If we had, this wouldn't have happened."

"Jade, you don't know for sure if anything's happened. You need to take a pregnancy test."

Her head jerks up and she grabs my arm. "Go get me one! Go to the store right now. I have to know. I can't wait until morning."

"Nothing's open. The drugstores closed at midnight. We don't have any 24-hour stores around here. But they open at six. I'll go then, okay? I'll go as soon as they open."

"What time is it now?"

"It's 2:30."

"So I have to wait three and a half hours? That's a long time."

"I know. But I'm right here." I hug her into me. "I won't leave your side."

She nods.

"Let's go back to bed." I help her stand up and she walks with me back to the bed.

We get under the covers and just lie there quietly. She's huddled against me, her cheek against my chest.

After a long period of silence, she says, "Are you mad at me?"

"Of course not." I try to pull away a little to look at her but she won't let me. She tightens her arm around my chest and keeps her head down.

"I'm mad at myself. So I understand if you're mad at me, too."

"I'm not mad at you."

"I screwed up, Garret. I wasn't thinking."

"You were sick. You weren't supposed to be thinking. You were supposed to be resting and getting better."

"I still should've thought about it. When I got better I should've thought about it and been more careful. Now it's too late and I'm pregnant."

"We don't know that yet."

"But what if I am?" She still won't look at me and it's hard to hear what she's saying with her face buried in the fabric of my shirt. "What are we going to do, Garret?"

"I guess we're gonna have a baby."

Saying it causes a bolt of sheer panic to course through my chest. A baby? Now? We're only 20. I'm not ready for a baby. And I know Jade isn't.

It's not like we couldn't handle having a baby. We have plenty of money. But it would change everything. And I don't mean stuff like how much sleep we get or how we spend our free time. I can handle those changes. What I mean is it would change how we live. Where we go. Who we trust. I worry enough about Jade. Add a baby to that? A helpless infant? Shit! I can't even imagine. I couldn't let it out of my sight.

We'd definitely have to move to a safer place. A place with a gate and maybe some armed guards. Even though nobody's bothered us and we're probably safe, it's different when you have a kid. There's that protective instinct that takes over and you'll do anything and everything to keep them safe. And that's exactly what I'd do. But I don't want to have to do that. Not yet. Not now. Then again, maybe I won't have a choice.

Six o'clock can't come fast enough.

Chapter 9

JADE

A couple hours ago I woke up to go to the bathroom. The toilet paper roll was empty so I reached in the cabinet to get a new one and saw a box of tampons sitting there. And that's when I realized I never got my period. I should've had it last week but it never came. I totally forgot about it. Everything was so crazy with William coming here and then I was stressing out about Walt showing up again and I had a paper due and a big exam for my chem class. Then Garret and I were out of town, so the week just went by and I didn't realize I was late.

After I saw those tampons, I raced into the kitchen and got the calendar we keep next to the fridge and a red marker from the drawer. I took them back to the bathroom and counted back to my last period. I counted again and again, hoping I'd counted wrong. But I hadn't. My period should've been last Tuesday. It's almost a week late and I'm never late.

I circled the date and just stared at it, wondering how this could've happened. And then wondering how I'd tell Garret. He trusts me to take care of this stuff. The not-getting-pregnant part of our relationship. I know he wants kids, but I also know he doesn't want them right now, while we're still in college. I don't want that either. That's why I should've been more careful. I was supposed to take care of this and I messed up.

When he found me in the bathroom, I wasn't ready to tell him. I couldn't say the words. And I didn't, until he forced me to. After I told him, I couldn't tell what he was thinking. He didn't really say much, other than to tell me that maybe I wasn't pregnant. Maybe I was just late. His reaction just confirmed he doesn't want this. It's not the right time. We're too young. We're still in school.

Now he's lying beside me, not saying anything. I wonder what he's thinking. How he feels about this. As for me, my emotions are all over the place; a continuous cycle of anger, disappointment, sadness, shame, and guilt.

The anger and disappointment are aimed at myself for causing the situation I was put in charge to prevent.

I'm sad because my life may soon completely change and I don't want it to. Growing up, I had to take care of my mom like she was a child and I was the mom. But now, I don't have to take care of anyone and I like not having all that responsibility. I love my life being just Garret and me and I don't want a baby coming in and changing everything. And that's what causes me to feel the shame and the guilt. Because it's not this baby's fault I screwed up. It's *my* fault and I have to accept that and get over it and be the best mom I can be. I just don't know how. I can't do it. I know I can't. I'm too messed up right now. I have too many issues I need to deal with before I can even think about being a mom.

As much as I've tried to get rid of her, my mom is still in my head. Not all the time, but enough that I know I'm not over my past. Which means there's no way I can be a mom. Not now. What if I did something bad? What if I hurt the baby? I've had nightmares about it. I had nightmares where the baby was crying and it was so loud and it wouldn't stop and I couldn't take it so I turned into my mom and starting screaming and throwing things at the crib.

"Jade?" Garret's rubbing my back as I cling to his chest.

I'm panicking now. Completely panicking as I think about being a mom.

"I can't do this, Garret."

"Do what?"

"I can't have a baby."

He's quiet, then says, "Well, if you're pregnant, then you're having one."

"I can't. I can't do it."

"What are you saying?"

"I just can't do it."

"What the hell does that mean?" He raises his voice and moves back, forcing me off him. "We're not getting rid of it!"

"That's not what I'm saying. I'll have it, but I can't be a mom."

"What? You're not even making sense."

"I can't ruin someone else's life the way my life was ruined. I won't do it. I'll leave the baby with you and then—I'll go away." Just the thought of that makes tears well up in my eyes, but I don't have another solution.

"That's crazy! You're not leaving me! And you're not leaving our baby. Why the fuck would you even say something like that?"

"I can't be around a baby. I don't trust myself. I'll get mad and I'll turn into her." Tears pour from my eyes as my mind replays the images from my nightmares. "I won't be able to stop."

"Jade." Garret sits up and pulls me into his arms. "Your mom was drugged and an alcoholic. That's what made her that way. You'll never be like her."

"You don't know that, Garret! I'm messed up because of her. Because of what she said to me over and over again. And how she treated me. You don't understand because you weren't there! You don't know what it was like!"

I struggle to get away from him, tears running down my face. He holds onto my shaking body, rubbing my back until I finally calm down enough to speak again.

"She made me this way and it all started when I was just a baby. In my psych class, we were learning how babies are affected by the smallest things. Like if you don't hug a baby, they're messed up for life."

"You'll hug the baby, Jade. I'm not worried about that."

"That's not the point. The point is that it doesn't take much to screw up a kid. And I guarantee I'll do it."

"Parents aren't perfect. They all make mistakes. And yet most of us manage to make it through our childhoods and come out okay, including you."

I push away from him. "Why aren't you listening to me? I can't do this, okay? You knew I didn't want to be a mom. I've told you this repeatedly."

"And it's a lie. I saw you with Caleb and I've seen you with Lilly. You want that, Jade. You want kids. You just won't admit it to yourself."

Sometimes I hate that he knows me so well. He's right. I love being around Caleb and Lilly and I love the idea of Garret and me having kids. But it's just an idea. A dream. It's not real life. In real life, I can't be a mom.

"Even if I wanted them, I can't have them, okay? I'm too messed up."

He puts his hands on my shoulders, his eyes on mine. "Okay, first of all, if you're pregnant, you're having one. *We're* having one. And second, stop saying you're messed up, because you're not."

"Yes, I am. I have so many issues, Garret. You don't know because I don't tell you about them. I don't want you to know."

He lets go of me and sits back a little. "What are you talking about? What issues?"

"I can't explain it."

"You need to explain it because I'm not letting this go."

I don't know what to tell him. I'm not even sure what all my issues are. I just know I have them and I don't know how to fix them.

"Just tell me what you're struggling with, Jade. Just one thing."

"I can't control my emotions sometimes. I get really angry or really sad and it just takes over and I lose control of it. That's why I have to run."

"Then we'll deal with that. We'll work on it together."

"We've tried and it doesn't work."

He sighs. "Then you need to talk to someone. A counselor. A psychologist. Someone who can help you get through this stuff."

"I did that after my mom died and it didn't work."

"You never gave it a chance. You said you only went a few times and that you wouldn't say anything."

"Because it doesn't work. I don't like talking to a stranger."

"I don't either, but *I* did it. Even my dad went to a counselor. And look how much he's changed."

"They'll try to give me pills. They'll drug me just like my mom."

"I won't let them." He moves the hair off my face and slips it behind my ear, leaving his hand there. "If you want, I'll sit in the room with you. I'll go to every session."

He has me considering it. It's not like I haven't thought about seeing someone. I just can't seem to make myself do it. I'd rather figure this out myself. Deal with my problems on my own. Except it's not working. I'm a lot better than I was a year ago, but deep down, I know there's still so much I need to work on. Mostly my anger. Anger at my mom for taking away my childhood and leaving me with all this pain that I have to try to cover up and pretend doesn't exist. Anger at her for leaving me when I had no one else in the world. Anger at her for saying all those hateful words that still linger in my head. I don't know how to get past all that so maybe someone else could help.

"Jade, would you just try it? Please?"

I nod. "Yes."

He hugs me really tight, like he's relieved I agreed to it. He probably wanted me to see a counselor a long time ago but didn't want to bring it up because he knew I'd say no. And I wanted to say no just now, but I feel like I need to do this. I at least need to try.

When he lets me go, I hold on to him and whisper, "I'm scared. Not just of seeing a counselor, but of having a baby."

"I know." He kisses my forehead. "But you shouldn't be. There's nothing to be scared of. I'm right here, and whatever happens you won't be going through it alone. You'll always have me. We're a team and we go through stuff together."

I sit back and see his face in the moonlight coming through the window. "Are you scared? Of having a baby?"

"I'm not prepared for it, but it doesn't scare me."

"Does anything scare you?"

"Yes."

"What?"

His eyes lock on mine. "Losing you. So don't you ever say you're going to leave me. Don't even joke about it. And if you really feel that way, talk to me. Don't just get up and leave one day. Don't do that to me. You promise?"

"Yes. I promise."

The room gets silent again and then he says, "Do you want to try to get some sleep?"

"I'll try, but I'm sure I won't. Did you set the alarm?"

"I set the one on my phone."

"Okay. Goodnight. I love you."

"I love you, too."

Hours later I'm still awake. I might have drifted off for a few minutes but I didn't get more than a half hour of sleep total. Instead I lie awake thinking about everything related to having a baby; being pregnant, giving birth, how to change a diaper, how to feed a baby, how to get a baby to sleep, how to fit a crib in our bedroom....

My mind never stops and then, finally, the alarm on Garret's phone goes off. It's 5:45.

Garret actually got some sleep so he's a little groggy. "It's time already?"

"Yeah. It's 5:45. Do you want me to make some coffee while you get ready?"

"No, I'll just go." He stumbles out of bed and puts on jeans and a sweatshirt. He yanks on some shoes, then he's out the door in the still-dark morning. He'll probably be the first person there when the drugstore opens.

I don't even know how pregnancy tests work. I know you pee on a stick and wait, but how accurate are they? And is it too soon to use one? Maybe I should look it up on the Internet. But then I'll be bombarded with ads and information about pregnancy and babies and I'll get even more nervous.

I don't know how Sara got through this. I really don't. If it weren't for Garret, I'd be going crazy right now instead of only half-crazy. And if I had to go through a pregnancy all alone? At my age? That would really suck. Sara's boyfriend was around when she was pregnant, so maybe he was somewhat supportive. Probably not. He sounds like a real ass. Leaving her with no money and not even wanting to see his son. And yet Sara managed to get through it all and now she's raising Caleb with no help from anyone. I don't know how she does it. She's amazing.

Garret returns with three boxes of pregnancy tests. "I didn't know which one to get so I got them all."

"I'll start with this one." I take one of the boxes into the bathroom and read the instructions. The box has two sticks so I pee on both of them and wait. I open the door and Garret's standing there, the color slowly draining from his face. Yeah, he's not scared. Whatever.

"I'm still waiting," I tell him.

He comes in the bathroom and we both stand over the sticks, which are sitting on the counter. And then finally, the results appear on one and then the other. I check the instructions again, just to make I'm reading the sticks right.

"I'm not pregnant!" I jump up and down.

Garret doesn't say anything, but the color returns to his face as he takes a deep breath and lets it out.

"Give me the other ones. I'm trying them all."

He hands me the other two boxes, then goes and waits in the bedroom.

I take the tests and get the same result. Negative.

"I'm so relieved." I collapse on the bed next to Garret.

"You should still go to the doctor."

"I will. I want a blood test to be absolutely sure."

"Not just that. I want you to find out why you're so late. Make sure there's nothing wrong."

"I'm sure there's not. My body probably just got off cycle when I didn't take that pill."

"I want you to go first thing Monday morning. I'll go with you."

I agree to it, and a few minutes later I fall asleep. I don't wake up until one in the afternoon.

Garret isn't in bed. I hear the TV on in the living room. The volume is really low, but it sounds like he's watching a football game.

I go in the bathroom and close the door. The test sticks are still there, lined up on the counter. I throw them all in the trash. Then I take a long hot shower and get dressed.

I feel better now that I've had some sleep and it's light out. For some reason, everything seems worse in the middle of the night when it's quiet and dark. Now it's bright and sunny and Garret opened the bedroom windows and a cool, fresh breeze is blowing in. I close my eyes and take some deep breaths.

"You want something to eat?"

I open my eyes and see Garret standing at the bedroom door.

"I'll just have cereal." I give him a quick hug on my way to the kitchen. "How long have you been up?"

"Since nine. I had homework for accounting. It's due tomorrow."

"Did you get it done?" I grab a bowl and fill it with cereal.

Garret gets the milk from the fridge. "Yeah, I finished it."

He walks back to the couch and sits in front of the TV. He's acting strange. Kind of cold and distant.

I take my bowl of cereal to the couch. "Who's playing?"

"The Cowboys and the Chiefs."

"You don't like those teams, do you?"

He shrugs. "Doesn't matter. It's still football."

I eat my cereal and he watches the game like I'm not even there. When I'm done eating, I take my bowl to the sink, then come back and sit next to him.

"You want to do something today?"

"Not really." He doesn't look at me. He just stares at the TV.

"Why not?"

"I just don't." He turns the volume up on the TV. The announcer says something as the crowd makes booing sounds. "That was a bad call. That guy was totally out of bounds."

"Do you want me to leave? You seem really into this game."

"Do whatever you want."

He's totally blowing me off and I don't know why.

"What's wrong? Are you mad at me?"

"I'm just trying to watch the game."

I snatch the remote from him and turn the TV off. "Why are you mad at me?"

"Give me the remote back." He holds his hand out.

"No. We're talking about this. Tell me what's wrong with you."

"Why? Are you saying you don't like it when I act like this and you don't understand why? When I don't tell you what's going on and you're left trying to guess?"

He's trying to prove some kind of point but I'm not getting it. I'm too out of it from last night.

"Just say it, Garret. Tell me what's wrong."

"It's frustrating, isn't it? When I leave you in the dark, wondering what I'm thinking?"

"Yeah, it is. So stop this and just tell me."

He moves back on the couch and turns to face me. "You're done hiding shit from me, Jade."

"I'm not hiding anything from you."

"Oh, really? Because last night you told me you had all these issues you're dealing with that you haven't told me about. Me. Your husband. Your best friend. The person you're supposed to tell everything to."

"That's because I—"

"And if that's not bad enough, last night you thought you were pregnant and you went and hid in the bathroom. You didn't even wake me up to tell me. I had to go in there and find you crying on the floor. And instead of telling me what was wrong, you told me to leave. And when I wouldn't leave, you made me guess what was wrong. You still wouldn't tell me. What the fuck does that say about us, Jade?"

"It doesn't say *anything*. I was just scared. I was afraid to tell you."

"Why? Why would you be afraid to tell me?"

I look down at the couch. "Because I thought you'd get mad at me. I was supposed to prevent that from happening and I screwed up."

"Why the hell would I get mad about that? Accidents happen. The pill's not a hundred percent. We have sex all the freaking time. Pregnancy is always a possibility and if it happens, it happens. This may not have been the best time to have a baby but we would've made it work." He puts his hand under my chin and lifts my face up to his. "Listen to me. I would never get mad at you for getting pregnant. And I would never blame you for it. So don't ever use that as an excuse not to tell me."

"It's not just that."

His hand drops from my face and he sits back and waits for me to continue.

"I couldn't tell you because I wasn't ready to. I needed time to think. I was a mess last night. I was scared and panicked and—"

"Which is why you should've told me, Jade. And why you should've woke me up as soon as you thought you might be pregnant. You shouldn't be sitting alone on the bathroom floor crying in the middle of the night when I was right there, just a few feet away."

It's true, and I don't know why I didn't go get him. I think it's more out of habit than anything else. I'm so used to not having anyone that when something like this happens, I shut down and turn into the old Jade. The one who did everything alone. The one who couldn't count on anyone. I've only had one year with the new Jade and 19 years with the old, so sometimes I find myself acting like her again.

Growing up, I was terrified of making my mom mad and I think I sometimes project that onto Garret. Like he's going to react like my mom did, and scream at me if I do something wrong. I know he won't, and yet part of me really did worry he'd get mad at me if I was pregnant.

"Jade." He waits until our eyes meet. "I don't know what else I can do to make you open up to me. I tell you all the time how much I love you and how I'll always support you and help you in any way I can. But it's like you refuse to believe me."

"That's not true. There's just some things you can't help me with."

"Like what?"

"I don't know. Just stuff I need to work out in my head."

"And you think this stuff doesn't affect me? You think it has nothing to do with me? You seriously think that?"

He sounds angry and frustrated. I can tell this has been bothering him for a while, but he hasn't said anything about it until now. He was probably afraid to because he knows I won't react well if he brings it up.

"Jade, ever since we got married, I've wanted to talk to you about us having kids. Just talk. That's it. But I can't, because I know you won't talk about it with me. You'll say you're not ready to, or that you have to deal with it on your own, or that it has nothing to do with me. But it *does* have to do with me. I'm part of this decision, Jade, and yet you act like I'm not."

"I told you when we were dating that I didn't want kids. This isn't a surprise to you. And now I'm starting to change my mind, but I'm not ready to make a decision. I don't know why you're rushing me to when neither one of us is ready to have a baby."

"I'm not rushing you. I just want you to talk about it. I want us to talk about it together, because this isn't only about you."

"I know it's not, but we *both* have to want kids. I can't make a decision based only on what *you* want."

"Yes. I know that. And if I knew you really didn't want kids, I would be okay with that. I could accept that. But I know it's not true. I know you're just telling yourself you don't want them because you're afraid to have them. And I'm not going to let your fears be the reason why we don't have a family someday. You can get over your fears."

"I'm not sure if I can."

"I *know* you can. I've watched you do it. When I first met you, you tried to act like you were so strong. Like you didn't need anyone. But once I got to know you, I could see you were just acting that way to cover up how scared you were to get close to people. I didn't understand everything going on with you back then, but when you finally stopped hiding behind your fears and let people in, you were so much happier. And now look at you. Your entire life has changed."

I nod, but don't say anything so he continues.

"And with the whole med school thing, you were so afraid to let people down. But once you got past that fear and dropped those classes and stopped pursuing something you didn't even want to do, didn't you feel better? Weren't you happier?"

"Yes. A lot happier."

"And don't you want that happiness to continue? Because it will, Jade. If you stop being afraid and if you deal with whatever's causing you to have those fears, you'll be even happier than you are right now." He moves closer to me on the couch and holds my hand. "If you had no fears about being a mom, does the idea of us having kids make you happy?"

I take a moment to think about it, but I don't need to. I know how I feel.

"Yes." I look at him. "I love you, and you're the best husband ever, and I know you'd be the greatest dad ever."

"But what about *you*, Jade? If you set your fears aside and you imagine yourself with kids, how do you feel?"

I close my eyes and picture it. I've done this before but my fears are always clouding the picture. If I let those fears go, it looks different. It *feels* different.

"I feel happy." I open my eyes. "Even last night, when I was thinking about having a baby, part of me was happy about it. Part of me wanted it." I look away, then back at Garret. "It's not like I don't think about this. I do. I think about it a lot. And in my head, I see us all together. You and me and our kids, and it feels right. It makes me happy. But then I see myself actually being a mom and I can't do it. I panic just thinking about it. And I don't talk to you about it because you can't help. And I don't just mean with the kid thing. I mean with all of it."

"How do you know that when you won't even give me a chance?"

"It's not that I—" I stop, not wanting to say it.

"Jade." He rubs my hand with his thumb. "Tell me."

"The truth is…I don't want you knowing. I don't want you knowing what goes on in my head. I don't want you knowing how hard I have to work to keep the voices from coming back. How hard I have to work to keep the memories from replaying in my mind."

"I want to know that stuff, Jade. I'm your husband. I *need* to know."

"I don't want you to. I don't want you thinking I'm that same broken girl from last year. Because I'm not. And I'm trying really hard to get past this. I don't want my mom to affect me anymore. I don't want her to have that kind of power over me. But then sometimes I feel like she still does and I can't make it stop."

"Jade, you should've told me you were going through all this. I want to be here for you but I can't when you shut me out. I know you say you don't want help, but dealing with that stuff on your own doesn't make you stronger. It makes you weaker because you just go in circles and never get past it."

I nod and slump down in his arms.

He wraps them around me and kisses the side of my head. "I love you. And I will do whatever I can to help you get through this. I don't care if it takes 20 years. Or more than that. I'm not going anywhere. Ever. So don't ever be afraid to tell me these things, okay?"

I nod again and wipe my eyes.

"But, Jade." He waits until I look at him. "I was serious about what I said last night. I want you to talk to someone. You've already tried doing this on your own. Now you need to try letting someone help you with this. Not just me, but someone else. A counselor."

"I'll think about it, but I'm not—"

"Jade, stop. I know you, and I know you could come up with a thousand excuses for why you shouldn't go, but I'm asking you to just try it."

I sigh. "Fine. I'll try it." I sit back and give him my annoyed smile. "You're just full of advice today, aren't you?"

He smiles back. "I can keep it going. We've got all day."

"No, I need a break. You're starting to make my head hurt."

"You want to go get something to eat? I'm sure that cereal didn't do much for you."

"I could eat something." I thread my hand with his. "Are you still mad at me?"

"No, but I *will* be if you keep shutting me out. We're going to keep talking about this stuff, Jade. This isn't a one-time thing."

"I know." I look down at our hands, then back at him. "Can I ask you something?"

"Go ahead."

"When you thought I might be pregnant, were you at all happy? Or were you just freaking out?"

"At first I was freaking out, but once I got past the initial shock and let it sink in that it could be a possibility, then yes, I was happy. The timing would've totally sucked but I knew we could handle it." He smiles. "And the idea of holding a tiny version of you in my arms made me very happy. Just think how cute she'd be."

"What if it was a tiny Garret?"

"I'd still be happy, but a tiny version of me wouldn't be nearly as cute."

"I disagree. I think a baby Garret would be very cute."

He hugs me into his side and kisses my head. "Maybe someday we'll find out."

"Yeah. Maybe."

Chapter 10

GARRET

*F*inally. Jade and I finally had a real conversation about kids. And about all the other stuff she'd been hiding from me.

I feel like we made real progress today. And it all started with Jade thinking she's pregnant. I still can't believe that happened. We were having such a great weekend and then all of a sudden, it switched course, heading down a completely different track.

But it ended up being good. We need to work on this stuff now and not wait. I feel like this was a huge step in moving our relationship forward. If Jade can finally deal with all the shit that holds her back, that holds us *both* back, we'll be even happier than we are now.

I always told myself I wouldn't push Jade to deal with stuff, but last night I'd had enough. When she hid in the bathroom and wouldn't tell me what was going on, I was pissed. I didn't think I was at the time. I was too focused on trying to figure out what was wrong with her. But later, when I thought about it, I was so angry at her. She thinks she's pregnant and she doesn't tell me? Her husband? What the hell?

And then when she acted like she wanted to get rid of it, I almost lost it. I seriously almost blew up at her. Luckily that's not what she meant, but then, when she told me she was going to leave the baby with me and disappear, I almost lost it again. It took everything in me not to scream at her and ask her what the fuck is wrong with her. You don't just up and leave because you're scared to be a mom.

After she said that, I knew I couldn't sit on the sidelines anymore. I couldn't wait for her to come to her own conclusion that she needed help. Professional help. If I continued to do nothing, I'd be spending the next few years watching Jade self-destruct. And I won't do that. She may hate me for making her see a counselor but I don't care. She's doing it. She's going to battle these demons from her past once and for all. I know that won't happen overnight. It's a process and it may take years, but like I told her, I'll never give up on her. I love her and I want her to have a full and happy life, but she'll never have that unless she deals with all the stuff from her past.

After our talk, Jade and I go out for a late lunch. When we get back, we take a walk on the beach. We go for about a mile, then turn around. As we're walking back, we see our neighbors, the ones who live in the house that was robbed. They look like they're in their fifties. Jade and I have never met them before. I've never even seen them before today.

"Hey." I wave at the guy. His wife didn't see us. When I waved she was already going inside the house.

The guy waves back at us.

"Let's go talk to him," I say to Jade.

We walk over there and the man comes up to me. "Are you one of my neighbors?"

"Yeah, we live in that one down there." I point to our house.

"I've seen you a few times on the beach. I wasn't sure if you lived here or were just visiting someone. I'm David." He shakes my hand.

"I'm Garret. And this is Jade."

He notices how young we are and gives us this look like he's trying to figure out our story.

I help him out a little. "We got married in July. We both go to Camsburg."

He smiles at both of us. "It's a good school."

"Yeah, it is. So do you live here year-round?"

"No, we just come here in the summer and a few weekends during the year. This is our vacation home. We like the area. It's quiet. Safe."

"Yeah, we thought so, too, until the robbery. But we're hoping it was just an isolated incident."

"There was a robbery?" He tenses up. "When did it happen?"

I'm confused. He doesn't know his house was robbed?

"Labor Day weekend," I tell him.

"Who was robbed?"

I look at Jade, then back at the guy. "Did you just buy this place?"

"No, I've owned it for 20 years."

"And you weren't robbed over Labor Day weekend?"

"That weekend we were out of town at a family reunion, but when we got back everything was fine. Nobody robbed us. Maybe you're thinking of someone else."

"A police officer came to our door and said you'd been robbed," Jade tells him.

He shakes his head. "No. It wasn't us."

I watch his face to see if he's lying, but I don't think he is. He looks like he has no idea what we're talking about. I know the cop who came to our door was fake but I assumed the robbery was real.

"I guess the officer was confused," I say. "It must've been someone else."

"I'm glad you told me. I might have to consider getting a security system."

I take Jade's hand. "We need to go, but it was good to meet you."

"Nice meeting you, too." He walks back to his house and Jade and I continue down the beach.

"He wasn't robbed?" Jade asks. "That doesn't make sense. That cop said it was the yellow house. There's only one yellow house on the entire beach."

"Wait until we get inside. I need to tell you something."

I wasn't going to tell Jade about the fake cop but I have to now. She needs to know what's going on. I should've told her as soon as I found out. What if the fake cop had stopped by when I wasn't home? Jade would've let him into our place. She thought he was a real cop. Shit, I didn't even think about that.

We get back and Jade goes to the kitchen to get some water. "What did you want to tell me?"

"That cop who came to our door wasn't a real cop. He was just some guy impersonating a police officer."

"When did you find this out?"

"On your birthday. I called my dad on the way to class that morning and he mentioned something about that police officer being really young. That's when I realized that old guy who came to our door wasn't a real officer."

"How did your dad know about the cop?"

"Ever since we heard about the robbery, my dad's had his people investigating it. He wanted to see the police report and find out more about the burglar. I told him that cop who came to our door was acting strange so my dad had the cop checked out as well. And it's a good thing he did or we never would've known that guy was a fake."

"Why didn't you tell me this?"

"Because it would've ruined your birthday."

"You could've told me later."

"I didn't want to scare you if it turned out to be nothing."

"Great. So you get to hide stuff from me, but I can't hide anything from you?"

"Jade, it's not at all comparable."

She rolls her eyes. "Whatever. Continue."

"My dad couldn't find the police report. Now that makes sense because apparently there was never a robbery."

"Then who was the guy in the white car? The one who got killed?"

"My dad said the cops arrested that guy and were holding him on other charges. But then you saw him on campus so either they let him go or someone paid his bail."

"What were the charges they held him on? What did he do?"

"They arrested him for robbing a convenience store, but he had a long record. He'd been charged with rape and attempted murder."

Jade shudders. "And that guy was right there when I was running that day. It was just him and me. He could've done something."

"That's why I keep telling you not to run alone. At least he's gone now. He must've been involved in some bad shit since someone wanted him dead."

"You said it was a drug deal gone bad."

"That's what I'm guessing, but who knows? It could've been anything."

"So going back to the fake cop, what does that mean? Why would a fake cop show up at our door to tell us about a fake robbery?"

"I have no idea. Maybe someone just wanted to scare us."

"Well, it worked."

"Nothing's happened for weeks so whatever this was, maybe it's over."

"I hope so."

I don't think it is, but since I don't know what's going on, I don't want to worry Jade. She has enough to deal with.

Monday morning, we go to Student Health Services right when they open. You don't need an appointment and Jade wanted to get this over with. The place is empty and she goes right in to see the doctor. She wanted to go in alone first so I'm sitting in the waiting room. On the table next to me there's a bowl of free condoms next to some brochures about STDs. I'm glad I don't have to worry about that anymore.

My phone vibrates just as I'm reading a sign that says 'All cell phones must be turned off.' I go outside to answer it.

"Garret? It's Harper."

"Hey, what's up?"

"I wanted to talk to Jade but her phone's off. I thought she didn't have class on Monday mornings."

"She doesn't, but she was sleeping in this morning. That's probably why her phone's off."

I'm not going to tell Harper what's really going on. Jade needs to tell her.

"Then I guess I'll try her later. I just wanted to see what she thought of Brook. You guys had lunch on Saturday, right?"

"Yeah, we did."

"So did they get along?"

I might as well be honest with Harper. I know she used to be friends with Brook, but I'm not going to lie for that girl. Harper should know the truth about her.

"Jade tried, but Brook ignored her the entire time. As soon as we sat down, she talked on her phone and she kept talking on it through our entire lunch."

"Really?" Harper sighs. "I can't believe she did that. She wasn't like that in high school. I mean, we weren't best friends or anything but she was never that rude."

"Well, she was rude on Saturday. She barely talked to Jade." I don't tell Harper that Brook flirted with me. She doesn't need to know that part.

"Garret, I'm so sorry."

"It's not your fault."

"It kind of is. I made you guys go out with them. How was Dylan? Was he rude, too?"

"No, he's a good guy. I'd met him before. I see him at the gym all the time. I thought we could be friends, but I don't think we can now that I've met his fiancé."

"Well, tell Jade to call me. I need to apologize to her. I feel really bad about this. I'll talk to you later."

"Yeah, see ya."

When I go back inside, a nurse is looking for me.

"Are you Garret?"

"Yeah."

"You can go back there now. Follow me."

She takes me to the examining room where Jade is waiting. She seems anxious to leave. She's got her coat on and she's clutching some brochures in her hand.

"What did the doctor say?" I sit next to her in one of the chairs near the examination table.

"She said I'm not pregnant."

"Did she say why you were late?"

"I told her to wait until you got here. She'll be back in a minute."

Moments later, a woman in a lab coat walks in. I introduce myself and then she says to Jade, "So I think there are several reasons why you're late. Missing that pill was one, but it also sounds like you've been under a lot of stress, not eating right, not sleeping well. And your weight is lower than it should be. If you combine all of that together, it makes sense you got off cycle."

She continues to explain how the pill works and how Jade could try a different one, or try a different type of birth control. I feel like we're in high school sex ed class. She gives us way more information than we need. The take-away is that Jade needs to gain weight, sleep more, and stop stressing. All things we already know. But at least it's nothing more serious than that.

"See? It was nothing," Jade says as we leave. "You didn't need to come with me."

"Jade, wait." We stop in front of a display of brochures. There's one from the student counseling center, which is in this building. I grab the brochure and hand it to her. "You should call them today. Get an appointment."

She goes through the door to the outside. "I don't need to. I changed my mind." She starts walking to the car but I grab her hand, stopping her.

"You're not changing your mind. We agreed that you're at least going to try it."

"I'm not ready to."

"If you don't do it now, you'll just keep putting it off. You're going. And I'm going with you." I get my phone out and call the number on the brochure.

"No, stop! Don't call them!" Jade tries to take my phone but I don't let her.

A woman answers and I make the appointment."

"Tomorrow at 4:15," I tell Jade as I put my phone away. "We'll meet outside the building after class." I take off toward the parking lot.

Jade follows behind. "Tomorrow? But that's so soon!"

"As long as we're out, you want to grab breakfast somewhere? I don't have class for another hour."

We reach the car and I hold the door open for her.

She narrows her eyes at me as she gets in. "You could've made the appointment for next week or the week after that."

I go around to the driver's side. "Breakfast or not? You didn't answer my question."

She reluctantly smiles. "Yes, I'd like breakfast."

Jade's not mad I made the appointment. She needed a little push. Just like I needed a push when my swim coach made me see a doctor about my shoulder. Sometimes you need someone else to force you to do the things you know you need to do.

I lean over and kiss her. "I love you."

"I love you, too." She rolls her eyes. "But you still annoy me sometimes."

"Good. That's why I'm here." I smile at her and wait.

"Are we going? Or are we just going to sit in the parking lot?"

"I need you to put your seatbelt on."

She rolls her eyes again as she puts it on. "See? That's annoying. I hate wearing my seatbelt."

"Get used to it because you're wearing it. I went to high school with a girl who died in a car accident because she didn't have her seatbelt on. She went straight through the windshield."

"Really? That's horrible."

"Yeah, it was. The whole school went to the funeral. It sucked. So you better be wearing your seatbelt even when I'm not in the car." I pull out of the parking lot.

"Where are we going for breakfast?"

"We'll just drive around and find a place. Oh, Harper called when you were in the doctor's office. I told her about Brook."

"What did she say?"

"She said she was sorry. She felt bad about it."

"It's not her fault."

"I told her that, but she still felt bad. I forgot to ask her how the babysitting went."

"Who did she babysit?"

"Lilly. I guess I didn't tell you. My dad had Harper watch Lilly on Saturday night. There was a party at my grandparents' house and they needed someone to watch her."

"I have to call her and see how it went." Jade checks her phone. "I forgot she has class now. I'll call her later."

We eat breakfast, then I drop Jade off at home since she doesn't have class until this afternoon. After my morning class, I call my dad and tell him what the neighbor said.

"That explains why there isn't a police report," he says.

"What do you think this means?"

"I'm guessing someone wanted to scare you. Make you think you're not safe."

"Who would do that? Roth? Someone else from the organization?"

"Maybe. You know how they like to mess with people."

"Do you think they've been watching us?"

"I don't know why they would. There's no reason to."

"Could you ask Grandfather?"

"I could, but he would tell me if he knew something like that. And besides, we're having a disagreement right now and I'd rather not talk to him."

"Did you get in a fight at his party the other night?"

"I guess you could call it that."

"What happened?"

"He left the party briefly and took me to his study and told me I had to convince you to take over the company. He wants you to work there next summer and start learning the business."

"He knows I don't want that."

"Yes, but your grandfather doesn't take no for an answer, which is how I ended up running the company years ago."

"What did you tell him?"

"I told him it will never happen. You don't want the company and you're not going to spend the summer there." He chuckles. "That didn't go over well."

My dad says it like he doesn't give a shit. It reminds me that he and I aren't that different. We both like to rebel and do what we want instead of what we're supposed to do. That's why he married my mom. Then when she died, he gave up fighting for what he wanted in life and ended up where he is now. But that doesn't mean his rebellious streak isn't still there.

"Are you not speaking to each other now?"

"It didn't come to that. I didn't want to fight with him at the party, so just to appease him, I told him I would ask you about the summer."

"I'm not working there."

"I know you're not. Don't worry about it. I'll handle my father."

"Did he even ask how I'm doing?"

"Actually, yes. He asked how you're doing in school. I told him I didn't know. How *are* you doing in school?"

"Good. A's and B's so far."

"And Jade's doing okay?"

"Yeah, she's back to getting all A's now that she dropped those other classes."

"Good. Well, I need to run to a meeting so—"

"Yeah, that's fine. I'll talk to you later."

Based on what my dad said, it sounds like my grandfather still wants nothing to do with me. Does he really think I'd go work for the company? I don't want any part of it. I've told him that many times. And if he really wanted me to work there, he should be calling and asking me himself. But instead he gives me the silent treatment.

My dad keeps saying my grandfather will accept me one day, but I'm starting to think that'll never happen.

Chapter 11

JADE

*M*y mind wandered all through psych class. I don't
even know what today's lecture was about. I kept
thinking about pregnancy and babies. And then I thought
about going to see that counselor tomorrow and I felt sick
to my stomach. At least Garret will be there. If I can't come
up with anything to say, I'll make him do the talking.

Then I started thinking about that burglary and how it
never happened and the fake cop who came to our door. I
don't even want to know what that's about. If I had to guess,
I'd say it's the organization trying to scare us and make us
think we're not safe. To let us know they're still in charge
and can get to us whenever they want.

The organization is all about faking stuff and making it
look real. Fake videos, fake photos, fake stories in the news.
Why not a fake crime and a fake cop? It's exactly what they
would do.

I'm sure Garret's thinking the same thing. He just
doesn't want to say it because he thinks it'll scare me. But
I'm not going to let it. The organization can't do anything
to Garret. It's over. His reputation was destroyed last spring,
so he'll never be able to be president. They have no use

for him now. If the organization is behind this made-up robbery, then it's just another mind game, like when Roth showed up the week before our wedding.

But if that's true, then why doesn't Pearce know about it? As a member, you'd think he would've at least heard something about it. Or William might've heard something. I know he doesn't know me that well, but I think if he knew they were trying to scare us, he'd tell me. Or maybe not. I'm still not sure if I can trust him.

I'm at the coffee shop now. I just sat down and Sara sees me and comes over to my table.

"Hey, I was hoping you'd stop by."

"So? How was your date last Friday?"

"It was okay." She's smiling, but doesn't seem that excited.

"It didn't go well, did it? Did he walk out on you? Because if he did, give me his number so I can call and yell at him."

"He didn't walk out. We spent an hour there. The first half hour was great. We have a lot in common. We like the same music. We have the same taste in movies. We got along really well."

"And then you told him about Caleb."

She sighs. "Yes. It's not like he reacted badly. He was just really surprised."

"What did he say?"

"After the shock wore off, he asked me about Caleb. But I did what you said and made sure not to overdo it on the Caleb stuff." She laughs. "Even though Caleb did the cutest thing the other day and I was dying to tell someone. But I didn't tell him. I just answered his questions and that was it."

"So what happens now? Are you going to see him again?"

"He suggested we just hang out as friends and see how it goes."

"That's good, right?"

"It's what I need right now, so yeah. As much as I'd love to have a guy in my life who's more than a friend, my focus needs to be on Caleb. And if I ever do get a boyfriend, he has to understand that. Otherwise it won't work."

"Garret and I were friends for months before we started dating. Sometimes I think it's better to start out as friends. It gives you time to get to know each other before you get more serious. So when are you going out with this guy again?"

"Friday night."

"Friday night is date night, Sara. You sure you're just friends?"

"Yes." She gets up and checks the counter for customers, then sits down again. "It's not a date. We're just going to an outdoor movie at the park."

"That sounds fun. Maybe Garret and I will go. What's the movie?"

"It's a comedy. I can't remember the name of it. Alex said I should bring Caleb but I don't know if I will."

"It was nice of him to suggest it."

"Yeah, it was." She smiles. "And I don't think he was just saying it to be polite. He acted like he really wanted me to bring him."

"I have an idea. Bring Caleb on Friday night, and Garret and I will be there and if you want some alone time with Alex, I'll watch Caleb for you."

"Hmm. I don't know. I don't want Alex to think I'm pushing him to be more than friends."

"He won't. I'll just come over and ask if I can play with Caleb. He won't think anything of it."

"You should talk to Garret first. He might want to do something else on Friday night."

"Sara, we're going. And we won't spy on you. We'll sit far away."

"You don't have to do that. I'm just friends with Alex, remember?"

"Yeah, but you still don't want Garret and me hanging around. You need time to get to know this guy."

"This is starting to feel more and more like a date. It's making me nervous."

"Relax. It's not a date. You're just going to the park and all you have to do is talk. It's just like when you had coffee with him last week."

"Yeah, but that was in the afternoon. This is Friday night. Like you said, Friday night is date night. I haven't been out on a Friday night with a guy since dating Caleb's dad."

"Hey, speaking of Caleb's dad, were you dating him while you were pregnant?"

"No. He dumped me as soon as he found out."

"So you had to go through your pregnancy all alone?"

"Pretty much. But he let me stay at his apartment until I saved up enough money to get my own. We didn't do anything though. It was strictly platonic. I slept on his couch."

"He made a pregnant woman sleep on the couch?"

She shrugs. "It was fine. I didn't care. It was better than being homeless."

"Was he around when Caleb was born? Did he go to the hospital with you?"

"No, but my mom was there. She was living with her boyfriend at the time. I called her and asked if she'd come to the hospital and, surprisingly, she showed up. But then right after Caleb was born, she left town and I haven't heard from her since."

"So when you were in labor, where was Caleb's dad? Just sitting at home?"

"It was during spring break. He went on a trip with his friends."

"I probably shouldn't say this since I don't know him, but I hate that guy."

She bursts out laughing. "Yeah, I hate him, too. I have to go back to work. You want coffee?"

"No, I'm going home." I stand up, slinging my backpack over my shoulder. "I just stopped by to say hi and see how your date went."

"I'll see you tomorrow." She goes over to the table next to me, where some students just sat down.

When I get home, Garret pulls in the driveway right behind me. I meet him by his car.

"Guess what we're doing Friday night?" I give him a kiss.

"Going to a movie?" He takes my backpack from me, then grabs his from the car and we walk to the door.

"How'd you know?"

"Because that's what we always do on Friday night."

I unlock the door and we go inside. "This time we're going to an outdoor movie at the park. Sara and Alex are going too."

"So it's a double date?" Garret drops our backpacks on the floor, then grabs me around the waist and pulls me to the couch, setting me on his lap.

"No, they're just friends."

Garret kisses my neck in the spot that always tickles.

I squirm, laughing. "Would you stop? I'm trying to talk to you here."

He sighs. "Go ahead."

"When they went out for coffee last week they got along really well, but when she told him about Caleb, he suggested they take things slow and just hang out as friends. She really likes him but she understands why he just wants to be friends, at least for now. Anyway, we aren't going to sit with them."

"Why not?"

"Because they need some alone time. And Sara's bringing Caleb to introduce him to Alex but we're going to watch him for a little while so they can be alone."

"You just said they're not dating. You don't need alone time if you're not dating."

"If they have some alone time, maybe they'll become more than just friends."

"Jade, are you trying to play matchmaker? Because maybe Sara doesn't want that."

"Oh, she wants it. She definitely wants it." I realize how that sounds and correct myself. "I don't mean sex. I mean she wants Alex to be more than just a friend."

"Are you sure it's not *you* who wants that?"

"Okay, so maybe I do, but she wants it, too. I know she does."

He rolls his eyes, smiling. "I swear, you just can't help yourself. First Sean and Harper. Now Alex and Sara. You want everyone to be a couple."

I loop my arms around his neck. "I just want them to be happy and in love, like we are. What's wrong with that?"

He's still smiling as he tucks my hair behind my ear. "Nothing's wrong with it. It's just funny that the girl who didn't even want a boyfriend last year is now married and wants everyone else to be."

"Yeah, well, that's your fault. You turned me into a hopeless romantic. I don't know how you did it, but you did and now I can't help myself."

He leans in and presses his lips to mine, giving me soft kisses as his hand moves behind my neck, gently massaging it. It feels really good. And I'd love for it to go farther but it can't. Not today.

I pull away from the kiss. "We need to stop."

He looks concerned. "It's too soon after what happened, isn't it? I'm sorry, Jade. Take as much time as you need."

"No, it's not about that. I got my period right before class."

"Oh. Well, that's good, right?"

"Yeah, it's good. The doctor said it might happen. But it means I'm off limits for the next few days, so don't be kissing me like that."

"Like what?" He says it over my lips, then kisses me, doing this thing he does with his tongue that always makes me want to have sex with him.

I push on his chest but he doesn't move as he continues the kiss. When I'm at the point where I'd normally be racing him to the bedroom, he pulls away and says, "You mean like that?"

I look at him, annoyed. "Yes, like that. Dammit, Garret! Why did you do that? Now I'll be thinking about sex until we can do it again."

"There are worse things you could think of. I think I did you a favor."

I roll my eyes at him. "Yeah, thanks."

"I need to go to the pool. You want to go with me?"

"No, I'll stay here. How long will you be gone?"

"An hour."

"I'll make dinner while you're gone so we can eat when you get home."

He gives me this wary look. "You're making dinner?"

"I thought I'd make pizza. We bought those new crusts last week. I want to see if they're any good."

"I could just bring home a pizza."

I punch him. "Are you trying to say you don't trust me to make a pizza?"

"Well, after the lasagna incident…" He's trying not to laugh. He's referring to his birthday dinner, in which I tried to make lasagna and it turned out so bad we couldn't even eat it.

I huff. "That was one time. And lasagna is very hard to make. Pizza is easy. I just have to put toppings on the crust and bake it. A child could do that."

"I don't know, Jade. Why don't I just pick one up from that pizza place by campus?" Now he's laughing and it's making *me* laugh.

"Hey! I used to make dinner for Frank and Ryan all the time and they never complained."

He slides me off his lap and gets up. "I need to go, but good luck with the pizza."

"You don't have to eat it, you know." I yell it since he's now in the bedroom. "I'll just make it for myself. You can make your own dinner."

"I'm kidding." He reappears with his gym bag, kissing me on his way to the door. "I'm sure dinner will be great. Love you. I'll be back soon."

"Okay. Have fun."

He leaves, but then comes right back in. "Here's the mail." He holds up a stack of envelopes. "You got a letter from your high school. What's that about?"

I jump up from the couch and take it from him. "It's probably from my algebra teacher. He wants me to speak at this event. I forgot to get back to him." I open the envelope and inside is a letter from my teacher, reminding me about the event and asking me to call him.

"I didn't know you were speaking at an event." Garret closes the door and drops his gym bag. "What's the event?"

"It's an afternoon of motivational speakers. It's for this organization that helps out young women who are struggling to move forward. Most of them came from homes like mine. This group helps them find jobs, or get whatever training they need for work. Stuff like that. My teacher is one of the volunteers. I need to call and tell him I'm not speaking."

"Why aren't you speaking?"

"Because I have nothing to say." I put the letter on the table with the other mail.

"You have all kinds of things to say. Call him and tell him you'll do it."

"Are you crazy? I hate public speaking. I get super nervous. And what would I say to these people?"

"Tell them how you got to be where you are. Tell them how you got to be valedictorian. And how working hard got you a scholarship for college."

"I didn't get the scholarship for working hard."

"My dad would've given you that scholarship even if Royce wasn't involved. You impressed him, and he's very hard to impress."

"Why would these girls want to listen to anything I had to say?"

"Because you're inspiring. Despite all the obstacles you had, you were still driven to succeed. You set goals and you met those goals. You stayed away from drugs and alcohol. You're a good role model. You're proof that if you work hard enough, you can do whatever you want."

"You really think I should speak at this thing?"

"Yes." Garret picks up the letter and hands it to me. "Call him right now and tell him. When's the event?"

"The Saturday after Thanksgiving, so we'll already be in Des Moines."

"Then you have no excuse not to go."

"I'm still nervous about speaking."

"I'll get you through it. You can practice in front of me. Do that thing they tell you where you picture the audience naked."

"You want me to picture you naked while I practice? If I do that, I won't practice. We'll end up having sex."

"Then we'll have sex right before you practice so you'll have no distractions." He smiles. "Now I'm really looking forward to these practice sessions. When can we start?"

I push him out the door. "Get to the pool."

While he's gone, I call my teacher and agree to speak at the event. He asks me all about college and where I'm living. He can't believe I'm married. But that's not surprising. Everyone's shocked by that. He was thrilled when I told him I'd speak at this event. He said I'm the most inspiring student he's ever taught. At first I thought he was kidding, but he was serious.

I don't get it. I don't find myself inspiring at all. Someone like Sara is inspiring. *I'm* not. But I guess I just can't see it when it's me and not someone else.

Now I have to find something to talk about for a half hour. That's right. I have to speak for an entire half hour! I thought it would be 10 minutes, 20 tops. But no, a full 30 minutes. When he told me, I almost backed out, but I pushed past my fear and agreed to it. It's all Garret's fault, making me face my fears. This sucks. I don't know how

I'm ever going to do this. At least I have a whole month to prepare.

After I get off the phone with him, I call Harper.

"Hey, it's me," I say when she answers.

"Finally. I've been trying to get a hold of you. Garret told me about Brook. I'm so sorry about that. She must've changed since I knew her. She didn't used to be like that."

"Don't worry about it. It's no big deal. So what's new with you?"

"I babysat Lilly last Saturday night."

"I heard. How'd it go?"

"She was as cute as ever. She might even be cuter now that she goes to school. Her stories are hilarious."

"What did she tell you?"

"She has this friend, Max. He wears a bow tie."

"Yeah, I know about Max."

"Lilly showed me his picture. So adorable. Anyway, Lilly said that boys his age smell really bad." Harper starts laughing. "And so she sniffed him one day and he must've smelled bad because she—" Harper's laughing so hard she can't finish.

"She what?"

"She sprayed him with air freshener! Oh my God, Jade, when she told me I was laughing so hard I was crying."

"Lilly did not do that."

"She did! Why would she even think to do something like that?"

Now I'm laughing just as hard. "Garret told her to. He thinks Max is trying to date Lilly so he told her to spray him with air freshener to keep him away. But I didn't think she'd actually do it."

"Well, she did, and she got in big trouble. Katherine wasn't around so Pearce had to go to her school and talk to the principal. Then Lilly was sent home for the rest of the day. And they confiscated the air freshener."

We're both laughing so hard we can't talk. I can't even breathe. After a while, we're able to speak again.

"So what was going on at Garret's grandparents' house? Was it a dinner party?"

"Yeah, it was for that guy who's running for president. Kent Gleason. So there was a ton of security there."

Garret didn't tell me the party was for Kent. I wonder if he knew that. I'm guessing he did but he wouldn't tell me because it involves the organization. I don't know how I feel about that. On the one hand, I don't like Garret keeping secrets from me, but on the other hand, I don't want to know about the organization. I want to pretend they don't exist.

"Did you meet our future president?" I shouldn't have said that. She might suspect something. Then again, Harper has no idea our presidents are hand-selected by this secret group.

"I saw him but I didn't go up and talk to him. I don't think he'll end up being president. He's too short. Aren't presidents usually tall?"

"Yeah, I think so," I say, relieved she didn't take my president comment seriously.

"Before dinner, they had a cocktail hour and I had to stand there waiting while Katherine showed off Lilly to some of the guests. If I'd known I'd be seen like that, I would've dressed up. I had on jeans and a sweater and everyone else was in evening gowns and tuxedos. I tried to hide off to the side but then this weird guy came up to me and introduced himself and I couldn't get him to go away."

"Who was he?"

"Some old guy. Well, not really old, but old to us. He's probably like 40. I think his name was Andrew. Anyway, he was flirting with me and he seemed mad when I didn't flirt back. I told him about Sean but the guy didn't care that I had a boyfriend. He asked me to go out with him after the party. He said we could take his private jet to Manhattan for the night. And yes, he meant for the entire night, like he assumed I would sleep with him."

"I wonder why he was there. That doesn't sound like the type of person Garret's grandparents would invite to their house."

"He probably wrote a big check to be there. It was probably one of those fundraiser dinners. Anyway, he was totally obnoxious. I can't stand guys like that. Always showing off how rich they are, assuming you'll do whatever they say just because they have money. I met guys like him all the time when I lived in LA. They're all over the movie business."

"What did Sean do while you were babysitting?"

"He took an extra shift at work. He's been working a lot of extra shifts lately. I think he needs the money."

When she says it, it makes me wonder if Sean's saving up money to buy Harper an engagement ring. I know he wants to propose to her, which means he needs a ring. But she doesn't want a ring. She's not ready for that. Yet Sean still doesn't know this. And Harper has no clue he wants to marry her.

"So anyway," Harper says, "there wasn't really anything to do at Garret's grandparents' house, so Lilly and I just watched TV. They only have one TV and it's in one of the living rooms at the other end of the house."

"How many living rooms do they have?"

"I don't know. Maybe three? The place was huge. Even bigger than my parents' house. And it was decorated in that old, rich-people style. Crystal chandeliers, tapestry rugs, ugly sculptures everywhere."

"I've never been there but that's how I pictured their house."

"Why haven't you been there? It's not that far from Garret's house."

"You know why. His grandparents hate me. That's why they didn't come to the wedding. They still won't talk to Garret."

"That's so stupid. I can't believe they act that way just because he married someone without money."

I have this urge to tell her I'm a Sinclair and that I have money now, but I can't. It would cause too many problems.

"I guess my dad's kind of acting the same way," Harper says, her voice quieter than before.

"What's going on with your dad?"

"He barely talks to me anymore. When I call him, he just says hi and puts my mom on the phone or my sisters. Even my mom hardly talks to me. We used to talk an hour a day and now I'm lucky if she talks to me an hour a week."

"Are they just busy?"

"No. It's Sean. They told me they don't want me dating him. And since I am, they're mad at me."

"When did this happen?"

"Last week. I didn't tell you because I wasn't ready to talk about it. And part of me thought maybe they were just in a bad mood that day and they'd change their minds later. But they didn't."

"Why don't they want you dating him?"

"They said he's not right for me. They said I should be with someone who's in college and has goals and will have a real career."

"Sean has a real career."

"No, he doesn't. He has a job. But he's working on his career and he's going to be really successful someday. The thing is, it doesn't matter to me that he didn't go to college. Not everyone has to go to college. And it's not like he just sat around and did nothing after high school. He went to culinary school and he's been working ever since. I like that he's a chef. It's creative and he's really good at it. When I first met him, my mom thought it was cool that I was dating a chef. But now she and my dad are being all judgmental, like Sean's not good enough for me."

"Just forget about what they think. Didn't you just tell me you weren't going to worry about your parents? That you were going to do what makes you happy?"

"Yes, but it's hard to have my parents mad at me like this. We've always gotten along really well. And now they barely speak to me." I hear her sniffling.

"I'm sorry, Harper. I wish I had some advice to give you but I'm not sure what to do. What did Sean say about it?"

"I can't tell him this stuff. It would make him feel bad. He already knows my parents don't like him." She sniffles again. "I don't want to talk about it. I should go. I have a huge test tomorrow and I need to study. I'll call you later."

"Okay, bye."

This whole thing with Harper's parents doesn't make sense. First they like him, then they don't. He didn't do anything to make them not like him so what's the deal? They hate him because he doesn't have money?

It pisses me off the way these rich people think people without money or college degrees are worthless. I'm really getting tired of it. And I've just about had it with Garret's grandparents. I want to call them up and yell at them to get over the fact that he married me and to have a relationship with their grandson again. I'd never actually do that, but it's tempting.

Chapter 12

GARRET

When I get back from swimming, I come in the kitchen with a paper sack and hand it to Jade. "I got you something."

She opens the sack. "Ice cream!"

"I stopped on my way home. It's that cookie sundae you like. That should help you gain some weight.

"Thank you!" She hugs me. "I'll put it in the freezer for after we eat." She leads me to the kitchen table. "Look. I didn't screw up dinner."

Her homemade pizza is sitting there, along with a big salad.

"I was kidding, Jade. I didn't think you'd screw it up. And even if you did, I'd still eat it."

She pulls my chair out. "Sit down. Let's eat."

"It's supposed to be the other way around." I pull her chair out, but before she sits down I bring her in for a kiss. "Thanks for dinner."

"Sure. How was swimming?"

We both take a seat at the table.

"Good. But the pool was crowded."

Jade places three slices of pizza on my plate and two on hers. "Oh, listen to this. Guess what your sister did?"

"You talked to Lilly?"

"No. Harper. She was telling me about babysitting Lilly last weekend. Anyway, Lilly sprayed that poor little Max kid with air freshener." Jade can barely say it, she's laughing so hard.

I smile as I pick up a slice of pizza. "That's my girl. Always listens to her big brother."

"Garret, she got in trouble. Your dad had to go to her school and take her home."

"What did Katherine say?" I'm trying to imagine the look on Katherine's face when she heard about this.

"She wasn't around. Maybe your dad didn't tell her."

"If she found out, she'd be so pissed. And if she knew I was the reason for it, she'd never speak to me again. You know, that's a good idea. I need to find a way to piss off Katherine enough that she never talks to me again."

"Hey, um, Harper said that dinner party your grandparents had was for Kent Gleason."

"Yeah? So?"

"Why didn't you tell me that?"

"You know why. I try to keep you out of that stuff. I try to keep *both* of us out of it. The less we know the better."

"But if it involved us, you'd tell me, right?"

"Why would it involve us? We're no longer part of that world."

"Yes, we are. We may not want to be, but we are. Your dad and my uncle are part of it, and because of that, we'll always have a connection to it."

"That doesn't mean we have to talk about it, or talk about what they do." I take a drink of my soda.

"Harper had some other news," Jade says.

"What is it?"

"She said her parents told her to dump Sean because he's not good enough for her."

"They actually said that?"

"Yeah, and since she's still dating him, they're barely speaking to her. I'm starting to really not like them. I don't get it. They seemed so nice when they were at our wedding. Well, nice to everyone but Sean."

"I know. They don't seem like the type of people who would be so judgmental about people without money."

The past few months I've been trying to figure out what's going on with Kiefer. Last spring he helped my dad make those fake videos we fed to the media to ruin my image. I don't think Kiefer knew we were doing it to destroy the organization's plan to make me president someday, but he knew we were purposely manipulating the media and he went along with it.

That's when I realized he'd done this before. And his close connection with my dad meant he'd probably done stuff for the organization before, too. I'm sure that's how my dad first got involved with him.

Last summer, Kiefer had a meeting with my dad and Mr. Roth, a high-ranking member of the organization, to discuss a project. At least that's what they said they were doing, but I think it was more than that. Someone at Roth's level wouldn't fly all the way across the country to meet with Kiefer about a project. It'd have to be bigger than that.

I'm thinking they offered Kiefer membership in the organization. They need people with his skills. People who can make videos that look real—real enough to put on the news and have people believe whatever story they're trying to tell. Kiefer's a movie director but he's also an expert in CGI, computer-generated imagery. He can use CGI to make it look like someone is somewhere they're really not. Like last spring, when I was supposedly trashing my dad's cars, Kiefer combined images of me with images of the cars so it looked like I was driving them. Then he added backgrounds to make it look like I was in different locations. The technology is so advanced now you can even make the person say things they never said. Just record their voice, put it in a software program and tell it what to say.

"I wonder if Kiefer was—" I stop because I didn't mean to say that out loud.

"Kiefer was what?" Jade's not going to let this go. She'll ask me until I tell her what I was thinking. I might as well. It's just a theory anyway.

"I was just wondering if maybe the organization offered Kiefer membership."

"They can do that? I thought you were born into it."

"You are, but my dad and some of the other members are trying to change that. They want to recruit people instead. People who want to be part of it and can offer something in return. And Kiefer can offer a lot. He has the skills they need to make stuff look real, like that video he made of Kent Gleason saving that kid on the beach. I think Kiefer's been working for the organization for a long time, which is how he got to know my dad. And William. And why he knew Arlin. So it wouldn't be that surprising for the organization to offer him membership. I think that's why Kiefer met with my dad and Roth last summer."

"So that's what the meeting in July was about? They were inviting Kiefer to become a member?"

"I think it was some kind of final interview. That's why Roth was there."

"I thought he came out here to scare us before the wedding?"

"That was just part of the reason. He had to do the interview somewhere, and instead of doing it in New York or LA, he picked the town where we were living and scheduled it right before our wedding. He knew exactly what he was doing. Playing his fucked-up mind games with us while also doing business for the organization. Those men he was with are both at Roth's level in the organization so I'm guessing all three of them were sent to interview Kiefer. But I think Roth was the final decision maker."

"When do you think Kiefer was asked to join?"

"I'm guessing last spring he went through the initial interview process and was told the requirements for membership, one of which is making sure his daughter doesn't date someone like Sean."

"Harper said her dad liked Sean when they were home over spring break, but then in May, he suddenly didn't like him."

"So that's when it must've happened. They probably invited him to be a member back then and told him the requirements."

"What about Kelly?"

"I don't think she knew until after the meeting last July. Kiefer probably waited to tell her until he knew for sure he was being offered membership, which is what I think happened at the meeting once Roth interviewed him and approved of him. Right after the meeting, Kelly decided she didn't like Sean, so the timing makes sense."

"How is your dad involved in this?"

"Like I said, my dad's been trying to change the rule that says you're born into the organization. He's on a committee that's looking into trying to recruit people instead. Maybe Kiefer is their test case. Their first recruit from the outside. And if he works out, they'll recruit other people. But I'm not going to ask him about it. Even if I did, he wouldn't tell me anything."

"Everything you're saying makes sense. I just don't want to believe it."

"That's why I didn't want to tell you. If this happens, if Kiefer becomes a member, you know what that means, right?" I don't wait for her to answer. "Harper will have to break up with Sean. She'll be paired up with a guy who's a member."

"They'll force her to marry someone? They can't do that."

"They can, and they will. If Kiefer wants to be part of it, he has to play by the rules. You know how it works."

"You really think Kiefer would do that to Harper?"

"All three of his daughters will have to marry members. Not just Harper."

"No. That can't happen. I can't watch Harper and Sean go through what you and I went through last year."

"Jade, I have no idea if this is true. It's just a theory."

"Yeah, but it makes sense. Why else would Harper's parents act that way to Sean? They used to like him and now they don't. And for no reason. Sean didn't do anything wrong. That has to be it, Garret. They offered Kiefer membership and he accepted. I just can't believe he and Kelly would want to be part of this."

"There's a lot of money involved."

"They already have a lot of money."

"Not this much. I'm talking billions, not millions. That type of money buys you power, the ability to influence people and control things. I told you, being a member has rewards. And financial rewards are just part of it. He'll have access to the clinic. His whole family will. That alone is a huge selling point."

"I don't want this to be true."

"If it is, there's nothing we can do about it. So don't say anything to Harper. We can't get involved in this, Jade."

"I know." She takes her plate to the sink.

I meet her over there. "We don't know anything for sure. We could be totally wrong about Kiefer."

"This is stressing me out. I need ice cream."

"Then it's a good thing your husband made a special trip just to get you some."

Jade spins around. "My husband is amazing."

"He is, isn't he?" I kiss her, then reach around her to the freezer and take the ice cream out.

Jade and I share the ice cream sundae. It's so huge it could feed three or four people. It reminds me of the Boxcar Bonanza we used to get back in Connecticut. I think that's why I keep getting it. It makes me think of that sundae, which makes me think of my mom because she used to get me that sundae every year on my birthday. And then I think of Jade, because I ordered that sundae for her on the first day we spent together. It's strange how food can evoke such strong memories. It's just a simple sundae. And yet it's not.

Later that night, when Jade and I are in bed, I notice she won't lie still. She keeps moving around and won't go to sleep.

I tuck her into my chest and kiss her. "What's wrong?"

"Nothing. I just can't sleep."

"Jade. No more hiding stuff from me. Tell me what's wrong."

"I'm really nervous about tomorrow. I don't think I can go to that appointment with the counselor."

"I'm going with you. It'll be okay."

"I can't talk to people about this stuff. I can't relive it."

"You don't have to tell her anything you don't want to. And if you don't want to talk about your mom, then talk about something else. Talk about other stuff you're worried about, like figuring out your major or what classes to take next semester."

"What if I don't like the counselor?"

"Then we'll find someone else. We'll keep trying different people until you find someone you like."

"Okay." Jade sighs, like she's relieved.

Did she really think I'd force her to go to someone she didn't like? I would never do that. I'd drive for hours to find the right person.

Jade flips around in my arms and faces me. "What happened when you went?"

"When I went to counseling?"

"Yeah. Were you nervous?"

"I was scared shitless. I was only 10 and I had to go alone. My dad dropped me off. I thought the guy was going to strap me down on a table and hook electrodes to my head." I laugh, because now it's kind of funny. "I had just watched a sci-fi movie where they did that to some old man so I thought for sure that's what would happen to me. But instead, I just sat in a room and talked to the guy."

"What did you talk about?"

"The first few sessions we just talked about sports. He was trying to get me to relax so that I'd talk to him about other stuff. Eventually I talked about the plane crash and my mom. I don't know how he got me to talk so much. He must've been really good."

"I'm still nervous about going."

"Don't be. I'll be right there with you and if you don't feel comfortable, we'll get up and leave."

"You promise?"

"I promise."

"I really *do* want to work on this stuff, Garret. I want to do it for me, but also for us. I don't want to go back to being like I was when we met." "You won't, Jade. You're not that person anymore."

She rests her head on my shoulder, her finger drawing circles on my chest. "But sometimes I feel like I am. When we moved here and school started, it was so much change all at once and I couldn't deal with it. So I started acting like I did last year; running all the time, pushing you away, hiding my feelings. But I can't do that. I don't want to be that person again."

I bring her hand to my mouth and kiss it. "There was nothing wrong that person. She just needed someone to love her and take care of her and listen to her. And Jade, that someone is still here."

She nods.

I keep hold of her hand and rest it between us. "I feel like I let you down, Jade."

"What do you mean?"

"I see you every day and I knew something was wrong but I didn't do anything, and I should have. Whenever you push me away, don't talk to me, go run for hours, it means you're hurting. And I know that about you and yet I didn't do anything. That's why I made that appointment tomorrow. I knew you'd be mad at me, and maybe you still are, but I had to do it because I don't know what else to do for you. I can be here for you and listen to you and love you, but I don't think that's enough. And I didn't know how else to help you."

"I'm not mad at you for making the appointment. I never would've done it myself. And you didn't let me down. You couldn't have because you didn't know what was going on with me. Even *I* didn't know. I still don't. That's why I have to talk to someone. The thing is, sometimes things are great and I think I'm over my past and moving on. But then something happens, like when I thought I was pregnant, and I can't handle it. I see myself turning into my mom and I panic. I've actually had dreams where I'm screaming at our kids and throwing stuff at them and telling them I hate them." Her voice cracks.

I hug her against my chest. "Jade, you should've told me that."

"I couldn't." She sniffles. "It doesn't matter. I'm going to fix this. I'm going to fix whatever's wrong with me."

"Nothing's wrong with you. You just need to work through some stuff. And I'll be right here beside you. You don't have to do it alone."

She looks up at me, and through the moonlight filtering through the blinds, I see her smiling, wet tears still on her cheeks. "I told you how much I love you, right?"

I kiss her forehead. "I love you, too."

We fall asleep. And the next day, after class, I meet Jade at Student Health. The counseling center has its own entrance on the other side of the building. There's a small waiting room and we check in at the desk.

A woman comes out of a room to the right of us. "Jade?"

"Yes." Jade and I are still standing at the check-in desk.

The woman goes up to Jade. She's about 45 with shoulder-length, straight brown hair and brown eyes. She isn't wearing much makeup and she looks like she works out a lot. She has on a blue sleeveless dress and her arms are really toned. She seems like someone Jade would like—casual, friendly, athletic.

"Hi, I'm Jennifer. Nice to meet you. Come on back."

"Um, he's coming, too." Jade points to me. "Is that okay?"

"That's up to you. If you're comfortable with him joining us, then yes."

"I want him there. This is my husband, Garret."

"Hi." I shake her hand.

"Hi." She seems a little shocked, as everyone does when we tell them we're married. "Follow me."

The room we go in looks like a living room, with a big couch and two overstuffed chairs and bookcases along the back wall.

"Have a seat." Jennifer motions us to the couch. Jade and I sit down and Jennifer sits across from us on one of the chairs. "So tell me about yourself, Jade."

"Um, what do you want to know?" Jade's doing the foot-tapping thing she does when she's nervous. And she's got a vise grip on my hand.

"What do you like to do for fun?"

Bad question. Jade struggles with that one.

"I don't know. Go to movies?"

"I like movies, too." Jennifer smiles. "So tell me how you met Garret."

Wow. She's good. She instantly knew to get off the what-do-you-do-for-fun question and move on to something else. And she picked a good topic. Jade likes talking about how we met.

As Jade tells her about it, I feel her hand relax. And then her foot stops tapping. She talks for a good 30 minutes.

When she's done, Jennifer says, "You mentioned you're from Iowa. Tell me about it. I've never been there."

Another good topic. Jade can easily talk about Iowa and her hometown of Des Moines. She talks until 5:30 and we were supposed to be done at 5:15.

Jennifer waits for Jade to finish, then says, "Well, you two probably want to get home." Another interesting technique. Instead of acting like we're the ones taking up her time, she acts like she's the one taking up ours. These psychologists have really upped their game since I went to one. Not that my guy wasn't good, but he wasn't *this* good.

"Would you like to come back on Thursday?" Jennifer asks Jade. "I have an opening at the same time, 4:15."

Jade hesitates. She looks at me, then back at Jennifer. "Okay, that works."

"Great, I'll see you then."

As soon as we're out of the building, Jade takes a deep breath. "I did it."

I hug her. "It wasn't so bad, was it?"

"No. She was nice. And she didn't ask me any stupid questions, except that first one about what I do for fun. Why do people always ask that? It's annoying. That question should be banned from ever being asked again."

She says it jokingly, which tells me the session went well and that she liked Jennifer. I think Jennifer will be good for Jade. She seems to have some tricks to use to get Jade to talk about stuff. And she's going to need them. Getting Jade to talk about her past is next to impossible, especially with someone she doesn't know very well.

When we get in the car, I turn to Jade and say, "So tell me, Jade, what do you like to do for fun?"

She laughs and shoves my shoulder. "I like to kill people who ask that!"

"You can't kill me because I'm taking you out for dinner. Where do you want to go?"

"The Mexican place downtown."

"Sounds good." I drive onto the street, heading toward the downtown.

"Can we get nachos?"

I reach over and hold her hand. "Why do you even ask that, Jade? Do I ever deny you nachos?"

"You haven't yet, but someday you might. You're always trying to get me to eat better."

"After repeatedly witnessing the immense joy that nachos bring to you, I promise you that I will never deny you nachos."

"They don't bring me immense joy. I just like them." She pauses, then says, "Okay, they bring me immense joy, but don't tell anyone that. It sounds weird."

"Lilly loves nachos almost as much as you do."

"Katherine lets her eat nachos?"

"Hell, no. She'd never allow it. But Katherine's been gone a lot with her boyfriend so my dad's been taking Lilly out for dinner. He took her to that Mexican restaurant by the house. You know the one we went to?"

"I thought you said he'd never eat there because it's not fancy enough."

"I said *Katherine* would never eat there, not my dad. Lilly loves the Mexican place. They've been there twice now. She's had the nachos both times."

"Is that mariachi singer still there?"

I laugh. "Yes, so when we're back for Christmas, I'm definitely taking you there for dinner. Maybe we'll take Lilly with us."

"Garret, do you think your grandparents will be at your house for Christmas?"

"They have to be. For Lilly's sake."

But if it weren't for Lilly, I know my grandparents wouldn't show up. They don't want to see me, especially my grandfather, who hates me right now.

I'm dreading Christmas. I know it's going to be bad. Katherine will be a bitch, as usual, and my grandparents won't speak to me. It'll pretty much suck.

"I'm sorry, Garret. About your grandparents."

"It's okay. They'll come around eventually."

After dinner, we go home and Jade goes out on the deck to do some studying. I stay inside and watch sports highlights from last weekend. It's football season and I love football and yet I've hardly watched any games.

My phone rings. I see it's Sean so I answer. "Hey, man, what's up?"

"If you'd call me once in a while, you'd know." He's kidding but he's right. I do need to call him more.

"Sorry. I'm a shitty friend. I'll buy you a case of beer next time I'm out there."

"You're underage, buddy." He laughs. "You're an old married guy but you can't even buy me a beer."

"Yeah, that's right. I always forget about that. I feel a lot older than 20. I'll give you some money and you can buy your own beer."

"When are you guys coming out here?"

"Not until Christmas, so you'll be waiting a while for that beer."

"I might need something stronger than beer."

"Why?"

"I'm going to propose to Harper at Christmas. And I'm already fucking nervous as hell."

"You don't think she'll say yes?"

"I don't know. That's why I'm nervous. One day she acts like she'd marry me in a heartbeat and the next day I'm not so sure. But by Christmas we'll have dated for over a year and we lived together all summer, so if she doesn't know by now that I'm the one, then she never will. And if she says no, then I figure it's better to find that out now than in a year or two. But I really hope she doesn't say no. I can't imagine being with anyone but her."

Shit. This really sucks. If Kiefer was offered membership, Sean will never be with Harper, even if she accepted his proposal.

"Did you already buy a ring?" I ask him.

"Yeah. I bought it last week. I spent more than I should have but I wanted to get her a really nice ring. I had to charge it, which means I'll be paying that thing off for the next 10 years at 18 percent interest."

"Sean, just pay it off. I'll loan you the money. You can pay me back when you can. It'll save you from paying all that interest."

"I don't like owing people money."

"The offer's out there. Just think about it."

That's just great. So now the poor guy's in debt from buying a ring Harper may not even want. Or may not be able to accept because she'll be forced to marry someone else. This is such a mess, but I don't know anything for sure, so for now I'm going to pretend everything's fine.

I hear Sean talking again. "I know you're going to tell Jade about this, but she won't tell Harper, will she?"

"No, she'll keep it a secret."

"So what's going on with you? You see the Patriots play last weekend?"

Sean and I talk sports for the next half hour. It reminds me that I need to find some more guy friends. Last week I started going to swim practice so I'm getting to know the guys there, but we don't talk much during practice. I'm friends with that Nate guy I met at the gym but we don't do stuff together. I just talk to him at class. And I talk to Dylan when I see him on campus. Kyle, a guy I met my first week here, keeps asking me to hang out but I always turn him down. I have nothing in common with him. He's quarterback of the football team and spends the majority of his time drinking and partying. That's not my scene anymore.

It's hard to find a good friend like Sean. Someone who's easy to talk to and would help you out if you needed it. Unfortunately, right now I don't feel like I'm being a very good friend to Sean. Not because I haven't called him, but because I think he's going to get his heart broken and I can't tell him.

Chapter 13

JADE

I'm out on the deck, studying, when Frank calls.

"Hi, Dad." I call him that sometimes. I call him Frank, too, but he likes it better when I call him dad.

"Hi, honey." He's smiling. I can hear it in his voice. "How are classes going?"

"Good. How's your house going?"

"It's almost done. Did you get the photos I sent?"

"Yeah, the house looks great. You did a really good job picking stuff out. I didn't know you had all those design skills."

"It wasn't just me. I had some help."

"From who? Ryan? Because I can't picture him picking out that tile and those paint colors."

"No, um, I had some help from a friend of mine. Karen."

Karen is his girlfriend that he's never told me about. Ryan tells me about her, but I'm supposed to pretend I don't know about her.

"Who's Karen?"

Frank clears his throat. "She's a woman I've been seeing." He hesitates, then says, "Romantically."

I almost laugh when he says 'romantically' but instead I try to act surprised and serious.

"I didn't know you were seeing someone."

"Jade, I know Ryan told you about her."

"He hasn't told me much. Just that she's a nurse and a widow and that you met her at the hospital."

"I met her last summer, but we didn't start dating until a couple months ago."

Hearing Frank say he's dating is just weird. It shouldn't be, but it is.

"And it's going well?"

"Very well. In fact, I've invited her for Thanksgiving. I hope that's okay."

"Of course it's okay. Why wouldn't it be?"

"You've never met her. It might make you uncomfortable to have her there."

"I think it's good you invited her. I'd like to meet her. And I like the idea of a big Thanksgiving with lots of people. I've always wanted that. And now with Chloe, Garret, and Karen, we'll have six people. That's a crowd compared to our usual Thanksgiving."

"Yes, our family's grown a lot the past year."

Family? Is he considering Karen to be family? Are they that serious? Maybe he just meant Chloe and Garret.

"Where does Karen work in the hospital? Or does she work in the clinic you go to?"

"She works at the hospital in obstetrics. She loves working with all the new moms and taking care of the infants. She never had children but she enjoys working with them. Karen's a very nice lady. I think you'll like her."

"I think I will, too."

"Oh, she wanted me to ask you if you'd like to take part in a Thanksgiving Day run. It's at a park in West Des Moines. She's running the 5K and asked if you'd like to run with her. I told her how you like to run. But Jade, don't feel like you have to."

"I'd love to. Tell her I'll do it."

"Thank you for agreeing to it. She'll be thrilled. She didn't want to do it alone."

"Do you have any other plans for while I'm there? Because I told my algebra teacher I'd speak at that event he invited me to. It's Saturday afternoon."

"Good. I'm glad you're doing that. And no, I didn't have any other plans. I thought we'd all just stay at home, play cards, watch movies, eat turkey."

What he's describing is exactly what I want. To be back with family and just be together at home.

"That sounds perfect. I'm really looking forward to Thanksgiving."

"I am too, honey. We missed having you last year."

We talk a little more, then we hang up and I go inside. Garret's watching a sports show on TV.

I snuggle up beside him on the couch. "I can't wait for Thanksgiving."

"You craving turkey?"

"No, it's not about the food, although I am looking forward to that. Ryan says Chloe's a really good cook. But besides the food, I'm going to run in this race with Frank's girlfriend and then we're going to spend the weekend hanging out at the new house, watching movies and playing cards and stuff."

Garret's laughing at me because I was talking really fast. "Slow down a minute. Now what was that about Frank's girlfriend?"

"Frank just called. He finally told me about his girlfriend. You should've heard him. I think he might be in love. He invited her over for Thanksgiving, so I'm thinking that's pretty serious. And she's running in a Thanksgiving Day race and I'm going to run with her. Do you want to run, too?"

"No, but I'll stand on the sidelines and cheer you on."

"This Thanksgiving is going to be so great."

He gives me a kiss. "You're finally getting into the holidays. I must be wearing off on you."

I spot his phone on the couch. "Were you just on the phone?"

"Yeah. Sean called."

I set his phone on the table and sit so I'm facing him. "What did he say?"

"Promise you won't tell Harper?"

"He's proposing, isn't he?"

"Yeah."

"When is he doing it?"

"Christmas."

I sigh. "And she's going to say no. Did he already buy a ring?"

"Yes, and he'll be paying it off for years, with 18 percent interest."

"This is so bad. See? I knew we should've said something to him. First he loses that job opportunity and now he'll lose Harper. He'll have nothing left."

"Maybe she'll say yes."

"She won't. She's already upset that her parents are giving her the silent treatment. Marrying Sean will make her relationship with her parents even worse. She won't let that happen. She'll want to fix it before she'll even consider marrying Sean."

"If we're right about Kiefer joining the organization, there's nothing Harper can do or say that will change her parents' minds. They'll still say they don't want her being with Sean."

"Maybe we're wrong about Kiefer. If he was invited to be a member last summer, then why is he taking so long to break up Harper and Sean? I mean, he just recently told her to break up with him but it's not like he gave her an ultimatum or anything."

"I know. I was thinking the same thing, which makes me wonder if this has nothing to do with the organization. Maybe her parents just decided they don't want her with someone like Sean. Maybe it's like she said and they want her with someone who's rich and has a college degree."

I wish that were true, because if it was, Harper and Sean could be together. Eventually her parents would come to accept him. But if Garret is right and Kiefer joins the organization, that's never going to happen.

On Thursday afternoon, I go back to see Jennifer. I only had that one session but I think I like her. She seems smart and I like that she's not one of those women who wears a ton of makeup and reeks of perfume. The counselor I saw after my mom died was one of those women. Her perfume was so strong it gave me a headache and she always wore purple eyeshadow and way too much blush. Jennifer has more of a natural, outdoorsy look and she seems athletic.

Garret came with me again, but next time I think I'll tell him to stay home. Now that I'm more relaxed, he doesn't need to sit in on all these sessions.

Today Jennifer asks about Frank and Ryan and I talk about them for the entire hour. It's good she's not forcing me to talk about my mom right away. If she did, I wouldn't come back.

Before we leave, I make an appointment for the same time next week. Afterward, Garret takes me out for dinner, just like he did the other day. He thinks he has to reward me for going to counseling, but really, I should be thanking him for making me go. I couldn't do it on my own.

Friday night we go to the park for the outdoor movie. Garret brought a sleeping bag to put on the ground and I packed a cooler with drinks.

Sara and Alex are already there when we arrive. They're sitting on a blanket with Caleb between them. They're talking and smiling, so that's a good sign.

"Let's set everything up over here," I tell Garret. We're standing off to the side, far away from Sara and Alex.

"Don't you want to say hi first?"

"We can't. If we do, we risk Alex telling us to sit by them and that will ruin the whole plan."

Garret's shaking his head. "You mean your matchmaking plan?"

"Yes." I toss the sleeping bag at him. "So get with the program."

"You haven't even met this guy. He could be a total jerk." Garret spreads the sleeping bag out and puts the cooler on top of it.

"That's why I need you to ask him some questions. We need to get to know him, figure out if he's good enough for Sara."

"Jade, I'm not getting involved in your little scheme."

"Come on. You're a guy. Take him aside and talk to him man to man."

"I'm just supposed to tell him to come talk to me? A guy he just met?"

"Make up an excuse. Go wait in line at the bathroom together." I point at the park shelter where the bathrooms are located. There's a line of guys standing on one side and girls on the other.

"Seriously, Jade? Guys do not go to the bathroom together."

"Then I'll take Sara aside and you can stay behind with Alex."

"And what exactly am I supposed to ask him?"

"Ask him what he thinks of Sara. If he thinks she's cute. Stuff like that."

"I'm not a 12-year-old girl, Jade. There's no way in hell I'm asking him that."

I smile and give him a kiss. "I love you, but you're not being very helpful. Let's go say hi before the movie starts."

Sara stands up as we walk toward her. "Hey, you made it."

"Yeah, we just got here." I turn to Alex, who's standing next to Sara. "Hi, I'm Jade. And this is Garret."

"Hi, I'm Alex." He shakes our hands.

He looks like she described; average height, dark hair, stubble on his face. He's thin and not very muscular. He's not my type, but from the way Sara's staring at him, I can tell she's attracted to him. She said he wears glasses, but he doesn't have them on tonight. He's wearing shorts and one of those vintage wash t-shirts in a light blue color.

Sara's wearing a red tank top and jeans. She's so short and small I bet she has to shop in the girls' department to find clothes that fit.

Caleb is sitting on a blanket, lost in his own little world, playing with his teething ring. He has more hair now than he did a few weeks ago but Sara can't make it stick down to his head. It's so thin it attracts static and sticks up all over the place. She's got him dressed in a white t-shirt and navy sweatpants. She has almost no money so she buys all his clothes at thrift stores or gets them for free at church giveaways.

The four of us talk for a few minutes and then Alex says, "You guys should grab the spot next to us before someone takes it."

"That's okay," I tell him. "We already set our stuff up over there."

Sara picks up her water bottle. "I'm going to go fill this."

"I'll go with you." I follow her, turning back to Garret and mouthing 'ask him' as we walk away. He gives me an eye roll and I laugh.

"How's it going so far?" I ask Sara.

"Great. We got here early and had a picnic. Alex played with Caleb a little so at least I know he's not totally freaked out by babies. He said he has tons of nephews and nieces so he's used to being around kids." She fills her water bottle at the drinking fountain.

"Do you want me to take Caleb so you guys can talk a little before the movie starts?"

"You don't have to. Caleb hasn't been fussy so Alex and I have been able to talk."

"Can I just borrow him for a few minutes? I need more baby experience."

She laughs. "You can borrow him whenever you want as long as you give him back."

When we meet up with Garret and Alex again, they're talking about sports. They seem to be getting along.

I pick Caleb up. "Sara's letting us borrow Caleb for a few minutes," I say to Garret.

"Practicing for when you have your own?" Alex jokes.

I smile. "Yeah, something like that."

"Take this in case you need anything." Sara hands Garret the diaper bag.

Garret and I go back to our spot. "That was so obvious, Jade. You need to work on your matchmaking skills."

"It wasn't obvious. I want to play with Caleb." I set him down on the sleeping bag.

"Alex knew you were trying to give them alone time. Guys aren't that stupid."

"He didn't seem to mind." I glance over at them. "And look how close they're sitting now. That was all my doing."

When I look back at Garret, he's holding Caleb on his lap. "You see that girl over there?" He points to me. "Never take her dating advice. You want advice on the ladies, you come to me."

"Hey!" I pick up Caleb's tiny hand. "Don't listen to him. I have good advice. If you ask Garret, he'll tell you to spray girls with air freshener, which you should never do by the way."

Caleb yawns really wide.

"I think we're boring him, Garret."

"He's just tired. You want to hold him?"

"No, you hold him."

Garret bounces Caleb and he starts that giggling and drooling thing he did when he was at our house. He's so adorable. And Garret is such a natural at this baby thing.

The movie starts playing on a giant inflatable screen. I look around and notice white lights are strung around some of the trees. The park is more crowded now with a mix of couples and families.

Garret turns to face the screen and I move next to him and lean my head on his shoulder. Caleb is still on Garret's lap, gnawing on his teething ring. For a moment, I imagine Caleb is *our* baby and I get this overwhelming feeling that I want that. I've had this feeling before but I always fight it, telling myself I can't have what I really want. But tonight I'm not fighting it. I'm letting myself feel it. And it feels really good.

Ten minutes into the movie, Sara comes over. "I can take him now so you two can watch the movie."

"I'm not done with him yet," I tell her. "Can we borrow him a little longer?"

"Sure. Come get me if you need me." She goes back over to Alex.

Garret sets Caleb in my lap. "I'm getting a soda. You want anything?"

"I'll take a water." Caleb's squirming as I try to hold on to him.

Garret sets the bottle of water next to me, then cracks open his can of Coke. The fizzing sound diverts Caleb's attention back to Garret and he reaches for him.

"Garret, I think he wants to sit with you. Can you take him back?"

"Nope." He sips his soda. "It's your turn. And you need the practice."

"I do? For what?" I give Caleb one of his toys, distracting him from Garret.

"For when we have kids. I can't hold them all the time, Jade. I have things to do and it's tiring on the arms."

"So now we're having kids?"

"You never know when the stork might drop one on your door. You gotta be prepared."

"The stork?" I laugh. "Garret, do we need to have the talk about where babies come from?"

He takes a drink of his soda. "I told Lilly about the stork and she believed me. Every time she saw one of those big white cranes, she thought it had just dropped off a baby at someone's house."

"Now that she's in school, some kid probably told her the truth."

"Yeah, probably."

"So how many kids do you think the stork's going to bring us?"

"I ordered three of them. Shipping and handling costs a fortune so get prepared to write a big check."

"I hope he doesn't bring them all at once."

"Yeah, that would suck. Although it would save on the shipping and handling costs since he'd only have to make one trip."

"I didn't know he took orders. I thought he just dropped them off."

"Sometimes he does, like when he surprised Sara with Caleb. But he also takes orders."

Caleb starts to fuss and cry a little. "You better take him." I hand him to Garret. "I think he's had enough of me."

"He's just tired or needs a diaper change."

I look over at Sara and Alex who are talking and laughing. "Should I take him over there? I hate to interrupt them."

Garret's searching through the diaper bag. "He needs to be changed."

"How do you know?"

"Because his pants are wet. His diaper's leaking."

"I'll go get Sara."

"Just change him yourself. You need to practice."

"Why? It's not like the stork's coming tomorrow."

"He might. His delivery schedule is very unpredictable." Garret hands me a diaper. He has a changing mat laid out on the sleeping bag and some baby wipes off to the side.

I lay Caleb down on the mat. He fusses some more as I take off his pants and wet diaper. "Now what do I do?"

Garret hands me a new diaper and takes the wet one from me. "Let me throw this out." When he comes back, he says, "Jade, you gotta hold the diaper over him or you'll get wet."

"How do you know? You've never changed a baby boy."

"No, but I've got the same parts as him and I know what they're capable of." Garret takes the diaper from me and grabs a baby wipe. "I'll finish up and you watch." Within seconds he's got Caleb in a fresh diaper.

I find another pair of pants in the diaper bag and put them on Caleb just as Sara stops by again.

Garret hands him to her. "He's all yours. Freshly changed."

"You didn't have to do that. You should've come and got me."

Garret gets up. "I'm going to go wash my hands."

Sara kisses Caleb, who's yawning. "I need to get him to bed. Alex and I are going to head out. But thanks for watching Caleb for me."

"Sure. He's a really good baby."

"Are you going to stay and watch the movie?"

"Probably, although we haven't really been watching it. We've been too busy playing with Caleb."

She smiles. "You guys will make great parents someday."

I shrug. "I don't know about that."

"You will. You guys really love each other and you're not afraid to show it. Kids pick up on that. It makes them feel safe and secure. I read that in a book, but it makes sense, right?"

"You ready to go?" Alex walks up and puts his arm around Sara's shoulder. Interesting. It could be a friend move. Or it could be more than that.

"Yeah, I just need to get his stuff."

"I'll get it." Alex picks up the diaper bag. "See you, Jade. Tell Garret if he wants to watch a game to give me a call."

"Okay. See you guys later."

As they walk away, I notice Caleb's already asleep on Sara's shoulder. He's even cuter when he sleeps.

"Did they leave?" Garret's back from the bathroom.

"Yeah. Alex said something about a game?"

"I asked if he wanted to meet at a sports bar sometime and watch a game."

"You never told me what you talked about with him."

"Let's see…we talked about how he thought Sara was cute, and how much we loved her outfit, and I asked him where she got those earrings. And then we discussed trends in nail polish colors."

I punch his arm. "Yeah, you're funny. What did you really talk about?"

"What do you think? Sports. That's what guys talk about."

"But you liked him?"

"I guess. I only talked to him a few minutes." Garret sits behind me, wrapping his arms around me and kissing the side of my face. "How long do we have to stay here?"

"I don't know. Why? You don't like the movie?"

"The movie's boring. You want to go back to my place?"

"Is there anything to do there? Because if I'm going to be bored, I might as well stay here."

"I guarantee you won't be bored."

"What do you have planned?"

He gives me a detailed description, whispering it in my ear.

I turn my head back and kiss him. "Your place sounds good. Let's go."

Chapter 14

GARRET

This morning we discovered we had no milk for breakfast. I knew we needed some when we left last night, but after I got Jade all worked up at the park we were in a hurry to get home. We hadn't done it for almost a week, so yeah, stopping for milk wasn't exactly on our minds.

We woke up at nine and I showered quick, then went to the store to get the milk. I also bought some strawberries and bananas in my continued attempt to get Jade to eat better.

My phone rings as I'm leaving the grocery store. I assume it's Jade calling, asking me to pick something up.

"Let me guess," I say when I answer. "You want donuts?"

"Garret?" I hear a deep voice on the other end of the phone.

"Who is this?"

"It's your grandfather."

I freeze, right in the middle of the parking lot. Someone honks at me and I get out of the way.

"Where are you?" He barks it at me. He was never in the military but you'd think he'd been a drill sergeant with his short abrupt speech pattern. He only talks that way when he's angry or annoyed, and it sounds like he's both of those things right now.

"I'm at the grocery store." I click the car remote to open the trunk.

"I'll call back later."

"No, wait!" If he hangs up, he'll never call back. "I can talk. Hold on a minute." I toss the bags in the trunk and get in the car. "Okay, go ahead."

"Is she there?"

"Who?" I can't think. He's making me nervous. My own grandfather makes me nervous. How fucked up is that?

"That girl."

"What girl? Jade?"

"The one you live with."

"Jade is my wife, Grandfather. You should know her name." I feel my anger rising, but I need to keep my temper under control. If he's actually calling me, we might have a chance to repair this relationship and I don't want to screw that up. "Jade's not here. She's at home."

"Have you spoken to your father recently?"

"Yes, just the other day."

"I assume he informed you of your summer job at the company."

So that's why my grandfather's calling me? To tell me what to do?

"I'm not working there. You know I don't want to take over the company."

"You're not taking it over, at least not right away. Your father is doing an adequate job with Kensington Chemical and he'll be in charge for at least the next 10 years, maybe 15."

Adequate job? My father's tripled the company's profits since he took it over. He's opened five new plants, doubled the workforce, been featured in tons of magazines. He's a huge success. And yet his father says he's done an 'adequate job.' My anger's ramping up again.

I take a breath and speak calmly. "Dad has done more than an adequate job. He works his ass off for the company and he's made it into one of the most successful companies in the world. You're way better off having him in charge than me."

"Your father won't be around forever. A succession plan needs to begin now. There's a lot to learn and you need to start learning it. I had your father working there when he was 16. You're 20. You're already behind."

"I don't think you understand. I'm not working at the company. Not this summer. Not 10 years from now."

"No, Garret. *You're* the one who does not understand." The volume of his voice goes up just enough to let me know he's angry, but not so much that it shows a lack of composure. He's all about control and not allowing others to dictate his emotions. "You were born into this family with certain obligations. Your father has indulged your juvenile behavior long enough. It's time to grow up and be a man. Accept the responsibilities that come with being a Kensington."

"It's just a name. It doesn't mean anything." As soon as I say it, I regret it. I try to take it back but it's too late.

"How dare you!" Now he's angry and he's not hiding it. "That name is a legacy! Most people would kill to trade places with you!"

"I'm sorry. I didn't mean to say that. What I meant was—"

"I don't want to hear your explanation." The phone goes silent. I think he might've hung up, but then I hear him say, "Garret, I'm extremely disappointed in you."

Fuck. That hurts.

And it shouldn't. I shouldn't care what he thinks of me. But I do.

"You had so much potential. You had opportunities handed to you that only a select few have ever been offered." He's referring to my being chosen to be president someday, which he considered to be a huge honor. "And you just threw it all away."

"It wasn't right for me. I didn't want—"

"Exactly. It's all about you, isn't it, Garret? It's always about what *you* want, instead of what's best for you and this family. You're a spoiled child. You don't deserve what you've been given. I blame your father for that. And the years you spent under the care of that woman who nearly destroyed your father's life."

I grip the steering wheel and force myself to breathe before I completely lose it. "Don't talk about my mother."

"I'm willing to give you another chance. You're young, which means you're naive and impulsive. And you're confused, due to a lack of proper discipline. Your father has failed you. But I will not allow him to continue to do so."

"What do you mean?"

"You will work at Kensington Chemical. You will accept your responsibilities and be grateful to have them. You will stop being a child and start being a man. You will leave—"

"Just stop!" My patience is used up. I can't listen to this. In this short conversation, he's managed to insult Jade, put down my dad, put down me, say bad things about my mother, and order me around like I'm one of his employees. "For the last time, I'm not taking over the company. I'm not working there. Not this summer. Not ever. I'm an adult. I have my own life now. And it's not yours to control."

The phone goes silent again. My heart's pounding hard in my chest. I've never talked that way to my grandfather. The silence continues. Then I hear him again.

"I will break you, Garret." His voice is eerily calm. It gives me chills. "I will break you, just like I broke Pearce. You, yourself, said he was a success. That was all because of me. He'd be nothing if I hadn't taken control and forced him to get his life on track. I had to break him, then build him back up. And I will do the same to you."

"I don't know what the hell you're talking about. What does that even mean?"

"Someday you'll thank me. Goodbye, Garret."

He hangs up. I'm still sitting in the car in the grocery store parking lot. I set the phone down and take some deep breaths, my head hung over the steering wheel where my arms are resting.

Someone taps on my window. I look over and see a woman with two kids and a grocery cart.

"Are you okay?" she asks. "Do you need medical help?"

I open the car door. "No, I'm fine. Thanks."

She nods, then walks to her car.

I need to get home, but I don't think I should drive right now. I'm boiling over with rage and my head is spinning, trying to figure out what the hell my grandfather meant.

I call my dad. "I need to talk to you."

"What's wrong? You don't sound like yourself."

"It's Grandfather. He just called me and I think he threatened me. I'm not exactly sure but it sounded like a threat."

"What did he say?"

I replay the conversation for my dad, word-for-word, because those words are now cemented in my brain. It's a conversation I'll never forget.

My dad lets out a heavy sigh. "I'll talk to him."

"No. Don't. I don't want him thinking I need you to fight my battles for me. I just need some advice on how to handle this."

"You have to cut him out of your life, Garret. I'm sorry to have to say that, but there's no other solution. If you let him in your life, he takes over. After last spring, I thought he'd given up on you. I didn't think he'd want you anywhere near the company given your negative public image. But I guess he figures in a few years all of that will be forgotten."

"So if I ignore him and don't speak to him, he'll let this go?"

"My father doesn't let anything go. If he wants something, he doesn't give up. But what's he going to do? He can't force you to work at the company."

"Why did you listen to him? I mean, when you were younger, why did you let him control you?"

I've never asked my dad that question. Our relationship in the past was so strained that we were never at a point where we could have an honest conversation. But now we are, and I've always wanted to ask him that.

"My father and I have a long history. He knows how to get in my head. He knows the right words to use and he knows my weaknesses. And his best weapon is that he fights on a psychological level. He rarely raises his voice. Rarely shows emotion. Yet he gets in your head."

"So that's what he meant when he said he'd break me?"

"My father had horses when he was growing up. That's why he uses that analogy. Once you break a horse he'll follow commands. He'll be loyal and won't step out of bounds. My father broke me years ago. I fought against him, but after your mother died, I had nothing left. And now I'm at the point where I've accepted my life and I try to get along with my father the best I can for my mother's sake."

I notice another call coming in. It's probably Jade wondering why I'm taking so long.

"Garret, I wish I could do something about my father, but he is who he is. He's always been this way. I can't change him. And after what happened today, I think it's best if you don't have a relationship with him."

"Then I guess I won't be coming home for Christmas."

"Don't be ridiculous. Of course you're coming home."

"But what about Grandfather?"

"He's no longer invited. It will upset my mother, and Lilly will be disappointed, but you're my son and I want you home for Christmas. I'm not letting my father interfere with that. You and Jade are coming here and you're spending the week with us, just like you planned. Nothing's changed."

"Have you told Katherine yet?"

"Yes, she knows you're coming. She keeps saying she's going to spend Christmas with her parents and take Lilly with her, but that's not going to happen. I'll make sure of it."

"Why does she keep trying to keep me away from Lilly? She never wants me to talk to Lilly on the phone. And now she doesn't want me to see her?"

He laughs a little. "Katherine has noticed that Lilly is becoming more and more like you every day. She swims constantly and the other day Katherine caught her in the game room playing that video game you used to play all the time. The race car one. And then she found Lilly in the gym trying to shoot baskets like you taught her. Katherine's upset because she thinks her little princess is turning into a tomboy."

"That's hilarious."

"I told her she's overreacting. Lilly still has her tea parties and plays with her dolls and wears pink all the time. It's just that now she prefers swimming to ballet. And she does those other things because they remind her of you. She still misses you a lot."

"Yeah, she tells me that all the time." I start the car. "I need to go. I'm at the grocery store."

"Let me know if you have any more trouble with my father."

"I will. I'll call you later this week."

When I get home, Jade's on the couch folding laundry. "What took you so long? I was getting worried."

"I got an unexpected phone call." I take the groceries to the kitchen and put the milk in the fridge. "When I was in the parking lot at the grocery store, my grandfather called."

She drops the shirt she was folding. "Seriously? What did he say?" She races over to where I'm standing.

"He told me I had to work at the company this summer, like I had no choice in the matter."

"That's it? He wasn't calling to make up? Did he say he's sorry for how he treated you?"

"Yeah, like that would ever happen."

"What did you tell him?"

"I told him I wouldn't do it. Then he lectured me about how it's my responsibility as a Kensington to take over the company, making sure to tell me what a disappointment I am to him."

Jade puts her arms around me. "I'm sorry, Garret."

I hug her back. "It's okay. If he's going to be that way, I don't want him in my life."

"Really?" She pulls back. "So you're not going to talk to him anymore?"

"I have nothing to say to him. He doesn't like my choices. He'll never accept me unless I do what he says, and I'm not going to do that. I'm not taking orders from him."

"You should tell your dad about this."

"I already did. I called him and told him what happened and he said I need to cut my grandfather out of my life. Otherwise, he'll keep trying to control me."

"What about your grandmother? Can you still talk to her?"

"I could, but it'll be awkward. She's loyal to my grandfather even if she doesn't agree with him." I let Jade go and open the fridge. "I don't want to talk about them. What do you want to eat?"

"I thought we'd have cereal since you got the milk."

"I need more than cereal. I'll make eggs. And I got us some fruit." I take the carton of eggs from the fridge, then get the skillet from under the counter.

"Garret." Jade stands next to me at the stove. "Are you sure you're okay?"

"I'm fine. I never expected him to come around."

She nods, but I know she doesn't believe me.

So maybe I *did* think he'd come around, but he didn't, and I can't change his mind. Now we'll never speak again. He lost his only grandson. And the sad thing is, I don't think he even cares.

Chapter 15

JADE

*G*arret doesn't talk at all during breakfast. I feel so bad for him. His grandfather basically just gave him an ultimatum: Work for the company or I want nothing to do with you. Who does something like that? Is having Garret run the company more important than having him as a grandson? Like they can't find someone else to take over the company in 20 years, or whenever Pearce steps down?

My phone rings as we're finishing breakfast. Garret motions to it. "Go ahead and get it. I'll clean up."

I pick it up and see it's Grace calling. "Hi, Grace. I was just going to call you."

"Honey, you don't have to call me every day."

"You don't want to talk to me?" I ask, kiddingly.

"I love talking to you. But I know you're busy."

"I'm not that busy. When am I going to see you again? You need to come visit me."

"Actually, that's why I'm calling. William will be in Los Angeles for work next week and Meredith is coming with him, so I wondered if this might be a good time for us to all get together."

"Like during the week?"

"No, next weekend. I was thinking we could all meet at my house in Santa Barbara. Everyone could stay over Saturday night and leave on Sunday. Unless you have plans. Sunday is Halloween. I wasn't sure if people your age celebrate Halloween."

"We don't have plans, but let me check with Garret." I run over and meet him at the sink. "Do you care if we go to Santa Barbara next weekend?"

He shrugs. "I don't care."

"Okay, we can go," I say to Grace. "What time should we be there?"

"Afternoon would be good. That will give me time to clean the house and air it out after being closed up for so long."

"I'll get there in the morning so I can help."

"Jade, I don't want to put you to work."

"Well, you'll have to because I'm getting there early. I want to spend time with you. I never see you."

"Okay, honey. Then what time will you be there?"

"We could be there around nine." I look at Garret as I say it. He nods in agreement.

"Wonderful. We'll have breakfast together out on the patio."

"Sounds good. So what else is going on? Do you have any plans for today?"

"I was just heading out to my bridge club, so I can't talk. I just wanted to ask you about next weekend."

"See? You're the one who's too busy to talk to me."

She laughs. "No, not at all. But I do have bridge club every Saturday."

We say goodbye and I follow Garret into the bedroom.

"So the plan is we're going to Santa Barbara and staying at Grace's house overnight. We're meeting William and his wife there."

"He's not bringing Walt with him, is he?"

"I don't think so. Why would he bring Walt?"

"It doesn't matter. Never mind." Garret takes his swim trunks and a t-shirt from the drawer. "So what about Halloween?"

"What about it?" I meet him at the dresser.

He kisses me. "We have to celebrate every holiday. It's tradition."

"We'll be at Grace's house in the morning but we could do something when we get back. What do you want to do?"

"I don't know yet. I'll have to think about it. I'll figure something out." He goes in the closet to get his gym bag. "We need to get ready. They want us at the pool an hour before the kids arrive."

Today is the swim class we volunteered to work at. It's all afternoon and since this is the first time we've done this, we have to get there early to go over how everything works.

When we get to the pool, we join the other new volunteers who are standing around waiting for instruction. Keith is in charge of the program so he goes over all the details and answers any questions. Then he introduces his wife, Lisa, and their two teenage sons, who are also volunteering. Their sons are on the high school swim team.

The people who have volunteered in the past show up a half hour later since they already know how this works. Most of the volunteers are from the men's and women's swim teams here at Camsburg. They arrive suited up and ready to go.

The kids arrive at one and Keith does a short welcome speech, then each volunteer is paired up with a kid. I'm working the snack table with Lisa but I also have to supervise a six-year-old girl in the locker room.

When they call off her name I go over and stand next to her. Her name is Emma. She has long red hair and her skin is covered with freckles. Her eyes haven't left the pool since she arrived. She looks scared to death.

"Emma, let's go to the locker room and you can change into your suit."

Her head jerks when I say it, like she didn't realize I was standing there. She grabs my hand, clutching it for dear life. The kid's got some strength. She's holding my hand so tight it hurts.

"You don't have to be scared." I lean down so I'm more on her level. "It's just water. It's fun. You get to splash around."

She shakes her head, like there's no way she's getting in the water.

"How about if you start by just putting on your swimsuit?"

She lifts her shirt up a little and I see she already has a bright yellow swimsuit on.

"Okay, well, we should probably put your hair up. Let's go in the locker room. Come on."

She walks next to me, so close she almost trips on my legs. I spot Garret next to a boy around eight who's kind of chubby with a buzz cut that makes his face look even rounder. He's staring at the ground and walking really slow, like he doesn't want to be here.

"Mrs. Kensington?" Emma is tugging on my shirt. I'm surprised she remembered my name. It didn't seem like she was paying attention when Keith was introducing the volunteers.

"You can just call me Jade." We're in the locker room now and I take her to the mirror to put her hair up.

"I need to go home."

"But you just got here. Don't you want to go in the pool?"

"I can't swim."

"That's why you're here." I point to some of the girls from the swim team. "Those girls are going to teach you how to swim. They're really good swimmers."

Emma's lip starts quivering and tears run down her cheeks. Crap! Now what do I do? All the other kids are running around the locker room, happy to be here, and I get the only one who isn't.

"Let's go sit down, okay?"

I lead her to one of the benches at the end of the locker room where it's quiet. She's still clutching my hand and crying.

"What are you scared of?"

"I'm gonna drown in the water and then it'll be all black."

"What's going to be black?"

"My sister said when you die everything's black. You can't see. It's like you're in the dark. And I don't like the dark. I'm scared of the dark."

"I don't know where your sister heard that, but she's wrong. When you die, there's light everywhere. It's so bright you have to wear sunglasses."

Her eyes get big and she puts all her attention on me. "Who told you that?"

"My mom did." It's a lie, but it sounds better than telling her where I really heard it, which was on a TV show about death. "But Emma, you're not going to die. You'll have your swim teacher with you the whole time and you'll wear these floaty things on your arms so your head stays above the water."

"Can you swim?"

"Yeah. I learned when I was your age. But I had to teach myself."

Actually, I'm surprised I didn't drown. A house down the street from mine had a small above-ground pool and one summer day I snuck into the back yard and jumped in the pool. It was only four feet deep but I was only six so not very tall. I couldn't keep my head above the water, but I was close enough to the edge that I was able to get out. It was scary, but I went back later that week and did it again. The owners were always at work during the day so I just kept sneaking into their back yard and using their pool. By the end of the summer, I learned how to swim.

"Can you get in with me?" Emma has stopped crying but she won't let go of my hand.

"I can't. I'm in charge of snacks. And I don't have my suit here."

"Please?"

"What if we just stick our feet in the water? Would you do that?"

She nods.

I put her hair up, then she takes her shorts and t-shirt off. Her swimsuit has a yellow ruffle at the bottom. It's cute.

We go back to the pool. All the other kids are in the water. A lot of them look scared, especially the younger ones.

I take Emma to the edge of the pool and we sit down. I put my feet in, but she scoots away from the edge.

"Try it, Emma. It feels good on your feet."

She inches toward the edge, grabbing the back of my shirt and holding on as she dips one foot in the water. Her lips turn up a tiny bit.

"Now try the other one," I tell her.

She grabs my shirt even tighter as she puts her other foot in the water. Her eyes are on the pool and I turn and see her looking at Garret, who's just a few feet away.

He comes over to us, along with the chubby boy with the buzz cut. "How's it going?"

"We're getting our feet wet. This is Emma. Emma this is Garret. He's my husband."

"Hi, Emma," he says to her.

She glances at him, but is too scared to say hi.

I peel her hand off my shirt. "Let's put some floaties on you, like that boy has on." I point to the kid next to Garret.

"This is Seth," Garret says.

"Hi, Seth." I smile at him, but he won't look at me when he says hi back. He's very shy.

"Is everything okay over here?" I turn and see Lisa behind me, holding a clipboard.

"Emma isn't sure she wants to get in the water."

"It looks like you're assigned to Haley." Lisa waves at one of the girls from the swim team. "Haley, I found her. Emma's over here."

Haley swims over. She's wearing a bright pink, one-piece suit and has pink and green ribbons weaved into her long blond braid.

Haley smiles really wide. "Hi, Emma. I couldn't find you."

"We took a little longer in the locker room." I turn to Emma. "I have to go now, okay?"

She shakes her head, keeping hold of my hand.

"Haley will take care of you. Look at her hair. It has ribbons in it."

Haley turns around to show her. "My friend did it for me. You like it?"

Emma smiles and finally lets go of my hand. "It's pretty."

Haley jumps out of the pool. "Let's get your floaties on." She takes Emma away.

Garret smiles at me as his hand touches my foot in the water. "I'll see you later."

The swim lessons continue and the kids start to have fun. Mid-afternoon, they break for snacks, then it's back to swimming. I talk to Lisa while the kids swim. She tells me about her sons and all the sports they're in. I like Keith and Lisa and their boys. They seem like a nice family. And Keith is a good coach. He really cares about his team. I don't think Garret would've ever fixed his shoulder if Keith hadn't talked him into it.

At five, it's time for the kids to get back on the bus to go home. I help Emma in the locker room and dry her hair for her.

"So did you have fun?"

She nods. "Haley's nice. I like her."

"And now you're not afraid of the water." I finish brushing her hair. "Okay, you're all set."

She hugs me. "Thank you."

I hug her back. "For doing your hair?"

"For letting me know it's not dark." She picks up her backpack.

"What?"

"Bye!" She waves at me as she follows another little girl out the locker room doors to the bus.

"She's cute, isn't she?" Lisa's next to me, picking wet towels off the floor. "She's still so sad, but I think today was good for her. She was smiling a lot."

"Why is she sad?"

"Her father was killed in a car accident last summer. The past few months have been difficult for her and her family."

"Oh. I didn't know."

Lisa drops the wet towels in a bin. "You and Garret are free to go. Keith and I will finish up here."

"Okay." I wait in the hallway for Garret, still thinking about Emma. So that's why she thanked me for telling her it wasn't dark. She didn't want her dad to be in the dark. Because the dark is scary and bad. No wonder her face lit up when I told her it was light.

Garret comes out of the locker room, his gym bag over his shoulder. "Ready to go?"

"Yeah." I turn to walk down the hall. My eyes are tearing up from Emma's comment and I don't want Garret to see.

"Hey." He steps in front of me. "Are you crying? Your eyes are all red."

"No, it's just the chlorine in the air. Sometimes it irritates my eyes."

He takes my hand. "I'm starving. You want to go eat?"

We go to a pizza place for dinner and as we're eating, he tells me about Seth. He said Seth gets made fun of and bullied all the time because he's overweight. He doesn't go to the pool in the summer because he's too embarrassed to be seen in swim trunks. And when he goes to the beach, he always keeps his t-shirt on and doesn't go in the water. That's why he never learned how to swim.

"How was Emma?" Garret gets his wallet out to pay the check.

"She was sweet, but really afraid of the water."

"You seemed to calm her down."

The waitress stops by and picks up the money Garret left.

"Emma's dad died last summer so she was asking me about death."

"What did you tell her?"

"She thought when you die that everything's dark, so I told her that it's not dark at all. That it's so bright you need sunglasses. And when she left, she thanked me. She didn't want her dad to be in the dark."

Garret reaches across the table and holds my hand. "If we ever have kids, you're going to be a great mom, you know that?"

I don't answer. I'm not ready to have another kid discussion. But I admit I liked being around them today, which surprised me because I usually don't do so well around kids. But I must be getting better at it because all the noise and chaos didn't really bother me. And I liked watching Garret teach Seth how to swim. He helped some of the other kids, too. He's really patient and a good teacher. As I watched him, I kept imagining him teaching our own kids how to swim someday and it made me smile.

Garret wakes me from my thoughts. "Let's get out of here."

"You want to go to a movie?"

"Let's watch one at home." He gets up from his chair, holding his hand out for me.

"Are you in a hurry?'

"Yeah, kind of."

"What are you in a hurry for?"

"I'll show you when we get home."

As soon as we walk in the house, he holds my face in his hands and kisses me, his tongue doing all kinds of yummy things that have me struggling to remain standing.

I guess this is why he was in a hurry to leave the restaurant, although I'm not sure what got him in the mood. Whatever it was, now he's got *me* in the mood, too.

"Can we go to the bedroom?"

"We can go wherever you want." He unbuttons my shirt as he kisses me. "I just need to have you." He slides my shirt off, letting it fall to the floor.

"Why do you need to have me?" I smile as he unhooks my bra, then takes if off and tosses it aside.

"Because you're hot." He kisses me as he walks forward, pushing me backward toward the bedroom. "And beautiful," he says in between kisses. "And sexy." We reach the bed and he lifts me onto it. "And all mine."

He slides my shorts and panties down. I flip over and toss the pillows aside and rip the comforter back. I feel Garret's hands on me, strong and firm around my hips. I remain on my hands and knees as he kisses my lower back. He must've got naked when I turned around because I feel his bare chest on my skin as his kisses move up my spine. We stay there a moment, then I flip back around and lie beneath him.

"You going somewhere?" He smiles.

"Just changing positions."

"But I like that one."

"I want this one tonight."

"And that one tomorrow?" He lowers his body over mine.

"Yeah," I close my eyes and smile. "That one tomorrow."

His lips brush against mine, then he kisses me as he inches in excruciatingly slow, and pulls out just as slow.

"Damn, you feel good." He says it in a deep, sexy voice.

I kiss him back and push my hips into him. Then it's an all out race to the finish. It's not that we're in a hurry, but sometimes when we get to this point, we can't slow down. Other times, we're able to control ourselves better, but tonight it's fast and furious.

We collapse on the bed, Garret on his back and me sprawled over his chest.

"That was fun," I say, a post-sex smile on my face.

"Always is." He strokes my hair. "You want to go to a movie now?"

"I guess we could. It's still early. What do you want to do *tomorrow?*"

"Make you pancakes."

I laugh. "At Garret's Pancake House? I don't know. I'm not sure I like their prices."

"You love their prices and you know it. So what kind of pancakes am I making?"

"Apple cinnamon."

"Interesting choice."

"What? It's fall, and you eat apples in the fall so I'm in the mood for apple-cinnamon."

"You sure it has nothing to do with the price?"

I hear him laughing and look up at him. "I wasn't even considering the price."

"Yeah, right."

"What are you trying to say?"

"The price for apple-cinnamon pancakes is shower sex, which we haven't had for a while. And I know that's your favorite place to do it."

"No, it's not. I like the bed just as much." I try to sound convincing.

"Just admit it, Jade. You like the shower. You like being wet."

I rest my chin on his chest. "Whatever. You like it, too."

"Of course I like it. Shower sex is a combination of my three favorite things; water, sex, and you. I love feeling your slick skin and your wet lips and—"

"Let's just do it right now." I jump off the bed, already turned on by his description.

He chases me into the bathroom and scoops me up in his arms. "You know you can't pay for the pancakes ahead of time."

"I'm not." I smile. "So we're doing this again tomorrow."

"You are seriously the best wife ever." He kisses me as he reaches in to turn the shower on.

I'm sure Garret thought that once we were married, I wouldn't want to have sex as much. That's the stereotype, right? The wife doesn't want sex anymore but the husband still does? Well, it's not true for me. I love being with Garret this way. And not just because he's hot and totally turns me on. It's more than that. The longer we're together, the closer we become. Our love just keeps getting stronger and that makes the sex even better. So yeah, we'll be doing this again in the morning.

Chapter 16

GARRET

I really need to get some studying done. It's Sunday afternoon and I spent all morning having sex with Jade. Well, not the whole morning. We took a break long enough for me to make the apple-cinnamon pancakes she wanted. And shit, they were a lot of work. I hadn't made them before. You have to shred the apples on a grater, which almost shredded my fingers off. I don't think I'm making those again. I'll switch those out for some other kind of pancake.

It's funny how much Jade loves this new tradition of ours. I didn't think I'd ever be able to replace Al's Pancake House. But she likes Garret's Pancake House just as much, mainly because of the prices. I was totally kidding when I made up that menu. I didn't think she'd go for it. But she did, and now she loves it. She keeps asking me when I'm going to have my 'buyer's choice' promotion, in which she gets to make up a price.

"Garret, your phone's ringing." I hear Jade calling me from the bedroom. I'm in the living room, trying to study even though I don't feel like doing it.

She brings me the phone.

I see Sean's name on the screen and answer it. "Hey, Sean. I swear, I was planning to call you today. You just beat me to it."

"Hey, Garret. Is Jade there?" Sean sounds serious. He never sounds serious. He's always joking around.

"Yeah, she's right here. Why?"

"Can you put me on speaker?"

"Is something wrong?"

"Just put me on speaker so I can tell you both."

"Jade, Sean wants to talk to us." I motion her to the couch. "I have him on speaker. Go ahead, Sean."

"Harper's in the hospital."

"What?" Jade yells it. "What happened?"

"She's okay. She's in pain but she's okay. She tore her rotator cuff. Like completely tore it. It's pretty bad."

"When did it happen?" Jade takes the phone from me.

"This morning. We were at the gym and she was using one of the weight machines and she heard a loud snap in her shoulder. Even I heard it, and I was two machines down from hers. After it happened she couldn't lift her arm. I took her to the emergency room and they ran some tests on her shoulder and found she'd torn her rotator cuff."

"But they're not keeping her in the hospital, right?'

"No, they're sending her home later today. The doctor is calling her parents right now. I'm in the waiting room."

"Does she need surgery?"

"Yeah, that's how they fix a full tear like that. It doesn't heal on its own. They're not sure when the surgery will be. For now, her arm's in a sling so she doesn't do more damage."

Jade starts firing off questions at Sean, mostly medical questions he can't answer. Questions about tendons and bones and ligaments.

Jade became an expert on shoulder anatomy when she found out I was having shoulder pain. My injury was caused by being shot in the upper chest, which damaged the surrounding tissue, so it's nothing like Harper's injury. But before I went to the doctor, Jade read everything she could about shoulder and chest anatomy so she could understand whatever the doctor was going to tell us. It wasn't necessary, but she didn't know any other way to help me and she was desperate to do something. I love how she takes care of me like that. I don't need her to, but I love that she still does.

"The doctor just left the room," Sean says. "I need to go back in there."

"Hey, so does this mean she's done with tennis?" I'm almost certain of the answer but I ask anyway.

"Yeah. She's done. Even after the surgery, the doctor told her not to play tennis because the shoulder is more susceptible to being torn again."

"When can I talk to her?" Jade asks.

"She told me to tell you she'll call you later. She's still in a lot of pain right now and the painkillers she's taking make her really tired. She'll probably fall asleep as soon as we get home."

"Okay, well, tell her we're thinking of her. She's not going back to the dorm, is she?"

"No, I'm having her stay at my place so I can take care of her. I'm taking the next few days off from work. I'm sure I'll get fired, but whatever. She needs me."

"You're a good boyfriend, Sean."

"Garret would do the same thing for you."

"I know he would." Jade smiles at me. "Harper and I are very lucky."

"I gotta go. I'll talk to you guys later." He hangs up.

Jade sets the phone down. "Do you think she'll be okay?"

"She'll be fine. Rotator cuff injuries are common with athletes. But she'll have a long recovery and a lot of physical therapy."

"But she can't play tennis anymore. She loves tennis. Being on the tennis team is the main reason she went to Moorhurst."

"Yeah, it's going to take a while for her to accept the fact that she can't play anymore. When you're an athlete and you can no longer do your sport, it's almost like a death. You mourn the loss of that part of your life. That's why I was freaking out when I didn't think I'd be able to compete on a swim team again. I wasn't ready to say goodbye to swimming."

"But you're getting better, right? You never talk about your shoulder anymore."

"Because I barely notice the pain. The physical therapy, and all the time I spend at the gym and the pool, is paying off. By next year I know I'll be competing again."

"I can't wait. I'm going to all your meets."

"Well, yeah, I would hope so." I lean over and kiss her. "You're my only fan. I need *someone* cheering me on."

"I'm also going to the pool with you while you train."

I'm smiling at her. "You want more pool sex, don't you?"

"No!" She playfully punches me. "I just like to go there and hang out with you. I find it relaxing."

I talk by her ear. "You'd be even more relaxed if we had sex."

"I don't think I can do that again. I'm too worried someone will walk in."

"That's why we need to hurry up and get a house so we can get our own pool."

"I don't want a house here. I don't really like this town."

"We wouldn't have to live here forever. Just until we're done with school."

"I'd rather keep renting. I don't want to buy a house, then have to sell it in a couple years. Besides, I thought we were going to *build* a house so we could make it the way we want it."

"We are. So when do you want to do that?"

"I don't know. When we talked about it last summer, I thought it'd be in maybe 10 years, after I finished med school and a residency and found a job. But now that I'm not doing that, maybe it could be sooner."

"How about after we graduate?"

"I don't know what we'll be doing for work so it's hard to say. We'll have to be close to wherever our jobs are."

"Jade, we're not going to have regular jobs where we have to show up at an office and sit in a cubicle from nine to five. We have money. We don't need to do that. Which means we can live wherever we want."

"Then what are we going to do for jobs?"

"We're going to be self-employed. Have our own business. Be our own boss."

"You're just deciding this for me?"

"Would you rather spend hours in traffic commuting to and from work, then sit at a desk all day? Be ordered around by a shitty boss and have to deal with office politics? Have only two weeks off a year and be told when you're allowed to take it?"

"All jobs can't be that bad."

"Most of them are exactly like that. Ask anyone. That's why most people hate their jobs."

"I don't know how to run my own business."

"That's why you have me. I can help you."

"But then I'll have to hire employees and I don't think I want to do that."

"You don't have to. Your business can just be you. A sole proprietorship. Lots of people have those."

"Wow. You really know a lot about this stuff. You must be smart." She smiles.

"Bringing out the insults again?"

"I just told you you're smart."

"Yeah, sarcastically."

"I know you're smart. I was just kidding. You're able to figure out that stock market stuff. That makes you practically a genius."

"Not really. But I'm pretty smart when it comes to business stuff."

"So what are *you* going to do after graduation? I know you want to start a company but what's it going to be? Have you decided?"

"Not yet, but I've been thinking that maybe I'll start with a nonprofit while I'm figuring out what the for-profit business will be."

"You mean like a charity or something?"

"Yeah, but it has to be something I feel strongly about. Like yesterday when we were at the pool I was thinking, why don't they have free classes like that all over the country? A lot of kids drown because they don't know how to swim. But a lot of them don't have access to a pool and don't have money for swim lessons. So maybe I'll start an organization that gives kids free swimming lessons."

"You should definitely do that. You could partner with colleges, like the program here does. Colleges usually have pools and most have a swim team."

"I need to think about it some more, but yeah, I'd like to do something like that. Something related to swimming. I'd actually like to have several businesses. Start one, and then when it's established, start another."

"You're going to be busy. Are you going to have any time left for me?"

"I'll always make time for you." I pull her onto my lap. "Now going back to the house, when are we going to build this thing?"

"Well, I guess if we're working for ourselves, we can build it after we graduate. We just need to figure out where in California we want to live."

"Maybe we should start taking trips on the weekends. Check out some areas."

"You're really in a hurry to do this, aren't you?"

"I don't want to finish college and then be stuck living in an apartment. We don't need to build the house right away but we should find some land to buy."

"Then Iet's start looking. We're still going to live on the beach, right?"

"Yeah, but it's hard to find land for sale along the ocean, which is why we need to start looking now."

"This is so exciting! I can't wait to build our house." She hugs me while still on my lap, pressing herself into my crotch.

"Hey, don't get me going again. I really need to study."

"It's just a hug."

I laugh. "Yeah, it's always just a hug."

"It's *your* fault. You're the one who taught me how to hug."

"I didn't teach you how to hug like *that*."

"I have no idea what you're talking about." She smiles at me as she gets off my lap. "I'll let you study. I need to study, too."

We study all afternoon and order takeout for dinner. Afterward, Jade says she's calling Harper so I go out on the deck to give her some privacy. I check the messages on my phone and as I'm doing that, a call comes in. It's Kyle, the football player. He keeps texting and calling me, trying to get me to do stuff with him. I know he's only doing it because of my dad. Kyle's a business major, like me, and he thinks if we become friends, I'll introduce him to my dad. The guy acts like my dad's a celebrity or something.

I usually ignore his calls but I decide to answer because otherwise he'll keep calling. "Hi, Kyle."

"Kensington, how's it going? You're a hard man to get a hold of. I've been trying this number for days."

Get a clue, idiot. I don't want to talk to you. I don't say that, but I want to.

"I've been really busy. Did you need something?"

"I just wanted to invite you to a party I'm having on Sunday."

"Is this a Halloween party?"

"Yeah, but costumes are optional. Stop by anytime after eight."

He always just assumes I'm coming to his parties. It's another reason I don't like him.

"And tell your wife she's invited, too."

The fact that he has to make that clear just shows how clueless he is. I'm married. I'm not going to show up without my wife at a party full of drunk girls wearing sexy costumes. Those parties are for single people looking to hook up. Everyone knows that.

"I don't think we can make it," I tell him. "But thanks for the invite."

"Come on, Garret. You never show up at my parties. Or *any* parties. This is college. Live a little."

Kyle reminds me of Blake, always pushing me to go to parties. I'm glad that asshole's out of my life. He probably flunked out of college by now. I still talk to Decker now and then but he doesn't mention Blake. And I don't ask.

"Garret, are you there?"

"I can't go to the party. I forgot that Jade and I are going to Santa Barbara this weekend to visit a friend of the family."

"On Halloween? That sucks. But hey, the party will go all night. Just stop by whenever you get back."

The guy doesn't take no for an answer. He just keeps talking. This is why I avoid answering his calls.

"I'll think about it. I have to go. I'll see you later."

I hang up before he can say any more.

Since he's the most popular guy on campus, Kyle's party will be huge. Jade would hate it. She loves Halloween, but going to a party like that is not how she'd want to celebrate it.

I'm not sure how we'll celebrate it. We'll probably get back from Santa Barbara late afternoon. Maybe we'll do like we did last year and I'll get some scary movies and load up on candy. Jade loved it when I had that party in my dorm room. I tried to decorate the place with some cobwebs and orange lights. I knew she'd never celebrated Halloween so I wanted to make sure she had the basics; cobwebs, candy corn, and every kind of candy bar I could find. I had so much candy. Jade was still eating it months later.

Most other girls would say that party was stupid or boring, but not Jade. She thought it was amazing.

That was such a great night. Just her and me. And then she stayed with me. Wrapped in my arms. All night.

Best Halloween I ever had.

Chapter 17

JADE

Sean texted me and said now would be a good time to call Harper. He said she's been asleep but just woke up and is watching TV at his apartment.

I call her. "Harper, how are you feeling?"

"I'm okay." She sounds either sleepy or depressed. I can't really tell. I hope she's just sleepy.

"You're not okay. You hurt your shoulder. How does it feel?"

"It's not a sharp pain. It's more like a constant aching. I don't even know how I did it. I was using one of the weight machines and my shoulder just snapped. My tennis coach said it might've been weak from overuse. I've been practicing my serve a lot."

"You talked to your tennis coach?"

"Yeah, right after I left the hospital. I told her what the doctor said. She was almost as disappointed as me."

"I'm sorry, Harper. I know how much you love being on the team."

"It's not just that. I can't play at all anymore."

"Is there anything I can do?" I'm sure there isn't, but I have to ask.

"You can tell Sean to stop babying me." Her voice switches to a much happier tone. Sean must have walked in the room. "He won't let me off the couch. He acts like I broke my leg or something."

"You were in the hospital just a few hours ago," I hear Sean say. He must be sitting next to her.

"Yes, but I can still walk." She laughs.

"Can you move your arm?" I ask her.

"I can, but I can't lift it above my head so it's going to be hard getting dressed."

"Which is why I'll be there every morning," Sean says.

"Sean thinks he's going to show up every morning at my dorm room and help me get dressed. But I told him I don't need him to do that."

"I'm doing it because I love you," I hear him say.

"You're so sweet." I hear her kiss him, then say, "Jade, I put you on speaker. Tell Sean to stop worrying about me."

"Jade, the woman's driving me crazy," he says.

"Yeah, it sounds like you have a difficult patient there."

"And now she's yelling at me because I took off work tomorrow to stay home with her."

"I don't want you missing work and getting in trouble," she says.

"You come before work, Harper. You know that."

Isn't that the truth? He gave up that great job offer for her. If she only knew.

"When can you go back to class?" I ask Harper.

"Tuesday. Tomorrow I'm seeing a specialist who will take a closer look at my test results and figure out when

I'm going to have the surgery. It sounds like it's going to be over Thanksgiving break."

"So you're having it done in LA?"

"Yeah. That way I can recover at home for a few days."

I hear the oven timer buzzing in the background. "Pizza's ready," Sean says.

"Sean made me one of his famous pizzas because I slept through dinner," Harper says. "And he rented a bunch of movies for me, too. All romance ones that he hates. He takes such good care of me."

"Garret's the same way with me. When I had the flu, he never left my side."

"How'd we find such great guys? And in the same town?"

"I don't know. Must be fate."

"Oh, I almost forget to tell you, I babysat Lilly yesterday. Don't tell Pearce. He's not supposed to know."

"Why not?"

"Because his wife was out on a date. That's why I was babysitting. Pearce wasn't home and Katherine needed someone to watch Lilly."

"Pearce knows she's dating someone. They have kind of an open marriage thing going. It's weird."

"It's not that weird. I mean, it is, but it's not uncommon. Everyone in Hollywood does that. Anyway, she didn't want Pearce to know she was going out. I think he's mad that she's never home with Lilly."

"Did you see Katherine's boyfriend?"

"I was upstairs when he got there, but I heard his voice when I was going down the hall so I peeked over the balcony and got a quick look at him. I recognized him as soon as I saw him. He's been to my house before for one of my parents' dinner parties."

"Who is he?"

"A senator from New York. You see him on the news all the time. He's the head of some committee in Congress that has something to do with the military. I don't know exactly what. I don't pay attention to that stuff."

"That sounds like someone Katherine would date. She likes powerful men and Pearce isn't powerful enough for her."

"She was gone all afternoon and didn't get home until seven so Lilly and I got plenty of girl time. I love Lilly's bedroom. It's all pink, just like mine."

"Did you go to her tea party?" I laugh.

"Of course. Everyone who visits has to have tea." She says it seriously, like Lilly always does. "And then we watched a princess cartoon and had dinner. Their cook, Charles, made the best mac and cheese."

"Hey!" I hear Sean yelling.

"The best after yours," Harper yells back. "You know I love your mac and cheese."

"Charles is a great cook, but not as great as you, Sean." I yell it so he can hear.

"He's bringing the pizza over, so I should go. But thanks for calling. I'll talk to you later."

"Okay, bye."

Garret comes in from the deck.

"I just talked to Harper," I tell him.

"How's she feeling?"

"She said her shoulder aches all the time. Is that how your shoulder felt, too?"

"No, I had more of a sharp pain."

"I wish you'd told me that. I hate knowing you were in pain all those months."

"I'm good now, so it doesn't matter." He sits next to me on the couch. "You want to give me another one of those hugs now?"

"What hugs?" I play innocent.

"The one you gave me earlier. One of your I-want-scx hugs?"

I try to hold my laughter in. "I've never heard of that kind of hug."

"You've not only heard of it, you've perfected it."

"So I'm good at it?" I climb on his lap, straddling him.

"You're very good at it."

"Then I guess I don't need to practice it."

"You should always practice." He puts his hands on my backside and pulls me into him. "If you don't, you won't be good at it anymore."

I practice the hug. And as predicted, it leads to sex. I guess I *am* good at it.

The next week goes by fast because I have a ton of home-work. I also have two more counseling sessions. During both of them, I spend the whole time talking about school and how I don't know what I want to do for a major. Jennifer gave me some worksheets to fill out that are supposed to assess your personality and help guide you to careers that fit you best. We still haven't talked about my mom. I know we will eventually but I'm putting it off as long as possible and Jennifer isn't pushing me.

I've been checking in with Harper several times a day. She's still in shock about the end of her tennis career. Like Garret said, it's a loss and it'll take time for her to accept it. Right now she's in the denial stage, acting like maybe she'll be able to play next year.

She's having the surgery the Friday after Thanksgiving. Sean is going to LA with her and will be staying at Harper's house until Sunday, which has Garret and me questioning our theory about Kiefer. If he really was joining the organization, there's no way he'd agree to let Sean stay at his house. And he'd be trying harder to break the two of them apart. I don't know what's going on with Kiefer, but for now I'm choosing to believe our theory is wrong and that Sean and Harper can be together.

Saturday morning, Garret and I go to Grace's house in Santa Barbara. As we're pulling in the driveway, I open the window so I can smell all the flowers. I love this house. The one in the Hamptons was nice, too, but this one is surrounded by flowers and their scent fills the air.

Grace comes outside when she sees us.

I go up and give her a hug. "You need to come here more often. I miss you."

"I've missed you, too, honey. It's good to see you again."

Grace gives Garret a hug. As she does, I notice she looks thinner and more tired than usual. Ever since Arlin died, she hasn't been the Grace I knew last spring. She used to smile all the time and was full of energy and would joke around. But now, it seems like it's an effort for her to smile. And her movements are slower, like she doesn't have the same energy level anymore.

She's in good health, so her lack of energy isn't because she's sick. I think it's because she's depressed. She lives at her house in Florida now and although she has some friends there, they only go out a few times a week. The rest of the time she's by herself, which is why I call her every day.

"Let's go inside," she says, looping her arm in mine. We go in the house, with Garret following behind us with our suitcase. "I slept later than I'd planned to so I don't have breakfast ready, but I have coffee made."

That's another thing that's changed. Grace sleeps late all the time now. She never did that before. She and Arlin used to get up at 5:30 in the morning. They'd have coffee and read the paper together. Now she rarely gets up before eight, usually later than that. And based on how tired she looks, I don't think she sleeps. I think she just lies in bed thinking about Arlin.

"Grace, I can make breakfast," Garret says. We're all standing in the kitchen and Grace is pouring us coffee.

"Yeah, Grace, let Garret make it. He makes really good pancakes and scrambled eggs."

Garret opens the fridge and takes out the carton of eggs and the milk.

She takes the eggs from him. "No, Garret. You just got here. I'm not making you work. Go sit down and relax."

He puts his arm around her. "It's not work. I make breakfast for Jade every day. So if I don't make it today, the whole day will feel off. You'd be doing me a favor if you let me make it."

She smiles. "The skillets are under the stove. I'm afraid I don't have any flour or sugar to make pancakes. I threw all of that out last summer when Jade and I cleaned out the pantry."

"Then we'll just have eggs and toast." He grabs the loaf of bread from the basket on the counter.

"I'm sorry I don't have more ingredients," she says. "I need to make a trip to the store. I was so tired last night after the flight that I just stopped and got eggs, milk, and bread and nothing else. After breakfast, I'll go to the store."

"I'll go," Garret says. "Just make a list." He cracks open some eggs in a bowl. "I always grocery shop on Saturdays, so again, you'd be doing me a favor by letting me go. Otherwise, like I said, my whole day will be off."

Garret made that up. He doesn't always go to the store on Saturdays. He just wants to help Grace out and give her and me some time alone.

When he does stuff like this, it makes me love him even more. I don't think he realizes how much that stuff affects me. He probably thinks I don't even notice. But I do. It reminds me that he's not just a great husband. He's also a great person. He cares about Grace as much as I do and he can see she's not doing well. So he offers to help without even being asked.

Grace smiles at him. "Then I guess Jade and I will take care of things here at the house. I have a grocery list already made out. I'll give it to you after we eat."

During breakfast, Garret asks Grace, "How long are you staying in California?"

"Until Wednesday. On Monday, I'm meeting with a real estate agent to sell some land I own about an hour north of here. I've been meaning to sell it but haven't gotten around to it."

"Is it investment property?"

"Actually, Arlin and I bought the land years ago thinking we would build a house there. It's right on the coast. It has a beautiful private beach." Her eyes drift to her plate and she sets her fork down. "We both fell in love with the land. We just never built the house. We talked about it many times but didn't do it." She clears her throat and dabs her mouth with her napkin. "And now, it needs to be sold."

It's obvious she doesn't want to sell the land. But Arlin is gone, and she's not going to build a house just for herself.

"How many acres?" Garret asks.

Grace looks up at him. "I believe it's four, but I'd have to check the paperwork again to be sure."

"Would you mind if Jade and I took a look at it?"

My eyes shift to Garret, but he keeps his gaze on Grace.

She was just about to sip her coffee, but sets it down. "Of course you can. You could have a picnic there if you'd like. That's what Arlin and I used to do. The land is up on a cliff so it offers a magnificent view of the ocean."

"On a cliff, huh?" Garret's mind is working. He's up to something. "So when are you putting it up for sale?"

"This week, hopefully. Why?"

He puts his arm around me. "I think I might buy it."

"What?" Grace and I both say it at the same time.

"It sounds perfect. Central coast. Four acres. Private beach. On a cliff. What do you think, Jade?"

"Um, yeah, we should check it out."

I wasn't ready to buy anything yet. We said we'd start *looking* for land, not buy some this weekend.

"Are you planning on building on it?" Grace asks him.

"Yes. Jade and I want to stay here after we graduate and we're looking for a piece of land we can build a house on later. What you described is exactly what we're looking for."

Her face brightens. "It would be wonderful if we could keep it in the family. I offered it to William but he prefers living on the East Coast. I would love for the two of you to have the land."

"How much do you want for it? And don't think you have to give us a deal because we're family."

"Garret, don't be silly. I'll give you the land."

"We're paying for it, Grace. Just tell us how much."

She waves her hand in the air, dismissing the idea. "Nonsense. You need the money from Jade's trust fund to build the house and pay for your future expenses."

"*I'm* paying for it," Garret announces. "We won't touch the trust fund."

I don't know how much Grace wants for the land but I know that four acres on the coast would cost at least a million dollars, if not more. Buying it would use up most of what Garret has in his account.

Grace puts her hand on Garret's arm and gives him her stern grandma look. "You're not paying me a penny. I would be absolutely thrilled if you and Jade took this land and lived on it someday. And if Arlin were here, he would be, too. He never wanted to sell that land and truthfully, I've put off selling it because I don't want to say goodbye to it. It's such a beautiful spot. I used to imagine the flowers I would plant there. I even plotted it out. I'm sure I have my flower map around here somewhere."

Garret holds my hand under the table and smiles at me. "What do you think? I know we haven't seen it, but something about it feels right."

I nod, smiling. "Yeah, it does."

He turns back to Grace. "Sold."

She claps her hands. "Oh! I'm so happy!"

I go around Garret and give Grace a hug. "Thank you, Grace. Really. This is a huge gift."

"I'm happy to give it to you. This feels like it was meant to be. The timing of you coming here right before I put it up for sale. The fact that the topic even came up is unusual. I hadn't even considered that you two might want it. I didn't know you'd be staying in California."

"We both like it here." Garret takes our plates to the sink. "So we decided to stay here after graduation."

"Have you told Frank that?" Grace asks me.

"No, but he knows I never planned to move back to Iowa."

"What about *your* family, Garret? You'll be so far from Connecticut."

"I can still fly out to see them. Or my dad and Lilly can come here."

Grace's smile keeps getting bigger. "I'm going to call the real estate agent and tell him I'm not selling the land. Then I'll call my lawyer and have him start the paperwork that will transfer it to your name."

She races off to the room down the hall that she uses as an office.

Garret pulls me into his side and kisses me. "So I guess we have some land."

"I guess we do." I smile as I think about it. "Did you see how happy Grace was? I haven't seen her that happy since our wedding."

"What about you? Are you happy?"

"Yes, but I think we're completely crazy for doing this. We haven't even seen the land yet. And now we have to live there. We can't disappoint her."

"Jade, we're living there. I trust Grace and Arlin. All of their homes are in beautiful locations, so if they loved this land as much as she described, I know we will, too."

"We'll go see it tomorrow, right?"

"Yeah, we'll stop on the way home."

"This is so crazy. We just decided to build a house in a place we've never been."

Garret and I finish cleaning up breakfast and a few minutes later, Grace walks back into the kitchen. "It's all set. The paperwork is underway. You will soon be landowners."

"Thanks again, Grace," Garret says. "That's very generous of you. Now do you have that grocery list? I should get going."

"Yes, I have it right here." She hands him a piece of paper she had sitting by the phone. "Let me give you some money."

He laughs. "No. I got this. You just gave us four acres of oceanfront property. I'm paying for the groceries. I'll see you guys later."

While Garret's at the store, I help Grace take the covers off the furniture and fold them up. Then I sweep the wood floors while she dusts. Grace has housekeepers at her other houses, but this house is smaller than those and she likes to do the work herself. Plus, it's good for her to get the exercise.

When we're done we go to the back yard and sit in the gazebo, which has flowers all around it.

"So what's Meredith like?" I ask Grace as she pours iced tea into some glasses. "She's not like Victoria, is she?"

"No. Not at all. She's very quiet. Very smart. She has a PhD in economics but never used it. She just enjoys learning. Sometimes she audits college courses in topics that interest her."

"How long have William and Meredith been married?"

Grace pauses to think. "It's been about 23 years, I think."

"That's a long time. They must've got married right after college."

"Yes, they were young."

I wonder if William was able to choose his wife or if Meredith was picked for him. When he talked about her that night we had dinner, it seemed like he really loved her. He smiled whenever he mentioned her and he had nothing but good things to say about her. So maybe he was allowed to choose her. I still don't know how all that works and I know nobody will tell me. But I know in order to be married to William, Meredith's father has to be part of the organization, which makes me kind of nervous to meet her.

"So William and Meredith never wanted kids?" I ask Grace.

She coughs a little on the iced tea she was drinking, then shakes her head as she clears her throat. "No. But they both love children."

She's acting kind of strange. Maybe it's a sensitive topic. Maybe they tried to have kids and couldn't.

"Does Meredith ever do anything with Victoria?" I ask.

"Rarely. They see each other at dinner parties or charity events but that's about it. They don't have much in common. They saw each other more when the girls were younger, but now the girls are too busy to have time for their Aunt Meredith or Uncle William."

"They don't have holidays together?"

"No. Royce and Victoria always used to take the girls on trips for the holidays. And William and Meredith would either come to our house or go to her parents' house for the holidays. This year, I'll be going to William's house for both Thanksgiving and Christmas."

"Maybe sometime you could spend the holidays with Garret and me."

"I would enjoy that." She winks. "Maybe when you build that new house."

"Yes. Definitely." I sip my iced tea.

She shuts her eyes, inhaling the air through her nose, then smiles as she opens her eyes again. "I love smelling the flowers. They smell different here than in Florida. They're the same flowers, but they have a slightly different scent. Perhaps because the air is so much drier here."

"Do you like living in Florida?"

She sighs. "I do, but it's not the same without Arlin. We used to spend all our time together when we lived there. We'd go golfing, take walks, play cards. It wasn't like at our house in the Hamptons, where Arlin would work on his sail-boat and I would read or do other things. So it's different being in Florida alone." She runs her finger along the bottom of her glass.

"Grace, why don't you move?"

She thinks I'm kidding and smiles. "And where would I move to?"

"Here. This house. You should live here instead of Florida. The weather is warm. You like it here. And I'm just two hours away."

"Yes, but I always spend the winters in Florida. That's the way it's always been."

"So do something different. Just because you did that in the past doesn't mean you have to keep doing it." I turn so I'm facing her. "Grace. I want you to move here. I'm serious. I want to see you more. I don't like having you so far away. And I don't think you like being down there all alone."

She doesn't respond, which tells me it's true. She doesn't like living there by herself.

"Would you consider it? For me? I promise I'll come visit you all the time. Every weekend if you want."

"Jade, no. You need to be at home, studying and spending time with Garret."

"Then every other weekend. Whatever. I just want you to live here. You *do* like it here, right?"

"I love it here. I always have. I've just never actually lived here for more than a few weeks. This was a vacation home. Arlin and I would stay here for a week and then leave. We'd come here three or four times a year."

"Could you see yourself living here for more than a few weeks?"

"I suppose I could. But I'd have to find a new bridge club."

"I'm sure they have them here. So what do you say? Will you do it?"

She pats my hand. "I'll consider it."

"What are my chances here? Like 50 percent? Eighty percent? I need to know how much harder I need to work to convince you."

"Well, given that you're part of the equation, I'd say there's a 90 percent chance I would agree to moving here. I'd love to be closer to you, Jade."

"Okay, I can work with 90 percent. That's easy."

She laughs and moves on to talking about something else.

I have to get Grace to do this. She's not happy in Florida. I'm sure she has a beautiful house there, but it's just a house and not a home when she's stuck there all alone.

Grace and I need to spend more time together. And unlike the rest of her family, I'm not just saying that. I actually *will* spend time with her. Not because I feel I have to, but because I want to. So before I leave tomorrow, I'm going to convince her to move to California.

Chapter 18

GARRET

When I got back from the grocery store, Jade and Grace were outside talking. I don't know what they talked about, but Grace was in a much better mood than when I left. She seemed really depressed when Jade and I got here this morning.

I'm not surprised Grace isn't doing well. In the past year, she's lost both her son and her husband. The only good thing is that she gained a granddaughter, but living in Florida, she never sees Jade. It's too bad she doesn't live here in California. It would be good for Jade to have her grandmother close by. And it would be good for Grace, too.

As Grace and Jade put groceries away, I go to the back yard and take out the patio furniture from the storage shed. I just put it away when we were here in August. I set the patio table and chairs where they were last summer, and the two big white chairs in a sunny spot that's surrounded by flowers.

I sit in one of the chairs and close my eyes and let the sun soak into my skin. I take a moment to imagine the house we're going to build. I can see it in my head and I can see us living there. And now that we have the land, we can start building it. Maybe we won't wait. Maybe we'll build it now so we can live there this summer.

I can't believe we got that land. When Grace described it, it was exactly where I pictured Jade and me living. I probably should've looked at it first, but I'm the type of person that goes with my gut. And my gut said this land was the right spot for our house. Sometimes you get a feeling you can't explain and you just have to go with it.

It's like when I met Jade last year. At first, I wasn't sure what to think of her. She wasn't very friendly and her constant insults got old fast. But there was something about her that drew me in. Not just the fact that she's beautiful. It was more than that. It was a feeling, a gut feeling, that told me I needed to give this girl a chance. And I did, and ended up falling in love with her.

Listen to your gut. It doesn't steer you wrong. That's what I always tell myself. And that's why I know this land is going to be perfect for us.

"Garret?" I open my eyes and see Jade there. "Were you taking a nap?"

"Just a short one."

"William and Meredith just got here. They're inside if you want to say hi."

"Yeah, I'm coming." I get up and follow her inside to the living room.

William, Grace, and Meredith are all sitting there.

William stands up. "Garret, glad you could make it."

"Yeah, it's good we could all meet like this."

His wife stands up. "I'm Meredith, William's wife. We've met before but I wasn't sure if you remembered me."

"Yes, I remember."

I met Meredith a few years ago at a summer party at Royce's house. Then I saw her a few other times at some charity events. She looks the same as always; straight brown hair, not much makeup. She's wearing a skirt today, with a short-sleeve sweater.

William is dressed in a polo shirt and casual, light-colored pants. He and his wife have more of a preppy, country-club look, whereas Royce and Victoria always dressed more formal, with him in suits and her in fancy dresses.

We all take a seat. Grace asks Jade a series of questions to get her to talk about herself. Jade doesn't like being the center of attention but she needs to talk because that's why we're here. William and Meredith want to get to know her.

"How do you like Camsburg?" Meredith asks Jade. Meredith hasn't said much since we sat down. It's mostly been William talking to Jade.

"It's okay. The classes are good. They're challenging."

"Did you like Moorhurst better?"

"Not really. But I do have a good friend who still goes to Moorhurst so I miss going there because of her."

"It's hard when you transfer like that. Sadie was just telling me how she'll miss her Georgetown friends when she transfers to Yale next semester."

"Sadie's going to Yale?"

Meredith glances at William, like she's wondering if that was a secret she wasn't supposed to talk about.

Grace answers. "Yes. Sadie is transferring there in the spring. I thought I mentioned that."

"No, I don't think so." Jade looks back at Meredith. "Why is she transferring?"

"I'm not sure." She nudges William. "What did she tell us was the reason?"

Now Meredith is afraid to speak. She doesn't need to be. We're all family. We all know what's going on. Sadie wants to be with Evan, her boyfriend. The guy who the organization picked to be president when their plans for me fell through. She wants to be first lady and she's going to make sure that she is by marrying Evan as soon as he'll let her.

"Sadie wanted to be closer to her boyfriend," William says. "Of course, that's not what she tells people. She has some excuse about how Yale suits her better than Georgetown, but we all know the truth."

"Now, William," Grace says. "You shouldn't spread rumors about your niece. Maybe Yale is indeed a better fit for her."

He nods. "Perhaps you're right, Mother."

Grace knows it's not true. She knows Sadie's true intentions. She just doesn't want to admit that Sadie's turning into the conniving, power-hungry person that her father was, and that her mother still is.

"Oh, William, I have some news to share," Grace says. "Jade and Garret are going to take the land I'd to plan to sell. They're going to build a house on it."

William smiles at us. "That's wonderful. Mother was very upset about having to sell it. I'm glad you two are interested in it."

At least he's not mad about it. I wasn't sure how he'd react to us taking the land.

"We're really excited about it," I tell him. "We were just getting ready to start looking for a place to build and then Grace mentioned she was selling this land."

"You aren't charging them for it, are you, Mother?" William asks her.

"Of course not. They tried to buy it from me but I wouldn't let them. I'm thrilled to be able to give it to them."

"This is excellent news. Now you won't have to deal with the hassle of selling it and the land will remain in the family. We need to celebrate." William stands up. "Mother, do you have some champagne? Or maybe some wine?"

"I have wine, but William, Jade doesn't drink."

"Then we'll celebrate some other way. Jade? Garret? How would you like to celebrate?"

Jade answers. "That's okay. We don't need to celebrate."

"We're Sinclairs. We like to celebrate things. And the fact that we're all here together is another reason to celebrate."

Grace gets up. "He's right. We should go out for lunch. I know of a nice little place on the water that has a jazz band on Saturdays. And they have the best desserts. When you're celebrating, you must have good desserts."

"I agree." William motions the rest of us to get up. "Let's go. We can take my car."

Every time I've been around William in the past, he's very serious and businesslike. Today he's being much more personable and laid-back.

We go to lunch at the restaurant Grace recommended. It's a casual place that serves mostly soups and sandwiches. The table we're sitting at has a great view of the ocean and as Grace said, there's a jazz band playing.

"Your father always loved coming here on Saturdays," Grace says to William.

We just finished lunch and the waitress dropped off the dessert menus.

"I can see why. Great views, live music, and a large dessert menu." He holds it up in the air.

Grace laughs and turns to Jade. "Your grandfather loved dessert. Sometimes he'd skip dinner and just have two desserts."

Meredith points at William. "It must be genetic because his son is the same way."

"There's nothing wrong with that." He kisses her cheek. "Two desserts never killed a man. Or a woman. Order two desserts, Meredith. I dare you."

"No, thank you. One is plenty."

"I'll order two," Jade says.

"Then I guess it *is* genetic," William says to Meredith. "Jade has a sweet tooth, just like her uncle and her grandfather."

Jade smiles really wide. It makes her happy to hear William include her as part of the family.

I put my arm around her. "Jade would have *three* desserts if I let her."

Grace sets her menu down. "I think I'll have two desserts as well. We're celebrating, so why not splurge a little? Garret, how about you?"

"He doesn't like dessert," Jade says.

Grace and William look at me in horror.

"I know, it's crazy," Jade says when she sees their faces.

"I don't know if we can let you in the family if you don't like dessert," William jokes.

Meredith leans closer to me. "I wouldn't worry about it. I hardly ever eat sweets and they let *me* in the family."

"Come to think of it, I don't think your father likes dessert either," William says to me. "Every time I've eaten with him, he skips dessert."

"Yeah, sometimes he'll eat ice cream but that's about it. He doesn't really like sweets."

William sets his menu down. "Well, there's clearly a genetic defect in the Kensington line."

Everyone laughs.

"Man, that's harsh, William." I pretend to be serious.

Grace shakes her head. "He's kidding. William, apologize to Garret."

I smile. "No, it's fine. And today I'm ordering dessert so it's not like I never eat it."

The waitress comes back, and when we order she looks at us funny because we're ordering so many desserts. She reads the order back to us just to make sure it's what we wanted.

When she brings the desserts, they're so huge they could be split between two people. But William and Jade are determined to eat both of their desserts. And they do. Grace takes one of hers to go.

As we're waiting for the check, Jade says to William, "Wouldn't it be nice if your mom lived out here instead of in

Florida?" She smiles at Grace. "Closer to her granddaughter who loves spending time with her?"

I wonder if Jade already talked to Grace about this because Grace doesn't seem surprised by the question.

William sits back and looks at his mom. "Actually, that's a good idea. The house here is much more manageable to maintain than the one in Florida. And you always complain about the humid weather."

Grace reaches over and rubs Jade's hand. "Jade and I have already discussed this and I told her I would consider it."

"You wouldn't need to do much for the move," William says. "Just pack up your clothes and have them shipped here. Why don't you try it for a month and see what you think? You can always go back to Florida."

We all wait for her answer.

She taps her hand on the table. "All right. I'll do it."

"Really?" Jade leans over and hugs her. "This is so great!"

"But once I get used to having my granddaughter close by, you know it'll be difficult for me to leave. I might just end up moving here for good."

Jade sits back. "I would love that."

"We need to celebrate again," William says. "Anyone want another dessert?"

We all laugh.

He holds up his water glass. "I guess we'll have to settle for a toast." He waits for the rest of us to raise our glasses, then says, "To my mother embarking on a new adventure in life." He looks right at Jade. "And to my niece, Jade, for making my mother smile like she hasn't smiled in a very long time."

We clink our glasses, then Grace says, "We're very blessed to have her in our lives."

I hold Jade's hand under the table and kiss her cheek. She's so happy right now. I've noticed Jade is happiest when she has family around her. She's happy when it's just her and me, but she's even happier when she has Grace around, or Frank and Ryan, or even my dad. That day before our wedding, when everyone was there with us, Jade couldn't stop smiling. Since she didn't grow up with a big family, she wants it now. And with William and Meredith, she can add two more people to that family.

I still have concerns about William. I feel a little better about him after spending some time with him, but I still don't trust him. I think I'll always be somewhat wary of him because he's involved with the organization.

In the afternoon we sit outside and talk. None of us want to go anywhere for dinner so we have Italian food delivered. Jade and Meredith set it up for everyone, buffet-style.

After dinner, William gets the fireplace going and we play cards. William and Grace are very competitive. They keep challenging each other regarding the rules while Meredith rolls her eyes, telling Jade and me that they do this whenever they play together.

When we're in bed later, I give Jade a kiss and say, "So what did you think of the family reunion today?"

"It was great. Better than I thought it would be. And I got Grace to move here, which was totally unexpected. I didn't think she'd do it." Jade backs into my chest and pulls the covers over us. "I know you don't like William, but I do. He kind of reminds me of Arlin."

"I never said I didn't like him."

"You think he's bad because of the stuff he's done. But your dad does the same things."

"Jade, I know that. I'm not judging him because of that. I'm just careful around him. That's all."

"But you don't need to be. Don't you think he's nice?"

"Yes, but I'm always extra careful when it comes to you." I tighten my arms around her. "I love you way too much to let anything bad happen to you."

"Nothing bad will happen to me. I feel like we're safe now. That guy we thought robbed the neighbors is dead and that fake cop hasn't shown up again."

"We still have to be careful, Jade."

She yawns. "I'm really tired."

"Go to sleep." I kiss her cheek. "And tomorrow we'll go see the place where we're going to live."

"I can't wait." She smiles, her eyes closed. "I love you."

"I love you, too."

In the morning, after we get ready, Jade and I go in the kitchen where William, Meredith, and Grace are all having coffee.

"I was just about to start breakfast." Grace pours us some coffee. "I was going to make eggs, but I thought you might want to make pancakes, Garret, since you weren't able to yesterday. Jade keeps saying you make great pancakes."

"Sure, what kind would you like?"

"I didn't know there were options. Jade, what kind should he make?"

It's Sunday, which is typically our pancakes-and-sex day. I know Jade is thinking the same thing because she's blushing.

"Jade, what kind would you like today?" I smile at her.

She smiles back. "Apple-cinnamon would be good."

I keep my eyes on her, imagining the shower sex we'll be having later.

Grace hands Jade some creamer for her coffee. "I'm sorry, honey, but we don't have any apples."

Jade spots the bowl of cut-up strawberries sitting on the counter. "How about strawberry-lemon?"

Shit, yeah. Finally. Outdoor sex. And I bet I know exactly where she wants to do it.

Grace opens one of the cupboards. "I don't have lemons but I have lemon extract. Will that work?" She hands it to me.

"Yeah, that'll work." Actually, fresh lemons are what's in the recipe but who the hell cares what the recipe says? I'm making those damn pancakes. I want the outdoor sex.

Jade helps me mix up the batter and when nobody's paying attention, she gets close to my ear and whispers, "I'll pay you for them later."

It gets me so worked up that if there weren't all these people here, I'd take her in the back yard and do her right now. But I can't, so I try to think non-sexual thoughts while I drop pancake batter onto the hot skillet.

The pancakes are a huge success. I didn't have the recipe but the basic batter is the same for all the different pancakes, so I had it memorized. Then I just added the lemon extract and chopped strawberries.

After we eat, Grace, Meredith, and Jade go outside to talk and finish their coffee. William and I offered to stay inside and clean up. When we're done I start to head outside but William stops me.

"Garret, can we talk for a few minutes?" He sits down at the kitchen table.

"Sure." I take the seat across from him. "What do you want to talk about?"

He looks out the sliding door behind him to make sure it's closed. "You're no longer involved with the organization. Is that correct?"

Why is he asking me this? He already knows the answer.

"Yeah, I'm out. For good."

He nods. "That's what I thought."

"Why did you ask me that?"

He clasps his hands together on the table and circles his thumbs. "I just overheard some things and it made me wonder. That's all."

That's all? He can't leave it at that. If he heard things, I need to know what the hell he heard.

"Yeah, you're going to have to explain what that means. What exactly did you hear?"

"I've heard your name being mentioned recently but I'm never there for the full conversation. I've only overheard bits and pieces so I don't know for sure what they're saying about you."

"Is my dad around when they're talking about me? Because maybe he's just—"

"No, he wasn't around."

"Maybe my grandfather was talking about me. He's trying to get me to take over the company and he often talks business with the other members."

"I don't see your grandfather anymore. He's been promoted, but I'm sure you already knew that."

"Yeah, I know."

"When they get to that level, we don't see them anymore. They're more of an entity, not a person. The upper tier."

I roll my eyes. "Is that what they call themselves? They actually have a name?"

"Informally, yes. It's not official." He looks back at the patio. Jade is laughing at something Meredith is saying while Grace sips her coffee. "Garret, are you sure you and Jade are safe?"

I tense up. "You think we're not?"

"I didn't say that. I just think it would be wise for you to invest in some extra security. That place you're living in is so out in the open. No security gate. No guards. You're a Kensington. There are always people who will want to come after you. I'm surprised Pearce allowed you to move there."

"I'm not part of his world anymore. I don't have to worry as much as he does."

"You're still his son, which means you still need to be careful. And Jade does, too."

"We are."

"I'm not telling you what to do. I'm just reminding you that you can never be too careful."

When he says it, it reminds me of Walt.

"What's the story with Walt? Why would you hire someone like him for your private security?"

William doesn't act surprised that I know the truth about Walt. He knows my dad would've told me about him.

"Walt is very good at what he does. And I only hire the best."

"You really want a killer working for you?" I didn't mean to phrase it like that, but it's what I was thinking and it just came out.

"Wouldn't you? I mean, if you were me?" He sits back casually in his seat. "People come after me, Garret. Not just because I'm wealthy but because of the things I'm involved in. I don't think I need to explain what I mean."

When I don't answer him, he continues. "Unfortunately, for people like me, and your father, there are times when it's either kill or be killed. And when it comes to that, you want the right people on your side. People who can do the job that needs to be done. It's not a choice, Garret. It's survival. You're just lucky you got out."

I didn't expect him to be so honest. My dad's never even been that honest with me. So does my dad have a guy like Walt working for him? If he does, I don't know who it would be. My dad has his own security team but I thought they were just guys he hired from a security company. But maybe they're guys like Walt. Guys who do freelance work for the organization.

I don't know much about that side of my dad's life. He keeps it hidden, or at least he tries to. I think William does, too, but just now I saw a glimpse of it. As William was talking,

I watched him, studying his face. The moment he alluded to the organization, it's like he became a different person. He looked at me with this blank stare and lost all expression on his face. It's like he turned off all emotion. Even his voice changed. It was deeper, more direct, almost angry.

My dad does the same thing whenever he talks about the organization. It's like he and William turn a switch and become someone else. Someone who does what he has to in order to survive. Someone who's able to set his morals and ethics aside just long enough to do whatever he's ordered to do. I don't like that side of my dad and I don't like that side of William either. Just sitting here and seeing him look at me that way is making me uncomfortable.

"Well, Meredith and I need to be going." He smiles and switches back to the other William, the friendly uncle I want to trust but can't. Not yet. Not until I know more about him. He has to earn my trust and he hasn't yet.

He moves his chair out and stands up, so I do as well. "I know we didn't have much time here, but I think it was good we got together like this."

"Yeah, I think so, too."

He puts his hand on my shoulder. "Keep an eye on Jade. Make sure she's safe."

I back away. "Don't say shit like that. You're basically implying she's not."

He shakes his head. "No, that's not what I'm saying. It's just that Jade doesn't know our world the way you and I do, and I don't want her taking risks. She needs to always be on guard. Even though you're not part of this, Garret, she needs to understand there are dangers in being a Kensington. Just like there are dangers in being a Sinclair. I want to make sure you haven't hidden these things from her. She needs to know the reality of being in a family like ours."

"She does," I assure him, even though I'm not sure if it's true. I'm always telling her to be careful, but at the same time, I don't want to scare her. I don't want her living in fear for the rest of her life.

William stands by the patio door and waves at his wife to come in. "Does Jade plan to tell Victoria and the girls who she is?"

"I don't think so."

"That's probably a good idea. It's best for the girls not to know what their father did. If Jade ever wants to meet her sisters, maybe she could do so without telling them who she is."

"Maybe. We'll see."

He opens the sliding door. "Meredith, we need to leave in a few minutes."

The three of them come inside and we all say goodbye.

I watch as William gives Jade a hug. He holds on to her a few seconds after she lets go. Arlin did that, too, so maybe it's just something Arlin taught him. Or maybe William really is worried about Jade. Maybe he holds on those extra seconds because he thinks he may not see her again. I'm probably reading too much into it, but after that conversation I had with him, maybe I'm not. Maybe he knows more than he told me.

Chapter 19

JADE

We left Grace's house around noon and now we're driving up the coast to go check out our land. We're almost there. This is so exciting. I can't wait to see it.

Garret's been quiet the whole time we've been in the car. I'm guessing he's just tired. We were up late last night playing cards with everyone. Grace and William are so competitive. It was funny to watch them.

"Hey." Garret reaches over for my hand.

"Hey, back." I smile. "Why are you so quiet over there?"

"I was just thinking."

"About what?"

He glances over at me. "You know you need to be careful, right?"

"Careful? What are you talking about?"

"I mean, like just in general, you know you need to always be aware of your surroundings. Don't trust people you just met. Stuff like that."

"Yeah, I guess."

"You can't say it like you're not sure. This is important. I need to know you're being careful and taking precautions."

"I don't understand. Are you saying I'm not safe?"

"No. It's just that William was talking to me after we cleaned up breakfast and he wanted to make sure you're being careful."

"Why does William care?"

"Because you're his niece and he worries about you and wants you to be careful. So are you? Like when I'm not around?"

"I was careful even before I met you. I never trust anyone. You know that."

"Yeah, but it's not just that. You can't take risks, Jade. Like going running by yourself when nobody's around. You can't do stuff like that. It's too dangerous."

"For anyone? Or just for me? You need to explain why you're saying this."

"It's dangerous for anyone, but especially you because you're a Kensington now. And that name comes with risks."

"Because of the organization? You keep saying not to worry about them."

"I'm not talking about them. What I mean is that having a lot of money attracts bad people. Everyone knows my dad has a shitload of money, which means they assume we do as well, which we do, but not anywhere near what my dad has. I'm just saying that bad people could come after us so I just want to make sure you're always being careful."

"You know I am."

"But sometimes you're not. Like when you went to check out that side exit on campus that day. You said there was nobody around and yet you went and checked it out anyway and ended up seeing two murders. If the shooter had seen you there, he would've killed you, Jade."

"I know." I say it quietly as I look out the side window. He's right. I need to be more careful. Sometimes I get a false sense of security living in a small town, but I can't do that. And even though I like to think I'm strong and could fight someone if I were ever attacked, or outrun someone who was chasing me, the truth is I probably couldn't do either of those things, especially if the person had a gun or a knife.

"I don't want to scare you, Jade, but you need to be aware of this stuff."

"I'll be more careful. I promise."

He brings my hand to his lips and kisses it. "You ready to see where we're going to live?"

I look over and see him smiling at me. "Is this it?"

"This is it." He pulls off the road onto the grassy field that will someday have a house on it. *Our* house. I can hardly believe it.

He parks and comes around the car and opens my door. "What are you waiting for?"

"You." I take his hand. "I want us to see it at the same time."

We walk through the field, and off in the distance I can see the ocean. I can smell its salty spray and hear the big, powerful waves crashing into the shore. Even though we already live on the ocean, this is different. This is permanent. I'll actually be living here for a very long time.

The field ends at the cliff. I peer over it and see the sandy beach right below us. "How do we get down to the beach?"

"We'll build some stairs." Garret stands behind me and pulls me into his chest. "Don't get so close to the edge."

"This is beautiful. It's just how I imagined it would look. Up high like this, looking out at the ocean."

"It's how I pictured it, too. I told you we'd like it."

"How did you know that?"

"I just had a feeling. I can't explain it."

"I like that Arlin wanted to live here with Grace. And now we're going to. There's something special about that." I spin around to face him. "When can we start building?"

"We have to do some research first. Figure out what kind of house we want. Find a contractor. But I thought you wanted to wait before we did that."

"We can wait. I'm just excited to get started."

"I'm okay with building it now if that's what you want. I was thinking about it yesterday and we could have it built by the end of May so we could live here this summer. But then it would have to sit here empty during the school year."

"We could come visit it. It's only an hour away. Or we could live here and commute to campus every day."

"That's a long commute. Let's think about it some more. We don't have to decide right now."

I look back at the field. "So how far is four acres?"

"I can't tell just from looking at it but it goes out a ways. We'll have to put up a big fence to keep people out. Maybe we'll do a stone wall like Harper's parents had. Nobody's getting through that thing. That was like a fortress."

"You think it's dangerous living out here?"

"It's isolated, so we'll want to have good security. That house we passed on the way here was so hidden by the gate and the landscaping that most people wouldn't even know there's a house back there. That's what we need. We need people to drive by and not know we're here."

It *is* really isolated. There are houses on either side of us but you can't even see them from here.

Garret sighs. "We forgot to get stuff for a picnic. We should've stopped at the last town we passed."

"We can come back and have one later. Garret, we should totally do that. We should come here every Saturday or Sunday and have a picnic on our land." I run around the open field, twirling with my arms out. "I can't believe this is ours! It's all ours!"

Garret's laughing at me. "I'll be right back. I need to get something out of the car."

I stop twirling and gaze out at the ocean. I go back to the edge of the cliff to get a better look. The view is amazing.

"Hey." Garret grabs me from behind. "What did I say about standing so close to the edge?"

"I wanted to see the ocean."

"You can see it without being this close."

I take a few steps back. "Is that better?"

"Yes. Now close your eyes. I got something for you."

"What is it?"

"Just close your eyes."

I close them and he turns me around. "Okay, you can open them."

I look and see that he has the sleeping bag we keep in the trunk spread out on the ground. And on it there's a bright orange plastic bowl filled with candy.

"Happy Halloween." He hugs me into his side. "It's the best I could do since we're out of town, but we can celebrate when we get home later. In addition to the candy, I got some scary movies for you."

I point to the candy. "When did you get all that?"

"I got it when I was out shopping yesterday. The grocery store didn't take very long and I wanted you and Grace to have time to talk. Plus, I had to get my sweetie some Halloween treats." He kisses my neck and it tickles.

"You're tickling me." I laugh as I squirm away and lie down on the sleeping bag.

Garret lies next to me. "The candy is our picnic food. That's why I went and got it from the car. Feel free to dig in."

I flip on my side and kiss him. "I'd rather do something else first."

He kisses me back. "Like what?"

"Like pay you for those pancakes you made this morning."

"I was hoping that's why you ordered those." He shoves the candy bowl off to the side and takes his shirt off. "You okay with doing it here? Someone could drive by."

"The road's way back there and nobody's driven by since we got here. But if you don't want to—"

"Are you kidding? I've wanted to since we did it in the park that day." He's undressing me as he says it.

I laugh. "Yeah, I can tell. You just got me naked in about 30 seconds. And yourself in about 15."

"I like the outdoors." He lies over me and covers us a little with the sleeping bag. "You're not cold, are you?"

There's a cool breeze but the sun is warm and there isn't a cloud in the sky.

"No, it feels perfect."

The wind blows some strands of hair over my face and Garret tucks it behind my ear. He smiles at me. "I love you."

"I love you, too."

"You know what?"

"What?"

"This is the first time we've done it on Halloween. So this isn't just outdoor sex. It's special Halloween sex."

I laugh. "I don't know what that means. Does it involve candy?"

He thinks for moment. "Yeah, it does." He moves off me to the side, then grabs a handful of candy from the bowl and drops it over my stomach.

"Why are you putting it on me?"

"So I can choose which one I want."

"I thought we were having sex."

"We are." He looks over the candy selection. "I think I'll have a chocolate bar. What do you want?"

"Something with peanuts."

He unwraps a miniature Snickers bar and puts it in my mouth. It's warm from the car and the chocolate melts as soon as it hits my tongue.

Garret pushes the other candy aside, then unwraps his mini chocolate bar and sets it on my lower abs, a couple inches below my belly button.

"Garret, I'm going to have messy chocolate all over me."

"No, you won't." He takes a small bite of the chocolate, his teeth lightly brushing against my skin. My breath catches at the feel of it. It tickles, but in a good way. A hot sexy way that sets off an explosion of sensations all up and down my body. He takes another bite and my stomach muscles tense up a little.

"Jade, just relax." His voice is low, soothing.

I breathe, my muscles relaxing as he takes the last bite, then slowly licks the melted chocolate off me. It feels so amazing that when he's done, I'm not ready for it to end. I want more. That chocolate bar was way too small.

"Have another one," I tell him in an urgent tone.

"Maybe I don't want another one." His mouth is back at my lips now, his chocolate-covered tongue teasing mine. He hasn't even touched me with his hands. Only his mouth. And yet a fiery heat is building inside me and tingling sensations are running up and down my core.

"I'm begging you," I whisper. "Have another one."

He smiles as he grabs another chocolate bar and unwraps it and places it in the same spot as before. He takes small bites until it's gone, his teeth grazing my skin. Then he slowly licks off the chocolate that remains. It's torture. Pure torture. The good kind. The kind that makes me want him so bad I can't wait a second longer.

He moves up my body, slowly, deliberately, his mouth lingering over my breast, igniting a surge of heat between my legs. I run my hands through his hair, gently tugging on it, signaling that I'm ready. I'm more than ready.

He gets my signal and continues up my body, leaving kisses the entire way until his lips finally meet up with mine. He enters me and I softly moan as his tongue slips in my mouth, all chocolaty and warm. His hand is warm, too, moving down my side, over my hip, then under me. He draws me into him and I feel him deeper inside me before he pulls out and thrusts into me again.

I'm so turned on, my body so revved up, it doesn't take long before I go over the edge, waves of intense pleasure coursing through my body. A few more thrusts and he's there, too. Then he lies on his back and holds me close to him.

I smile. "So that's Halloween sex?"

"Yeah. Did you like it?"

"I liked it so much I'm not waiting a whole year to do it again." I pull the sleeping bag around us.

"The rule is that you can keep doing it until the candy is gone. After that, you have to wait until next Halloween." He nods toward the bowl. "Did you notice how much candy I got?"

"I did, but maybe we could get some more on the way home. I really don't want to run out."

We lie there and end up falling asleep for an hour. When we wake up, we get dressed and take everything back to the car.

"I hate to leave," I tell him as I pick out some candy to eat on the drive home.

"We'll come back. Like you said, it's only an hour away."

I take one last look before I get in the car. The long grass is swaying in the breeze and I can see even bigger waves forming way out in the ocean. I never get tired of watching the waves.

Garret's waiting for me in the car. I get in, buckling my seatbelt. "This is really ours?"

He picks my hand up and kisses it. "It's really ours."

"Wow." It's all I can say.

On the way home, we stop at the store and load up on more candy. Garret tells me he was joking about the candy rule, saying he'll lick chocolate off me whenever I want. But I'm not taking any chances so I get 10 more bags of it. Besides, I figure you can never have enough candy.

"So we're watching scary movies tonight?" I ask Garret as I'm unpacking the suitcase. We're home now and he's sitting on the bed, scrolling through his phone while I toss clothes in the laundry basket.

"That's the plan, unless you want to do something else."

"Too bad we don't have a Halloween party to go to."

He looks up from his phone. "Jade, you hate Halloween parties. Everyone gets totally wasted at those things. You were at the one last year. You know how they are."

"I was too distracted to notice. I had a lot going on that night."

That was the night I read my mom's letter, then went to the Halloween party and saw Garret with Ava, and drank for the very first time. So yeah, I wasn't really paying attention to the party.

As I walk over to the dresser, Garret catches my waist and pulls me over to the bed and onto his lap. "Even though that night didn't start out so great, it ended well." He holds my hand, rubbing his thumb over my knuckles. "We had our first sleepover that night. You were so angry and so sad. I just wanted to make everything better." He gives me a kiss. "So I held you in my arms that entire night and never let go."

"It's a good thing you did. I couldn't be alone that night. I felt like everything was spinning out of control. But being with you made me feel like things would be okay. I loved that night. I didn't tell you that back then because I was too embarrassed to say it. But I loved it."

"So I guess this is the anniversary of our first sleepover."

"Actually, it was last night. That party we were at was the night before Halloween."

"Damn, we didn't get to celebrate it."

"How do you celebrate that type of anniversary?"

"By having another sleepover." He puts his lips to my ear. "But this time, we don't just sleep."

I kiss him. "I say we still celebrate it, even though it's a day later."

"Then we'll celebrate it tonight."

His phone vibrates on the bed. I pick it up and see a text message from Kyle. "Is Kyle still trying to be your friend?"

"Yeah, but only because he wants me to introduce him to my dad. I keep ignoring him, but he's relentless. He never gives up."

"His text says there's a party tonight. He left the address."

"I told him we're not going. Just delete it."

"Maybe we should go, just for an hour or so."

"Jade, the place will be packed. It'll be loud and people will be spilling beer on you."

"But it's Halloween. I feel like we should go out, even if it's just for an hour. Plus, we haven't gone to a single party since we got here."

"Because we don't go to parties. Parties are for people looking to get drunk and hook up. They're not for married people."

"I still want to go. I want to see people in their costumes."

"Only the girls will be wearing costumes and most of them will be practically naked. Is that really what you want to see?"

"Garret, come on. Stop trying to talk me out of it. I just want to go for an hour. Please?"

He sighs. "Fine, but we're going early, before it gets too crazy."

"Listen to you." I kiss his cheek. "You sound like an old man."

"No. I sound like a man who's been to these parties before and knows how out of control they can get. Guys get drunk, they get into fights, bottles get thrown, people get hurt. I don't want you around that shit."

"That's why we won't stay long. Maybe I should get a costume. I've never dressed up for Halloween."

"What kind of costume?"

I shrug. "I don't know. Maybe a witch or a pirate costume. Let's go to the store and see what they have left."

"Jade, you don't need to dress up. We're only going for an hour."

I slide off his lap and stand between his legs. "That doesn't mean I can't wear a costume." I tilt my head and smile. "Maybe I'll get one of those sexy cheerleader costumes. The ones with the really short skirts?"

"There's no way in hell you're wearing something like that to a party. Guys would be all over you."

"I'll get a different one for the party. The cheerleader costume is only for you. A little Halloween present. What do you think?"

The corners of his mouth slowly rise. "Shit, yeah. I'd love to see you as a cheerleader."

"Then let's go shopping."

We go to a strip mall that has a costume shop that's only there during the Halloween season. I spot the cheerleader costumes and find the one I want. It has a super-short red skirt and a tiny white shirt that ties in front and only covers your boobs, leaving your stomach exposed.

"I'm getting this one." I hold it up. It's in the package so you can't see the actual costume but there's a photo on the front of a girl wearing it.

Garret smiles as he eyes the package. He takes it from me and heads for the register. "Let's go home so you can try it on."

"Wait." I laugh and grab his arm, making him stop. "Calm down. That's for later. Let's see if there's anything less revealing for the party tonight."

"Forget the party. We've got better things to do."

"That doesn't take all night. We have time for both." I drag him to another aisle that has costumes that cover more skin. But all the costumes are lame. I don't want to dress like a hotdog or a crayon or a clown. And that's all they have. The women's costumes are either super sexy or really juvenile. So I decide to just get the cheerleader costume for my private Halloween party with Garret.

We stop for dinner and get home around seven. Kyle's party starts at eight.

"Try on your costume," Garret says the minute we walk in the door.

"I'll put it on after the party."

"The party isn't for an hour. Come on, Jade. You said it's my Halloween present. You can't make me wait until later. Halloween's almost over."

"Okay, but I'm only trying it on. That's it." I take the bag and walk to the bedroom.

He follows me in there. "Yeah, got it."

I go in the bathroom and put it on and, holy crap! How can girls go out in public wearing this? The skirt barely covers my butt and it hangs really low on my hips, like a bikini. I have to tie the front of the top in a double knot to keep my boobs from bursting out. I pull my hair up into a high ponytail to complete the look, then go back in the bedroom.

"What do you think?" I spin around.

Garret raises his brows and smiles. "Yeah, that'll work."

"What do you mean?" I ask, innocently.

His eyes wander over my body. "Damn. That's fucking hot. You can't just wear that on Halloween. You've got to wear that for me all the time."

"You want me to just walk around the house in a cheerleader costume?"

"You won't be wearing it for very long." He comes over and tugs at the knot holding my top together, releasing the first knot, which loosens the other one.

"What are you doing? Garret, I told you I was just trying it on."

"And I'm helping you take it off." He kisses me as his hands slide over the back of my skirt, his fingers lifting up the fabric and brushing against my butt. He talks against my mouth. "You're not wearing anything under this."

"Nope." I smile.

"Shit, Jade. You're killing me." He yanks his shirt over his head, then undoes his belt and drops his shorts and boxer briefs to the floor.

I'm still smiling. "You just thought you'd get naked?"

"Yeah." He kisses me as he says it. "I gotta change before the game."

"What game?"

"The football game. I'm the quarterback, remember?"

Just imagining him as the hot quarterback totally turns me on. I would've loved seeing him play football in high school. I've always had a thing for athletes but never dated one before Garret.

"Maybe you should get to your game," I tell him.

"I should do the cheerleader. *Then* go to the game."

His hand returns to my shirt, his finger playfully outlining the fabric, which is just barely covering my breasts. "I like this shirt."

"Yeah, I figured you would." I have to admit, it *is* damn sexy. And now I just want him to take it off. But instead, he kisses the area he just outlined with his finger, while his thumb circles over my nipple.

I tip my head back and clutch his shoulders. "Now *you're* the one killing *me*."

"It's only fair." He gives one last tug to the knot and my shirt falls open. His mouth moves to my breast while his hand slides up my thigh, under my skirt.

The earlier Halloween sex was really hot but this might be even hotter, maybe because I'm not worrying about people driving by. I push on his chest trying to get him to the bed. He doesn't move.

"Garret. The bed."

His lips move back up to my mine. "You said you didn't want to do it until later."

He does this to me all the time. Makes me ask for it, beg for it.

Forget it. I'm going to make *him* beg this time.

I stop kissing him. "You're right. We'll do it later."

"You sure about that?" His hand is still under my skirt doing all the things he knows drive me crazy.

"No." I smile. I'm so weak when it comes to this. "I want it now."

"I thought so."

He lifts me up and backs me against the wall. The sex is hard and fast and steamy hot. So hot we have to have shower when we're done.

The cheerleader costume was 40 bucks, which I thought was way too much for hardly any fabric. But after what we just did? It was worth every penny.

Chapter 20

GARRET

When Jade told me she wanted to get a costume, I figured she'd get one of those long black dresses with the crooked hem that come with a witch's hat. So the cheerleader costume was a huge surprise. I didn't think Jade would go for something like that. She always said those types of costumes make girls look slutty, but I guess she changed her mind. Or else she thinks they're only slutty if you wear them in public.

Once I saw her in that costume, I couldn't wait to get her out of it. I admit, the cheerleader thing does turn me on. Big time. Which explains why I had sex with so many cheerleaders back in high school. So seeing Jade in a cheerleader costume? Shit, I could barely control myself. She looked so fucking hot. She's definitely wearing that again.

After the sex and the hot shower I'm so relaxed I just want to lie on the couch and watch movies all night. But she's making us go to this party and I have no idea why. I know she won't like it.

We arrive at Kyle's place around 8:30. People are standing out on the lawn, drinking, and some of the girls are dancing to the music that's blaring from the wireless speakers on the porch. I spot a girl wearing the same cheerleader costume that Jade bought. It looked a thousand times better on Jade.

Kyle comes out of the house as we're walking up the porch steps. "Kensington, you actually came."

"Yeah, we thought we'd stop by."

Kyle's wearing a black t-shirt, a bandana around his head, and a patch over his eye. "Go on inside. The keg's over by the bar. And Niki's mixing drinks for people. She made some kind of Halloween cocktail."

I don't know who Niki is—maybe his girlfriend? Or girl of the week? Kyle doesn't date girls for very long.

The inside of the house is already crowded. The music is so loud you can feel the bass thumping through the floor. In the middle of the room people are dancing, if you want to call it that. It's mostly girls in skimpy costumes waving their arms around while guys grind up against them.

I'm not judging here. I've been those guys. I'm just over it now. I've already lived this scene many times.

"So what do you want to do?" I have to practically yell it for Jade to hear.

"You want to dance?"

"It's too crowded."

"But you're good at it. Come on." She waves her hands around like the other girls are doing, but it doesn't look right. I'd never tell her this, but Jade's not a very good dancer. She has no problem with slow dancing, but faster, club-style dancing? Not so good.

"You're not dancing." Jade puts her hands behind my neck and sways side to side.

"Yeah, I don't feel like it tonight."

"Garret." Someone says it from behind me. Jade lets me go and I turn to see Nate there.

"Hey, Nate. I didn't know you were friends with Kyle."

"We're more like acquaintances. I go to his parties sometimes."

"Nate, this is Jade. Jade, this is Nate."

"Hi." Nate shakes her hand. "So you're the wife?"

"That's me. And you're the one who plays five hours of video games every day?"

"Three hours, not five." He shoots me a look. "Don't be making up shit about me, Kensington."

I shrug. "Hey, man, I've heard from multiple sources that it's five hours a day."

"Yeah, well, I'm trying to cut down." He notices someone behind me. "I gotta go. I'll see you guys later."

I look back and see him chasing down some girl with red hair wearing a devil's costume.

"Hi, Garret." A girl steps between Jade and me and gets right in my face. It's Brook, but I couldn't tell at first because she has a mask over her eyes, like the kind you wear at masquerade balls. She's holding a drink in her hand and her breath smells like rum. Yeah, she's so close I can smell her breath.

"Hi." I back up and hit a wall of people. "Where's Dylan?"

"He didn't come. He says he's too old for college parties. Sometimes I think he's just too boring for me." She leans forward and I move to the side before her breasts collide with my chest.

Jade taps Brook on the shoulder. "Hi, Brook."

Brook checks behind her and turns around. "Have we met? You look familiar."

Seriously? This girl is such a bitch. I don't know why Harper was ever friends with her.

"We had lunch together," Jade says. "I'm Jade *Kensington*." She emphasizes the last name. That's my girl.

"Oh, yeah. Harper's friend."

"Yeah. And Garret's wife."

Jade goes around Brook and over to me. I put my arm around her and kiss her.

Jade smiles at Brook. "So have you talked to Harper lately?"

"No, but my mom talked to her mom just the other day. She said Harper did something to her shoulder."

"She tore her rotator cuff and—" Jade stops, because Brook is waving at someone in the crowd and not even listening.

"I have to go. Tell Harper I said hi." Brook holds her drink in the air and squeezes between the people next to us, trying to get through.

When she's gone, Jade says, "She doesn't seem like someone who's ready to get married. She was totally hitting on you again."

"Not just me." I see Brook in the crowd, latched onto one of the football players, rubbing her chest against his bicep and talking really close.

"What do you mean?" Jade follows my gaze and sees Brook, who is now saying something into the guy's ear. He smiles and jerks his head toward the hallway that leads to the bedrooms.

I watch as Brook and the guy head back there. "Poor bastard."

"Which one? That guy? Or Dylan?"

I laugh. "Both of them. Thank God I found you and don't have to deal with girls like her anymore." I lean down and give Jade a kiss. "You want to get a drink?"

"I'll take a soda if they have any."

"Aren't you coming with me?"

"It's too crowded. I'll just wait here."

I'm not sure if I want to leave her. The bar has a long line. It'll take forever to get a drink. But I'm tall enough that I'll be able to see her from the bar.

"I'll be right back. Don't move."

Jade starts dancing again and waves at me to go. I laugh as I walk away. She really needs to work on her dance moves.

A new song starts and enough people migrate to the dance area that I'm able to quickly sneak through to the bar.

The bar looks like a tiki hut. It's one of those portable bars that people set out on their patio. Sitting next to it on the floor I see two big white coolers. One of them has cans of soda so I grab a couple Cokes and head back toward Jade. Except now I can't see her. She's so short and the people around her are tall. Plus, she's wearing black, which half the people in here are wearing.

I make it through the crowd and see her in the same spot where I left her. A guy is talking to her. He's standing way too close and as I approach them, the guy puts his arm around Jade and stares down at her breasts.

Great. Now I have to kill him. Okay, so I won't actually kill him but it's not like the thought didn't cross my mind.

"Get your hands off my wife." I give Jade the soda but my eyes are on the guy. He's about my height but he looks older than me. He's probably a senior.

"Your wife?" He takes his time removing his arm.

Jade holds up her hand, showing off her ring.

"No, shit?" The guy laughs. "Fuck. I thought you were joking."

"Thanks for the soda, honey," Jade says to me as she imitates what Brook did with the football player, pressing her breasts against my arm and rubbing my chest with her hand.

The guy turns and walks the other way.

Jade laughs. "Did you see his face?"

"What did he say to you?"

"He said I was a good dancer."

That just confirms the guy was hitting on her.

"You ready to get out of here?" We've only been here 20 minutes but it feels like it's been an hour.

Jade looks around at the crowded room as drunk people stumble past us, their drinks spilling out of their cups. "Yeah, let's go."

I knew she wouldn't like being here. I don't either. We're totally out of place. College parties aren't for married people. I used to love parties like this, but now I have no interest in them.

As we're walking to the car, Jade takes my hand. "Your Halloween parties are way more fun."

"You mean the one I had last year?"

"Last year *and* this year."

"We didn't have one this year."

"Yeah, we did. Maybe it wasn't a party but it was still fun." She swings our arms as we walk. "The chocolate. The costume."

"And we still have to celebrate our sleepover anniversary."

"See? Way more fun than some college house party. I don't know what I was thinking."

We're at the car now and I open Jade's door, but she doesn't get in.

Instead, she gives me a hug. "I love you."

I love it when she does stuff like this. When she just hugs me out of the blue for no particular reason. Or kisses me. Or tells me she loves me.

"I love you, too."

"We're still watching scary movies, right?" She gets in the car.

"It wouldn't be Halloween without them."

When we get home, we only watch one of the scary movies. Jade's too sleepy to watch any more. But she perks up when we head to the bedroom to relive our first sleepover, which this time involves a lot less sleeping.

This was a damn good weekend. Jade got to hang out with her relatives, we were given a piece of oceanfront property, and we spent most of Sunday having amazing sex.

The next few weeks are uneventful, which is nice for a change. No school drama. No family drama. Nothing. Jade and I just go to class and spend our nights studying, watching TV, and having sex. We're finally getting into a routine that seems to work for us.

During the week, I've been meeting Jade a couple times for lunch, but other than that I don't see her much on campus. Since dropping those classes she has such a light class schedule that she spends more time at home than at school.

Jade's counseling seems to be going well. I think she even likes going. She said in the last few sessions she started talking about her mom. She doesn't tell me any more than that, which is okay. At least she's finally opening up to Jennifer.

I've been going to the gym and the pool a lot more, trying to get my shoulder back in shape. I saw the doctor last week and he said that, according to the tests he ran, my shoulder's finally healing. It definitely feels better. My range of motion is back and the pain is almost gone.

Now the physical therapist wants me to focus on building back strength in my chest and shoulder muscles, which means I have to work out a lot. I go to the gym in the mornings before class and the pool late afternoon. That way Jade and I are able to spend our evenings together.

Everything's going so well that it almost seems like we're due for something bad to happen. I hate to say that, but given all that's happened the past year, it's always in the back of my mind.

I did get a little on edge during the election a couple weeks ago. When I saw Kent Gleason up at the podium, waving to the crowds before his acceptance speech, I had flashbacks of being at the meeting last March, being told I'd be president someday. As I watched Gleason give his speech, I kept thinking that could've been me in 20 years; standing at a podium, with gray hair, a phony smile, and a wife I didn't choose.

I didn't even vote. It's bad, I know. But what's the point? I knew Gleason would win. Jade voted, but only because she wanted to vote for the politicians in the local races. I told her those elections are probably rigged, too, but she still went and voted.

It's now the Friday before Thanksgiving. I'm done with class for the day and sitting out on the deck. Jade's out with Sara and Caleb at the park. Jade used to only see Sara at the coffee shop, but lately the two of them have been doing stuff when Sara gets off work. Sara will never replace Harper but she's still a good friend. Jade and her get along really well.

I flip through my phone messages and decide to call Sean. I've been calling him every few days instead of waiting for him to call me. We mostly talk football and now we've added basketball since the season just started.

As I'm getting ready to call him, my phone rings. Speak of the devil. It's Sean.

I answer it. "Hey, man, you read minds or something? I was just about to call you."

"You got a minute? Or actually, you got more than a minute?" Sean doesn't sound right. His voice has a serious, heavy tone.

"Yeah. I'm just sitting outside waiting for Jade to come home."

"Does she know?"

"Know what?"

"Then I guess she doesn't."

"What's wrong? Did Harper get hurt again?"

"No. Her shoulder's the same as it's been."

"Then what is it?"

I hear him take a deep breath. "Fuck."

"Sean, what's going on?"

"Harper, uh…" He pauses. "She broke up with me."

Shit. I shouldn't be surprised, but I am. Actually I'm kind of shocked. I thought Harper would fight harder against her parents. She keeps telling Jade she doesn't care what her parents think and that she loves Sean and isn't breaking up with him. And so far, her parents haven't tried that hard to break them up, so I thought maybe my theory about Kiefer joining the organization was wrong. But if so, then why would Harper do this?

I get up and go inside so I can hear him better. "What the fuck happened?"

"Exactly what I'd like to know."

"Did you have a fight?"

"No. Everything was good. She's been practically living at my place ever since she hurt her shoulder. And then she just breaks up with me."

"When did she tell you this?"

"Earlier today. She came here after her morning classes and told me. Then she packed her stuff and left. I tried to get her to talk to me, but she wouldn't. She just left."

"What was her reason? She had to have given you a reason for doing this."

"She said we needed some time apart. She said she's confused and needs time to think."

"So this isn't a break-up. She just wants some time apart."

"Garret, you and I both know what that means. That's just a nicer way of telling me she's breaking up with me."

He's right. I was just trying to stay positive for him.

"What did she say she needs to think about?"

"Something about how she thinks she's too young to be in a serious relationship. How she isn't sure if she sees a future with us. Who the hell knows? By that point, my mind was all over the place. I wasn't really listening."

"Sean, I'm sorry. I don't know what to tell you."

"At least her parents will be happy. They showed up yesterday."

"Why? They'll see her next week when she's in LA."

"They wanted to meet with the doctor she'll be seeing when she's back here after the surgery. They'll probably decide he's not good enough for their daughter either."

"Have you seen her parents since they got there?"

"No. The three of them went to dinner last night. I wasn't invited. Of course they didn't bother to tell me this until after I'd asked my boss for the night off. Now I have to work double shifts this weekend. Guess it doesn't matter. I don't have a girlfriend anymore. My weekends are free."

"This sucks, man."

"Yeah, tell me about it. Hey, you know anything about pawning engagement rings?"

"Sean, don't sell it. Keep the ring."

"Why? So I have a constant reminder of her? No, thanks. Besides, I need the money to help pay it off. I know I won't get much for it at a pawn shop but at least it's something."

"How much was the ring? You don't have to tell me if you don't want to."

"It was $10,000."

Shit, that's a lot of money for Sean. It's probably half of what he makes in a year.

"Just let me give you the money to pay it off."

"I told you I can't take your money. I don't want to feel like my best friend bought my girlfriend's engagement ring."

"Yeah, but she's not your girlfriend anymore." I sigh. "Sorry, that came out wrong."

"No, you're right. She's not. It just hasn't sunk in yet." He gets quiet, then says, "Let me think about the money. Maybe I'll take you up on the offer."

"Just don't sell the ring."

"Garret, I don't need it anymore."

"You don't know that. Harper could change her mind. Maybe she really does need time to think. She's been going through a lot. Not being able to play tennis anymore is a big deal. When I hurt my shoulder and thought my swimming career was over, I fucking lost it. I was yelling at Jade, then I wouldn't talk to her. We were fighting all the time." It's a bit of an exaggeration, but Jade and I did fight. "And the thing was, none of it was her fault. She didn't do anything wrong. I was just pissed about not being able to swim and

I took it out on her. Harper might be going through the same thing."

"I guess it's possible. She *has* been really down ever since they told her she can't play tennis. And she's really nervous about the surgery next week."

"Which is why you can't sell the ring. Let her have the surgery and recover for a week or two and then talk to her. See if anything's changed."

"I want to be there for the surgery, but if I show up at the hospital her parents will be pissed. What do you think I should do?"

"I don't know. I can't decide that for you. If it were Jade, there's no way I wouldn't be there, even if she told me not to. But she doesn't have parents to yell at me."

"If she did, would you still go?"

"Yeah. I would. I love her too much. I'd have to be there."

"I feel the same way about Harper." He pauses. "Fuck it. I'm going. Which means I've gotta scrape up some money for a hotel room. I won't be staying at the Douglas mansion."

"You can stay at my dad's apartment."

"He has a place in LA?"

"It's downtown in one of those hi-rise buildings. The doorman can give you the key."

"That would be awesome. You sure your dad would be okay with that?"

"I'll ask him, but I know he won't care. It's not like he'll be using it over Thanksgiving."

"Shit, it's after seven. I was supposed to be at work 10 minutes ago. I gotta go."

"I'll let you know about the apartment."

"Okay, thanks."

"And Sean, call me anytime, okay? Even if it's the middle of the night. Doesn't matter."

"You're a good friend, Kensington."

"See ya, Sean."

I call my dad. He's probably having dinner but I'll leave him a message. It rings eight times and then he finally answers.

"Hello, Garret."

I hear noise in the background. Maybe the TV? I can't tell.

"Where are you?" I ask him.

"In the game room. Lilly and I are playing your race car game. I was in the final lap when you called so I couldn't answer right away."

"I'm winning!" I hear Lilly yell.

My dad laughs. "Yes, honey, but you practice a lot more than I do."

I hear Lilly again. "I could beat you, too, Garret!"

"Since when did she get so competitive?" I ask my dad.

"She's a Kensington. It's in the genes." I can hear him better now. He must've gone out in the hall. "So are you just calling to check in?"

"Actually I wanted to ask if Sean could use the apartment in LA next week. He'll be there for Harper's surgery and he needs a place to stay."

"I don't think it's a good idea, Garret."

"Why? I already told him he could stay there."

"Harper's parents don't approve of him, and as you know, we're good friends with the Douglas family. If they found out I was enabling Sean to be there for the surgery when I know they don't want him there, it could cause problems."

"What the hell? That's ridiculous. First of all, they don't have to know he's staying there. And second, since when are you such good friends with Kelly and Kiefer?"

"We're becoming more involved with them. That's all I can say."

If he can't tell me, then it means this involves the organization. So I was right. Kiefer's been asked to be a member, which means he has to get Sean out of Harper's life. Shit. I was really hoping that wasn't true.

"Dad, Sean is my best friend."

"I know he is, and I'm sorry but I can't help you out here. Just give Sean some money and have him stay at a hotel."

"When there's an apartment sitting there empty?"

"Garret, you know how this works. This isn't about me. I would be more than happy to let Sean stay there, but I can't, given the circumstances."

"Why is he doing this?"

"Who are you talking about?"

"Kiefer. Why is he doing this? And who asked him to?"

"You know better than to ask those types of questions."

"I just don't understand it. I don't know why he wants to do this, especially knowing what it means for his daughters."

"It's complicated. Just leave it alone. And tell Jade to stay out of it."

"You know she won't do that."

"Then it's your job to convince her to let this go."

"I don't think I want to. This is stupid. Why can't Sean and Harper just be together?"

"You know the rules."

"They're already breaking the rules by letting Kiefer in, so why not break the rule that says Harper has to marry—"

"We can't talk about this. Just give Sean some money so he can get a hotel."

"He won't take money from me. I'll have to figure something else out."

"I'm sorry, Garret. I really am."

I hear Jade's car in the driveway. "I gotta go. I'll call you next week before you leave."

"We're not going. We're staying here for Thanksgiving."

"Why aren't you going to St. Croix?"

Katherine decided she wants to stay here in town. She didn't tell me this until yesterday. If I'd known, I wouldn't have canceled all my meetings on Friday."

"Why does Katherine want to stay home?"

"She wants to spend the weekend with the man she's seeing. She's with him right now. That's why Lilly and I are having pizza and game night."

"You're eating pizza *and* playing video games? I swear, sometimes I don't even know you're my dad."

He chuckles. "Yes, I've changed a little the past year, haven't I?"

"Just a little."

"Daddy, would you play with me, please?" Lilly yells it from the game room.

"I'll be right there," he yells back.

"I'll let you go. Tell Lilly she's going to need a lot more practice if she thinks she's going to beat me in that race car game."

"I will. Goodbye, Garret."

Jade walks in the door. She's not going to like what I'm about to tell her.

Harper broke up with Sean. And Kiefer's joining the organization.

So much for everything going well. I knew it couldn't last.

Chapter 21

JADE

I walk in the door and see Garret sitting on the couch.

"I was hoping you'd be home." I drop my backpack on the floor and race over to the couch, curling up next to him and giving him a kiss. "What do you want to do tonight? It's Friday night, date night. Want to see a movie?"

"Sure. But first I need to tell you something." He's got that serious look on his face. I hate that look.

"Something's wrong. What is it?"

He turns so we're facing each other. "Sean called."

"Yeah? So?"

"Harper broke up with him."

I bolt up from the couch. "What? Are you serious?"

"She went to his apartment and told him earlier today."

I slowly sit back down. "Did she give him a reason?"

"She said she was confused and needed time to think."

"About what? Whether she wants to marry him? She already knows she wants to marry him. She just isn't ready yet. So what does she need to think about?"

"Nothing. She just said that to let him down easy. She broke up with him, Jade. They're not getting back together."

"Of course they're getting back together. This is just a stupid fight. I'll talk to her. Call Sean and tell him not to worry. They'll be back together by Sunday."

"Jade, it's not going to happen. Her parents are there."

"In Connecticut? Why?"

"Sean said they wanted to meet with Harper's doctor but I think Sean is the real reason they're there."

"What do you mean?"

"They need this to end. They need Harper to break up with Sean before Kiefer can join the organization."

"No." I slump into the couch. "This isn't happening. Tell me this isn't happening."

"I just talked to my dad. We were right, Jade. They asked Kiefer to be a member."

I close my eyes and take a moment to breathe because I'm starting to feel like I can't. This is all too similar to last year. The organization interfering with lives, destroying them.

"Jade." Garret strokes my hair. "I know this is bad, but there's nothing we can do. So I need you to stay out of this."

I open my eyes just as Garret leans over to kiss my forehead.

"I want to do something, Garret. I want to fix this."

"I do, too. But we can't risk it. I'm trying to stay off their radar. I don't even want them thinking about me."

"What if I just—"

"Jade. No. If either one of us does anything to interfere with their plans for Kiefer, they'll find out. They'll come after us."

"It's not fair they're able to do this. To control people like this. Someone needs to do something."

"Jade, look at me." I lift my head and he locks his eyes on mine. "We are not going to get involved in this. As much as I want to see Sean and Harper together, there's no fucking way in hell I'm risking our relationship for them. I need you to promise me you won't either."

I nod.

"That's not enough. I need you to say the words. Promise me you will not get involved."

"I promise." I don't think he believes me, so I say it a different way. "I love Harper and Sean, but I would never, ever do something that would jeopardize what you and I have together."

"Good." He rests his forehead against mine. "I really needed to hear you say that."

"How's Sean doing? How did he sound?"

Garret sits back. "Sean's a fucking mess. He sounded lost, confused, hurt. Part of him is still in denial, the other part's in shock. He didn't get any clues, any warnings this was coming. He thought everything was going great. And then she just walks in and tells him it's over."

"Are you mad at Harper?"

"I shouldn't be, but yeah, I guess I am."

"What was she supposed to do? Her parents obviously forced her to do this."

"I get it. It's not her fault. It's just that if you'd heard Sean today, it wasn't the Sean I'm used to. The guy's always smiling and happy. But today he sounded like his life was over. So yeah, even if it's wrong, I can't help but be pissed at Harper. But I'll get over it."

"What's Sean going to do with the ring?"

"Sell it at a pawn shop. I told him not to, so I hope he listens to me."

"Why would you tell him not to sell it?"

"Because they might get back—" He tips his head back. "Shit. I told him that before I knew what was going on. I told him Harper might change her mind. Fuck."

"Garret, you didn't know. And maybe he should keep the ring. Just in case."

"I'm sure he'll end up selling it. He needs the money. That's the other thing. He's going to LA for Harper's surgery and he doesn't have money for a hotel. I offered him the apartment but my dad said Sean can't use it."

"Why?"

"Because he'd be helping the enemy, meaning Sean. My dad has to show his solidarity with the plan. I get why he has to do it, but now I have to find Sean a different place to stay. Or get him to take my money for a hotel."

"Sean shouldn't be going to the surgery. He'll end up getting in a huge fight with her parents."

"He doesn't care about that. The woman he loves is having surgery. He's going. If you were in the hospital, there's no fucking way I wouldn't be there. I don't care who I had to fight with to get in that hospital. I'd still be there."

"You would?" I smile. "Even if I'd broken up with you?"

"Yes." He threads his hand with mine. "You still don't get it, do you?"

"Get what?"

"I'll never stop loving you." He looks me right in the eye. "If you broke up with me tomorrow or next week or next year, I'd still love you. For the rest of my life, I'll love you. You have my heart, Jade. I can't get it back. It's yours now."

I reach over and hug him. "Where do you come up with this stuff? I really need to start writing this down. Put it in a scrapbook. Or frame it."

He gives me a kiss. "Do you want to get out of here? I need a break from all this Sean-Harper stuff. It's depressing."

"I need to call Harper. I'm sure she's a mess right now. I'm surprised she hasn't called me." I get up and check my phone. "No messages."

"She's with her parents. She probably doesn't want to call you with them around."

"But I'm worried about her. I need to call her."

"Jade. Remember the promise you made me."

"Yes. I won't interfere. I just need to know she's okay. Well, I know she's not okay, but you know what I mean." I call her phone but it goes right to voicemail so I leave a message asking her to call me.

Garret and I go to a movie, then out for dinner. I can't stop thinking about Sean and Harper. I always imagined them getting married and having kids and all of us hanging out 20 years from now, and even years after that. It was a nice dream, but dreams don't always come true.

When we get home I watch TV while Garret checks his phone.

"Any messages from Sean?" I ask him.

"No. He had to work tonight."

"I'm sure he didn't feel like going to—"

"What the fuck is this?"

I turn around and see Garret in the kitchen, staring at his phone.

"What's wrong?"

"I got a message from a PR agency in LA wanting me to be their client. And I think I have a voicemail from them." He holds the phone out. He has it on speaker and I hear a woman's voice.

"Garret, this is Wynona Stiles. I'm a publicist at Halstine, Callahan, and Witz, one of the premier public relations firms in Los Angeles. I'd love to speak to you about our services. We handle the publicity for Shalise Halloway, who you may know from the daytime drama, Creston Hills. Shalise's daughter, Brook, recently called me saying you were in need of a publicist. I would love to speak to you about that. I'm familiar with the unfair portrayal of you in the media last spring, but if you hired us, I guarantee we could turn your image around within a few months. The whole country will love you when we're done with you. And just to show you how powerful our reach is, check the news the next few days. I think you'll be pleased with our results. Just imagine what we could do if you were our client. Call me at..." She leaves her number.

Garret slams his phone down on the kitchen table. "Who the fuck does Brook think she is? I met the girl one time—twice, whatever—and now she's setting me up with a publicist?"

"Garret, calm down." I meet him in the kitchen. "Just call that lady back and tell her you're not interested."

"I will, but she said they already did something." He goes to the living room and picks up the remote and starts flipping through channels. "Do a search for me on the Internet and see what you find."

I get my laptop and bring it to the couch and sit next to him.

"Jade, look." He's pointing at the TV. At the corner of the screen, there's a photo of him with the words 'No longer a bad boy?' under it.

It's one of those celebrity news shows and the host says, "Garret Kensington, one of the stars of the reality show, *Prep School Girls*, has reportedly traded in his wild nights in Vegas for a more quiet lifestyle. The rumors are that Kensington is now attending a private college in a small town somewhere along the California coast. Our sources didn't identify the town or the college but did say Garret hasn't been seen at parties and is no longer drinking or doing drugs. We reached out to Pearce Kensington, Garret's father and CEO of Kensington Chemical, but he declined our request for an interview. In other celebrity news..."

Garret throws the remote down. "That's just fucking great. Just what we need. All that work we did last spring destroyed because Brook can't stay the hell out of our business."

"What do you want to do?"

"I'm calling her. Do you still have her number?"

"Yeah, it's in my phone. I'll go get it. Here." I hand him the laptop. "I found some articles about you online. It's the same story we just heard. That PR agency must've put out a press release about you."

As I'm going to get my phone, Garret's phone rings. I pick it up from the table and see it's Pearce calling. "Garret, it's your dad."

"Answer it and put him on speaker."

"Hi, Pearce." I bring the phone over to Garret.

"Hello, Jade. Is Garret there?"

"You're on speaker, Dad." Garret's searching for more articles online. "Have you seen what they're saying about me?"

"Yes. That's why I'm calling. We need to figure out who did this and shut it down."

"I know who did it. It's a girl who goes to school here. Brook Holloway. Her mom's an actress on a soap opera. Brook called her mom's publicist and the publicist did this. She's trying to get me to be her client."

"Brook went to high school with Harper," I tell Pearce. "That's how we got to know her. We had lunch with her a few weeks ago and she told Garret he needed a publicist to turn his image around. He told her he wasn't interested but she didn't listen."

"She'll listen if my attorney calls her," Pearce says.

"Dad, just let me handle it. If you get your lawyers involved, this might turn into something bigger and we don't want that. I can get Brook to back down."

"Are you sure?"

"No, but let me try before you do anything."

"You need to do this soon, Garret. Don't wait."

"I won't. I'll call her right now."

"Let me know how it goes. If she won't back down, I'll take care of it."

"Okay. Bye, Dad." Garret ends the call and looks at me. "Do you have her number?"

I pick up my phone and start reading it off.

"Wait. Let me use your phone." Garret holds his hand out. "I don't want Brook having my number."

"Dylan already has it. I'm sure she went through his phone and took it already."

"Yeah, you're right. I'm sure she did." Garret calls her and she answers almost immediately. She probably thinks he's calling to thank her for what she did.

"Brook, it's Garret Kensington." He doesn't have it on speaker so I can't hear what she's saying. "I got a call from your mom's publicist and I gotta tell you, I'm really pissed off right now. I told you I didn't want a publicist or a PR agency and you still went out and got me one."

He's quiet as she talks, but he's pacing the floor. He puts his hand up. "Brook, stop. I don't need you to tell me what's best for me. I'm more than capable of handling my own life. And I don't give a shit about fixing my image. I don't want this media attention. I came here to be left alone and now I'm going to have people following me around."

He listens again. "Yeah, I know you didn't tell them where I live, but if someone really wanted to know, they could figure it out. Or a Camsburg student might see one of those news stories and tell the media where I am, if they haven't already." He pauses as she talks, then says, "Brook, listen to me. I'm not joking around here. I need you to end this. Can you do that for me?" He waits. "Yeah. Okay." He sets the phone down.

"What did she say?"

"She said she'd call the publicist and tell her not to send out any more press releases."

"Do you believe her?"

"No. That's why I'm calling the publicist myself." He picks his phone up again and calls her.

"Garret, it's midnight."

"I'll leave her a message."

He does, and then puts his phone away and sits on the couch. "You want to watch a movie? I'm too pissed off to sleep."

"Did Brook say she was sorry or anything?"

"I don't want to talk about her. I'm trying to relax. But no, she didn't say she was sorry. I didn't think she would. And I don't need her to. I just need her to end what she started."

"Garret, even if people thought you'd changed and weren't the guy you were last spring, they wouldn't try to take you again, right? I mean, they can't. They let you go."

"I'm not taking any chances. We've gotta stop this."

"Are you saying they'd—"

"Jade. I'm not saying that. I just want people to leave us alone. I don't want photographers following us around and I don't want people knowing where we live."

I sigh and lean into his side. "This has been a really crappy night. First Sean and Harper and now this thing with Brook."

"I know." He kisses my forehead. "You gonna fall asleep?"

"Probably." I lay my head on his chest. "I love you."

"I love you, too."

On Saturday morning, I flip through the TV channels and can't find any stories about Garret. So maybe Brook actually listened for once.

After breakfast, Garret goes to the gym. I'm waiting for him at the coffee shop. Then we're going to run errands and have lunch.

I've called Harper seven times and heard nothing back. I called her again just now, from the coffee shop, but it went straight to voicemail.

"So Alex asked me over for Thanksgiving dinner." Sara scoots to the end of the booth and leans against the wall, putting her feet up on the seat. She just went on break so she met me in the corner booth so we can talk.

She went out with Alex last night. Even though they're just friends, they've been going out every Friday night. And they see each other almost every day. He stops by the coffee shop, or he meets her at the park when she takes Caleb there, or she goes to his place for dinner. They clearly want to be more than friends but they're taking it slow.

"Where's the Thanksgiving dinner?" I ask her. "At his apartment?"

"No, at his parents' house."

"He wants you to meet his parents? That's serious."

"It's really not. He has a huge family. They might not even notice I'm there. He's got three older sisters and two older brothers and they're all married and his sisters have kids. So they'll all be over, along with his aunts and uncles and cousins. I think he said 40 people will be there. Maybe more."

"Wow, that's a lot of people. Did you tell him you'd go?"

"I told him I'd think about it. But I think I want to go. It'd be nice to have an actual meal on Thanksgiving instead of canned soup or a peanut butter sandwich."

"Where do they live?"

"Sacramento. Alex wants us to ride together but he's staying overnight so then I'd have to do the same. His parents don't have room for everyone so he's staying at a hotel. He offered to let Caleb and me stay with him since I don't have money to get my own room, but...I don't know."

"What's the problem? You don't want to stay with him?"

"I just don't want things to get weird between us. Everything's going great and I don't want to screw it up."

"How would it get screwed up? Are you planning on moving past the friend stage while you're at the hotel?"

"No. I'd never do that with Caleb there. It's just that it might be weird being in the same room all night. We'll have separate beds, but still."

"It's not weird. I think you're worrying too much. Unless you think Alex is going to try something."

"He won't. He made it clear that won't happen."

"Like ever? Or just next week?"

She laughs. "Just next week."

"So it *will* happen at some point?"

Her cheeks blush. "Well, I hope so. I know Alex would like that."

"Have you kissed him?"

She smiles. "Yes."

"When did it happen?"

"A couple weeks ago."

"Weeks? And you didn't tell me? Sara, you're supposed to tell your girlfriends this stuff."

"I didn't want you thinking I'm a bad mom, kissing guys when I should be taking care of Caleb. When I was a kid I hated when my mom brought her loser boyfriends over and made out with them right in front of me. I'm not going to do that to Caleb."

"First of all, it's one guy and he's not a loser. And I'm sure Caleb was asleep when this kissing was going on, right?"

"Yes. But still."

"Kissing Alex doesn't make you a bad mom." I smile at her. "So does this mean you're officially dating now?"

"No, we're just friends who kiss." She checks her phone. "I only have two minutes left. Let's talk about you. What did you do last night?"

"Movie and dinner, like we always do."

"Oh, I forgot to tell you. Some guy was in here the other day asking about you."

"A guy from Camsburg?"

"No. He said he's from out of town. He didn't say where."

"What did he look like?"

"He was a big guy. A little taller than Garret. Dark brown hair, brown eyes. He had a suit on. He looked kind of important."

Whenever I hear about guys in suits lurking around, I panic and assume it's someone from the organization. But why would this guy be looking for me at the coffee shop? The organization could easily find out where I live.

"Sara, you need to tell me anything you remember about this guy. How old do you think he was?" It comes out rushed and Sara looks at me funny.

"Is everything okay? You seem nervous."

"I'm fine. So how old was he?"

"Early to mid-twenties? I don't know. I'm not good with ages."

"And what exactly did he say?"

"He asked if I knew Jade Taylor. I said no because that's not your last name. I thought he meant someone else. But then he showed me a photo of you."

"And what did you say?"

"I told him you're married now and that your last name is Kensington."

"How did he react?"

"He seemed surprised. He said he didn't know that you and Garret got married. He thought you were still just dating."

So he doesn't know I married Garret? Everyone in the organization knows that, so is the person playing dumb? Or are they not connected to the organization?

"How does he know Garret?"

"He said they went to school together."

"What school? High school? College?"

"He didn't say." She gets up. "I have to go. My break is over."

"Wait. Are you sure you can't remember this guy's name? Was it a common name, like John or Matt or Jeff?"

"It was kind of common. Jeff, Jake, Jared. Justin! That's what it was. Justin. He didn't say his last name."

I don't know any Justins, and Garret's never mentioned anyone named Justin.

"Sara, if that guy comes in here again asking about me, don't tell him anything, okay? Don't tell anyone else either."

"Um, okay." She stares at me like she knows I'm hiding something. "I have to get back to work."

An hour later, Garret meets me at the coffee shop and we run some errands, then go out for lunch. While we're eating I tell him what Sara said.

"Do you think this guy's a member? And if he is, why would he be looking for me instead of you?"

"He's not from the organization. If they want information on someone, they don't walk up to a waitress in a coffee shop and ask her questions. They use surveillance or they use their connections to find stuff out."

"Then I don't know who it would be."

"How does this guy know you?"

"Sara didn't say. But she said he knew you from school."

"I knew a Justin back in eleventh grade but he didn't come back for senior year. His family moved to France for his dad's job."

"Were you friends?"

"We played football together but we weren't really friends. And he wouldn't know about you."

"He would if he ran into someone you know, like Decker. Or Blake." I shudder just saying his name. "You don't think Blake would send someone after me, do you?"

"He better not. I'll fucking kill him."

"I'm getting really nervous about this. Why is someone you know looking for me?"

"We don't know what this is about, so let's not overreact here. If this guy's trying to hurt you, why would he be giving all that information to Sara?"

"So she'd trust him and tell him what he wanted to know. He could've been lying about all that."

Garret takes a moment to think. "Until we figure this out, don't go to the coffee shop unless I'm with you. Go to the library between classes. And if you're home alone, don't answer the door. For anyone."

We get back to the house around two. We're doing homework for the rest of the afternoon. But as soon as I pick up my psych book, Harper calls.

"Harper? I was worried about you. You didn't call me back."

"Jade, I—" There's silence, and then I hear her sniffling and taking shaky, uneven breaths. She's crying.

"Harper, are you—"

"I broke up with Sean." She says it fast, then starts sobbing. An all-out sob where she can't catch her breath.

Hearing her this upset makes *me* cry, too, but mine are slow, silent tears. Garret walks by with his laptop, stopping when he sees me.

"It's Harper. I'm okay." I mouth the words, waving him on.

He nods and goes out to the deck to give me some privacy.

"Jade, I didn't know what to do." She gets the words out, then continues sobbing.

"About Sean?"

"They said—" She stops to blow her nose. "They said they'll disown me."

"Your parents? If you don't break up with Sean?"

"Yes. Well, my dad is the one who said it. My mom just sat there and listened. I don't think she wants this. I think this is all my dad. But she's going along with it so she's just as bad as he is."

"What do they mean when they say they'll disown you?"

"They said they'll stop paying for college and that I'll have to move out of their house." She sniffles. "And they said they won't talk to me anymore."

"Harper, I'm really sorry."

"I had to break up with him, Jade. I didn't know what else to do. I hate my parents right now but I can't lose them. I still want them in my life. So I had to do it. I felt like I didn't have a choice." She takes a shaky breath. "His face... when I told him...I hurt him so bad, Jade. I hurt the person I love more than anything." The sobbing begins again.

My own tears continue to fall and I get up to find a tissue. "Harper, I'm so sorry."

I don't know what else to say to her. If I didn't know what was really going on, I'd be asking her all kinds of questions. Telling her this will all work out. Telling her everything will be okay. But I can't say any of that.

When she's able to speak again she asks, "Did Garret talk to Sean?"

"Yes."

"What did he say?"

"That he was confused. He didn't understand why this happened."

"Everything was so perfect, Jade. We've been living together ever since I got hurt. And I wanted to make it permanent. I was just about to tell Sean that I wanted to move in with him next semester. I was finally ready for that next step."

"Harper, I'm really sorry." I say it again because I don't know what else to say.

She sniffles. "Why aren't you getting more upset about this? I haven't called you because I was sure you'd yell at me and tell me how I'm making a huge mistake. I know you want Sean and me to be together. We talked about it all last summer. And now you're not even trying to get me to stay with him."

Crap. How do I explain this? I can't tell her what I know.

"I'm just trying to be supportive. This is your decision. I can't tell you what to do."

"You always tell me what to do. And I do the same to you. If it weren't for me yelling at you about all the things you did wrong in your relationship with Garret last year, you two probably wouldn't even be together. You may have hated me at the time, but it's what friends do. We keep each other from making stupid mistakes."

It's almost like she wants me to force her to change her mind. Like she's dying for me to talk her into getting back with Sean. But I can't do that. I can't get involved in this. I promised Garret I'd stay out of it.

"Harper, talking about this will only make it harder. I'm not going to make this any worse for you."

"How did Garret get his dad to change his mind?"

"What are you talking about?"

"Last fall, Pearce kept trying to forbid you two from seeing each other. But then he accepted you. Why? What changed?"

I can't tell her that, either.

"I don't know. I think he just realized how much Garret and I love each other and he gave up trying to keep us apart."

"My parents know how much I love Sean, but they don't care. They only care about themselves. And what really pisses me off is that they let my sisters date whoever they want. Kylie's dating someone and they have no problem with him."

"Your sisters have boyfriends now?"

"Just Kylie. She's dating some guy who works at one of the movie studios. I can't remember which one. Anyway, he's from New York and just got his MBA and now he's working in the finance department at the studio. Oh, and get this. Kylie's only been on a few dates with him and my parents invited him over for Thanksgiving dinner. So I guess my parents only hate *me* and not my sisters."

This makes no sense. Harper's sisters are only supposed to date guys who are part of the organization. So is this guy a member? He must be.

"Jade, I have to go. My mom will be back any second. She's staying here until Tuesday and then we're flying back together."

"Where's your dad?"

"He had a meeting to go to in New York and then he's flying home. With my mom here, I probably won't be able to call you again until I'm back in LA. And then I'll be getting prepped for surgery so I guess we'll just talk after Thanksgiving."

"Okay. But call me before then if you want to talk."

"I will. Bye, Jade. Happy Thanksgiving."

"Yeah. Happy Thanksgiving."

I go out on the deck and tell Garret what Harper said.

"Why would the rules be different for her sisters?" I ask him.

"They're not. That guy Kylie's dating is a member. He has to be. Otherwise her parents wouldn't be inviting him to dinner. Kiefer probably set them up."

"It sounds like Harper has no idea what's really going on. But they have to tell her eventually, especially if they're going to force her to marry someone."

"That's not going to happen right away. They have plenty of time to tell her."

"But she needs to be told now, not later. She doesn't understand why they're doing this. And I don't either. They can see how upset Harper is, and I know they love her, so why are they doing this? Is it really just for the money?"

"You need to let this go, Jade. Don't get involved. And don't ask questions."

Don't ask questions. The number one rule. I've been told it so many times now you'd think I'd never ask another question ever again. But when I can't explain something, like this thing with Harper, my mind just keeps coming up with questions. But they'll have to remain there, unanswered. Because finding the answers isn't worth the cost to get them.

Chapter 22

GARRET

*L*ast weekend pretty much sucked. Jade and I tried not to think about what's going on with Harper and Sean. We tried not to talk about it. But that's nearly impossible to do when something bad like this happens to your best friends.

Sean called me Sunday night after he got off from work. It was 2 a.m. his time, 11 here. He couldn't sleep. He hasn't slept more than a few hours since the break-up. He sounded like a totally different person. His voice was hoarse, monotone, lifeless. And then he cried while we were on the phone. The guy fucking cried. And he wasn't drunk. It didn't last long, but still. It was bad. I didn't know what to do or what to say. I was basically useless.

I know how it feels when you think you've lost the person you love most in this world. It shreds your heart. Rips at your gut. Makes you feel like you're missing part of your soul that you'll never get back.

That's how I felt when I thought I lost Jade. After we said goodbye in the woods last May, I went back to my house, locked myself in my room, and completely shut down. I didn't eat. I didn't sleep. All I did was think about Jade, and how I'd lost the person who meant everything to me. The only person who ever really understood me. The person I'd given my heart to, fully and completely, without hesitation.

Thinking I'd lost her forever hurt so fucking bad. I wouldn't wish that kind of pain on anyone, but definitely not my best friend. So what do you say to someone who's going through that? The truth is there's nothing to say. There wasn't a single word that would've helped me when I thought I'd lost Jade. The only thing that would've helped would've been getting Jade back. And luckily, a week later I did.

Sean hung up around midnight, my time, and it took me a while to fall asleep. When I got up this morning, I felt like shit, not only from the lack of sleep, but from the fact that I can't do anything to make this any easier on Sean.

I took a long shower, which usually wakes me up, but today it didn't. I still feel half asleep and I'll be late to class if I don't hurry up. I dry off and go back in the bedroom, the towel around my waist. Jade is still asleep. I usually let her sleep in, but she has stuff she wants to do this morning so she told me to make sure she doesn't sleep too late.

I go over and sit next to her on the bed. She's on her side, snuggled up under the blanket looking cute as ever. I lean down and kiss her cheek.

She smiles. "Hey."

"Were you already awake?"

"Kind of, but I pretended not to be so you'd kiss me."

"I'd kiss you even if you were awake."

"I know, but your wake-up kisses are different than your other kisses and I wanted a wake-up kiss."

I sit up. "What's a wake-up kiss?"

"It's a kiss you only use when you're trying to wake me up. It's softer than your other kisses."

"And what are my other kisses like?"

She rolls onto her back. "Some are slow and sexy. Some are really quick. Some are gentle. It depends on what kind of mood you're in."

"My kisses aren't that different."

"They are. You have all kinds of kisses."

I lean down and give her my slow, sexy kiss. Then I remain by her lips, my eyes on hers. "What kind of kiss was that?"

"A teasing kiss. You're teasing me because you don't have time for sex, but that kiss made me want it and now I have to wait until we get home tonight."

I laugh. "Okay, I admit it. I do have different kisses. And you're right. I was teasing you just now. Heating you up for later."

"You're so mean." She laughs and pushes me away.

She goes in the bathroom while I go to the closet to find some clothes. I throw some jeans on and as I'm putting on my shirt, Jade comes out of the bathroom and walks up to me.

"Are you okay?" She does the buttons on my shirt as she looks up at me.

"Yeah. I'm good."

"Are you sure?"

She's asking because today is the anniversary of the day my mom was killed in the plane crash. This day always sucks, but not nearly as much as it used to. Ten years have passed and a lot has changed in those 10 years, especially the past year. Having Jade in my life has changed how I feel about this day. Instead of thinking about my mom being dead, I imagine her watching over me, seeing me with Jade, and being happy that my life turned out this way.

Having my dad back in my life, being a real father, has also helped. This day is hard on both of us, but neither one of us would admit it. My dad used to pretend this was just another day and I used to spend the day drinking. But now that we have a relationship again, we talk about my mom more, and although we haven't talked about her death, I think if I mentioned it, he'd talk about it. That just shows how much things have changed between us. Just a year ago, he would've yelled at me for even saying my mom's name.

I wonder how he's doing today. I never would've asked him before, but I feel like I can now. I feel like I should.

Jade finishes the last button. I take her hands from my shirt and kiss her. "I'm going to call my dad and see how he's doing."

"I thought he wouldn't talk about it."

"I don't need him to talk about it. I just want to make sure he's okay."

She hugs me. "I think that's a good idea."

"I have to get going. I'll see you tonight."

"Can you meet for lunch?" She follows me to the living room

"No, I have physical therapy at noon." I grab my backpack and take my keys from the hook on the wall.

"Okay, then have a good day." She walks me to the door. "I love you."

"I love you, too." I kiss her goodbye, then go out to my car. As I'm driving to campus, I call my dad. He's probably at work. I always forget the time difference.

"Hello, Garret," he answers.

"Hey, are you at work?"

"No. I stopped somewhere first." His voice is quiet. He sounds sad. Really sad. Shit. I didn't expect that. He rarely shows emotion, even on days like today.

"Where did you stop?"

"At that pancake place your mother used to like. That run-down diner."

"Al's Pancake House?" I can't believe he'd go to that place. He hasn't been there since she died.

"Yes, that's the one. Remember how she used to make us go there on Saturday mornings?"

"Yeah. It was one of her favorite restaurants. I took Jade there last year."

"I didn't know you'd been back there."

"Jade and I went every Sunday. She really liked that place."

"I didn't stay long. I just had coffee. The menu hasn't changed. I remember when we first went there and your mother—" He stops because his voice was shaking, almost like he was about to cry.

Fuck. I don't know how to respond. He always acts like he's over her death. But he's clearly not. Is this day always this hard for him? Or is every day this hard? He never tells me so I don't know. Maybe it's just hitting him harder this year because he's been opening up more. Letting himself feel shit instead of shoving it away.

I pull into a parking lot and turn the car off. "Dad, talk to me. What's going on?"

He's quiet, but then says, "Ten years. I can't believe she's been gone that long. It seems like just a few years ago we were—" He clears his throat. Shit, he almost cried again. Or maybe he is and he doesn't want me to know.

I had no freaking clue he felt this way. I assumed this day was difficult for him but I didn't know *how* difficult. He's never let me know. After she died, he was devastated, but he tried to hide it from me. The only time I saw him cry was when he told me what happened. I was only 10. He tried to be strong for me, but he broke down in the middle of telling me about the plane crash. He could barely say the words. And I didn't want to hear them. I yelled at him to stop talking. I was so angry that I started hitting him and kicking him, like it was somehow his fault. He picked me up and held me so tightly that I eventually gave up fighting him. When I saw him crying, it scared me. I'd never seen him cry, so when he did, I knew what he'd told me was true. That she was gone and never coming back.

After that, I never saw my dad cry again. But in the weeks following, I'd hear him in his room, sobbing. I tried to go in there to be with him, but he locked the door so I couldn't. He shut me out from that point forward. He pretended he'd moved on even though he hadn't. And because he didn't deal with his own grief, he couldn't help me deal with mine. That's why I ended up going to counseling.

Now all these years later, I find out he's still grieving. I wish I'd known that. Maybe I could've helped him. Maybe we could've helped each other instead of suffering in silence, or in my case, drinking until I passed out.

I don't know what to say to him. Nothing I say will make this any easier. At least I have Jade to help me get through this day. My dad has no one.

"Dad, I'm sorry. I should've come out there."

He clears his throat again. "No, that's not necessary."

"Maybe not, but I still think I should've been there. Or you could've come out here. We should be together on this day."

He sighs. "Perhaps you're right. Perhaps we need to stop ignoring this day and honor her somehow."

"Yeah, I think we should."

"Are you doing okay? I know how much you miss her."

"I'm okay. It helps to have Jade. And it helps that you're actually talking about it."

"I'm sorry for that. I shouldn't have ignored it like I did all those years. It was just difficult for me. Pretending it didn't happen was easier."

"I know." I used to be pissed at him for not acknowledging this day but I'm not anymore. I get why he did it. This day is even harder for him than it is for me. I just didn't know that until today.

"Garret, you should get to class."

"Don't worry about class. I can be late." I check my watch. Class starts in ten minutes. "Where are you right now?"

"In the car, heading to the office."

"Maybe you should take the day off."

"I can't. I have meetings all afternoon. I have another call coming in. I should get going."

"Call me later if you want to talk."

"You as well."

"I love you, Dad."

"I love you, too, son." He hangs up. I can tell it's still hard for him to say those words. Last summer he told me his parents have never told him they love him. I assumed my grandfather had never said it, but I thought my grandmother would've, at least once. But she never has.

I feel really bad for my dad, especially today, and especially after hearing how much he still misses my mom. My mom meant everything to him. She was probably the first person who ever said those words to him. That she loved him. She told him that every day.

I shouldn't be surprised my dad still misses her this much. He loved her more than anything. He'll never find that kind of love again. He won't let himself. That love was just for her and he'll never open himself up again to love someone else that way. It's sad because he's not that old and he has a lot of years left that he could share with someone. But even if he found someone he wanted to be with, the organization wouldn't allow it. He's stuck with Katherine, who's now dating someone else.

My dad's life basically sucks. He's forced to run the company and follow orders from the organization. His wife is an uncaring bitch. And his parents treat him like shit. Lilly and I are the only good things in his life but now I never see him, so all he has is Lilly. I need to call him more. It seems like I only call him when I need something, but I need to start calling him just to talk and see how he's doing.

I arrive at class just as it's starting. After class I meet with my group for a project we have to do. I go to physical therapy at noon, then grab lunch and check messages as I'm eating. There's an email saying my 1:30 class is canceled.

My lack of sleep is catching up to me so I decide to go home and take a quick nap before my other class, which is at three. Jade won't be home. She usually goes to campus around one on Mondays and studies at the library before class.

When I get home, I open the door and drop my backpack on the floor. I'm so freaking tired I can barely keep my eyes open. The blinds are partially shut and the dim light of the room makes me even sleepier.

"Hello, Garret."

I freeze when I hear the deep voice. I instantly assume it's a burglar with a gun aimed at me. I slowly turn my head to the right and see that it's not a burglar.

It's my grandfather.

Chapter 23

GARRET

*M*y grandfather is here. Sitting in my living room.

"What the fuck?" I'm breathing fast, my heart beating a million miles a minute. "You scared the shit out of me! What are you doing here?"

How the hell did he get in here? The door was locked.

"I expected a better greeting, given that I travelled all the way across the country to see you."

My grandfather is sitting up, tall and straight, in the white upholstered chair at the far end of the couch. His legs are crossed and he has one arm resting at his side, the other one raised slightly, his hand rubbing his chin. He's wearing a black suit, a white shirt, and a light gray tie. His suits are specially made for him and cost thousands of dollars. I rarely see him wear anything other than a suit.

"I don't—how did you—" My thoughts don't come out of my mouth right because they're a jumbled mess in my head. I'm still trying to comprehend this. My grandfather is in my living room. Uninvited. He broke into my house. And now he's acting like I should be happy to see him.

"Garret, do you need a moment to collect your thoughts before we begin?"

"Begin what?"

"Our discussion. That's why I'm here. I need to talk to you."

"You flew all the way out here to talk to me? Why didn't you just call me?"

"Because I wasn't getting through to you over the phone. And the things I'm going to tell you need to be said face-to-face."

Great. This should be good. What's he going to tell me that can't be said over the phone? That he's cutting me out of his life? Never wants to see me again? I don't need that to be done in person.

"How did you get in here?"

"I walked in the front door. You should really invest in some better security."

Since when does my grandfather know how to disable an alarm system? And get past two deadbolts?

"Sit down, Garret." He motions to the chair on the other end of the couch that faces the chair he's sitting in.

I sit on the couch instead. "I have class later so we don't have much time to talk."

"You don't have class. Your classes have been canceled for this afternoon."

"No, just the one class was canceled. My other one's not. Wait—how did you know my class was canceled?"

"Because I'm the one who canceled it. Both of them. Check your phone if you don't believe me."

I get my phone out and check for any new emails. One just came in, saying my finance class was canceled.

"How did you do that?"

"That's not what we're here to talk about. Turn your phone off and put it away."

I do as he says, then lean back on the couch, crossing my arms over my chest. "If you're here to tell me you're cutting me out of your life for good, you could've just called. Sent a letter. Even an email would've sufficed."

"I'm not cutting you out of my life, Garret. Quite the contrary. I want to see *more* of you. I want you more involved with the family again."

I'm confused. He breaks into my house and cancels my classes just to tell me he wants me back in his life? Like he couldn't have called first? Done this after class?

Whatever. I've never understood him. No need to try to do so now.

"I want that, too, Grandfather. But in order for us to have a relationship again, you have to accept Jade. She's my wife. She's part of our family now."

"People do not become part of our family because of a piece of paper you obtained at the local courthouse. Being part of this family is a privilege reserved for only a certain few. Like Katherine."

"Jade is a Kensington. If you don't accept that, then you're not accepting me. This won't work if you continue to treat her like an outsider."

He uncrosses his legs, then crosses them again on the other side. "Let's discuss your future, Garret."

Here we go again. Another lecture about taking over the company. So I guess he isn't here to make amends.

"I don't know exactly what went on last spring but I know you didn't do all those things. Trashing hotel rooms. Destroying your father's cars. Being with all those women. It doesn't make sense that after all that, you just became this model citizen, living in a small town, going to college, involved with only one woman."

He refuses to call Jade my wife. Or even say her name. It pisses me off but I try to remain calm and focus on the stuff he said about last spring. I don't want him figuring out what really went on.

"I hit rock bottom," I say matter-of-factly. "And after that, I changed my life. I didn't want to be like that anymore."

"Or…you faked that behavior to ruin your image so you could get out of being president." A smug smile crosses his face. "But you would never do such a foolish thing, now would you, Garret?"

My heart stops. Like completely stops. And then I breathe again.

"Of course I wouldn't. How would I even do something like that?"

"You'd need help. Help from someone powerful. Maybe someone like Arlin Sinclair?"

I feel my pulse speed up but I keep my breathing steady. "What are you talking about? I barely knew that guy."

"You knew him quite well. Our family has been friends with the Sinclairs for years. You had a relationship with his granddaughter, Sadie. And if I'm not mistaken, Arlin's wife, Grace, attended what you considered to be some sort of wedding ceremony last July."

Shit. How did he know that? My dad wouldn't tell him. Did Roth? He was at the hotel. Maybe he saw Grace there. Or did Roth have someone spying on the wedding? Or maybe Lilly told him Grace was there. She probably did. But how does my grandfather know about Arlin? Or is he just saying that to see my reaction? If he knows what Arlin did for me, does the rest of the organization know, too? If so, they would've killed him. They would've caused that heart attack he had.

So does my grandfather know my dad was involved in what happened last spring? He doesn't act like he does, so maybe not. Arlin did most of the hands-on work, not my dad.

"If Arlin was such a good friend of the family," I say, "then you shouldn't accuse him of things he didn't do, especially since he's dead now and can't defend himself."

"The point is that I'm going to fix the mess you made last year. I will restore your public image so that you can enter society again and be seen as a leader."

"I don't need you to do that. I'm not worried about my image."

"Which is why I will worry about it for you. But you will do your part to ensure that your image is restored. We'll go over the plans for that at a later time. For now, let's discuss your education. In the spring semester you will be transferring to Yale, where I attended and where your father attended. You will—"

"Wait, what? I'm not going to Yale. I'm going to school here. At Camsburg."

"You're going to Yale. I've already spoken to the people in charge and you've been accepted for the spring semester."

"I never even applied. How could I be accepted?"

He doesn't answer the question but I'm sure the answer has to do with his connections. Not just as an alum, but as a member of the organization.

"In the summer, you will be working at Kensington Chemical, as we discussed."

"I already told you I'm not doing that."

"You will work there full-time, including weekends, and you will learn the business alongside your father."

"Dad's in on this? He told me he didn't—"

"This isn't his decision. I'll speak with your father later. As I was saying, you will learn the business this summer and continue to learn it by working there every summer until you graduate college. If you choose to pursue an MBA, like your father did, I will allow that, but I will pick the school."

I roll my eyes. "Yeah, I don't think so."

"Garret!" He says it like he's commanding a dog's attention. "This is not a joke. Therefore I expect you to take it seriously."

"Actually, it *is* a joke because I'm not doing any of the stuff you just said."

"You will do what I tell you to do." His jaw clenches and his hand grips the arm of the chair.

"No. I won't." I stand up. "And I'm done listening to this."

"Sit down!" He yells it. He rarely yells, so the fact that he did so just now shows that he's really pissed.

I sigh and sit down again. "I'm sorry I'm such a disappointment to you, Grandfather, but you can't control my life. I'm an adult and I make my own choices. And I've chosen to live here and go to school at Camsburg."

"After we're done here, you will do as I say."

"It's not going to happen, so you might as well leave."

He's silent, and then says, "I tried to make this easy on you, Garret. I tried to take care of any obstacles standing in your way so that you wouldn't have to make a decision. It would've been made for you. But then the plan fell through, which caused me to re-evaluate how I wanted this to play out. The objective is the same, but the means to get there has changed. I decided to take a different approach. One I should've used with your father, but back then I hadn't considered it."

He's rambling on and I have no idea what he's saying. He's not even making sense.

"I don't understand what any of this means."

"You would choose to work at Kensington Chemical if you had nothing else. No other distractions. No obstacles."

"What obstacles? What are you talking about?"

And then, like someone shoved it in front of my face, I see the piece of paper. The one I was given last March when I went to that meeting and learned about the organization's plan for my future. I told them I wouldn't do it, and then they handed me a piece of paper. It was an order to kill my mom. But they didn't use her name. They called her an obstacle.

I stare back at him. "Jade is not an obstacle."

I'm breathing hard, my chest moving in and out. I'm sure he notices. I'm trying to control my emotions, not let him affect me, but I can't do it.

He appears calm and relaxed. "She's destroyed you, Garret. Just like that woman destroyed your father."

I don't know what he's trying to tell me, but I can't listen to him put down Jade and my mom. And hearing him call my mom 'that woman' just sets me off.

I shoot up from the couch. "It's Rachel! Just say her fucking name! You never say her fucking name! And she didn't destroy my father. She was the best thing that ever happened to him. Just like Jade is the best thing that's ever happened to me."

He chuckles. "It's amazing how similar you are to your father. Weak. Easily manipulated. Unable to see the big picture."

I want him out of my house. Out of my life. Forever. I don't know why I ever thought I could have a real relationship with him.

I sit back down. "Let's just get this over with. Finish what you were saying. So Jade is an obstacle? An obstacle to what? My working at the company? I wouldn't work there even if I'd never met Jade."

"That's why you need an incentive. A push. And I will give you that in a moment. But first, let me finish telling you about your future. Pearce may have told you that I've been promoted. And in that position, I have greater influence over decisions. Despite numerous objections, I was able to convince the members to reinstate your membership in the organization provided that you meet certain criteria. You will spend the next few years working on the various things you will need to do in order to fulfill that criteria. It will involve a great deal of work on your part, but I'm confident you can do it."

"Are you serious?" I shake my head. "No way. I'm never joining that group. I don't care what the benefits are or how much money is involved."

"And that brings us back to the incentive. As you said, the girl you're currently living with—"

"Jade. Use her name or I'm leaving."

"Jade." He clears his throat. "Is an obstacle that keeps you from moving forward. And I tried to take care of that obstacle so you wouldn't have to choose."

"What did you do?" I tense up, my heart thumping harder.

"There was a burglary in your neighborhood."

"No, it never happened. Someone faked the whole—" I stop. He's obviously telling me he's involved. But how? Why?

"Yes. I had to make it look like there was a burglary because the man I hired didn't finish the job. Just when he was about to do it, you installed those security cameras and he wouldn't go through with it. He didn't want to get caught and end up in prison. But you'd seen the man around your property and I didn't want you getting suspicious and telling your father. I know how he looks into these things. So I needed you to think the man was just a random burglar who ended up robbing your neighbor. That police officer who came to your door was just an actor."

"Why would you need to fake a robbery?"

"I just told you why. Your father—"

"No, you said the guy didn't finish the job. What job?"

"The man I hired is a criminal. He has a history of violent crime. He had no problem taking the job. I didn't even have to pay him that much."

"Pay him to do what?"

"Break into your house. Make it look like a burglary. Make it look like he didn't realize she was home. She sees his face, he panics and shoots her in the head. Then he messes up the place to make it look real, takes a few valuables, and leaves. It's the classic home invasion plan. It's been done many times and it almost always works."

"You're not serious." I'm looking at his austere expression, not able to believe how any of this could be true.

"I'm very serious. You're the one who wasn't taking this conversation seriously. Perhaps now you do."

"You're making this up just to scare me. You wouldn't hurt Jade. You're my grandfather. I know you wouldn't do something like that."

"Sacrifices must be made for the greater good, Garret. Just look at your father. Look how successful he became after the plane crash. After that woman was finally out of his life. I shouldn't have waited so long. I should've done it years earlier than that, but—"

"No!" I stand up and go behind the couch and start pacing the floor. "No. No. No."

I can't breathe. My head is pounding. This can't be real. None of this is real.

And that man. The one sitting here in my home. He can't be my grandfather. There's no way. My grandfather has done bad things in his life, but he isn't evil enough to do something like that. It's not possible.

"You didn't do it." I'm still pacing, my eyes on the floor, shaking my head. "You couldn't do that. Not to your own family. *They* did it. The organization. Not you."

"You're right. They executed the actual plan. But it was my idea."

I stop pacing and look at him. "What are you saying? Their punishment wasn't to kill her?"

"Your father's original punishment for marrying that woman was going to involve the company. But I was not going to stand by and let them destroy the company my grandfather founded and built from the ground up. So I offered them an alternative. A punishment that was more fitting to the crime. They agreed to it, but they wanted it done right away. At the time, your father had only been married a few months. That wasn't long enough. So I told them to wait. I wanted Pearce to suffer for not obeying his father. I wanted him to spend every waking moment wondering what his punishment would be, and if it would involve that woman. If he was smart, he would've divorced her. If he had, maybe she would've been spared."

I remain behind the couch, far away from him. If I get any closer, I might kill him.

"Why? Why would you do that? He's your son! He loved her! And *I* loved her! And you killed her! You killed my mother! You sick, fucking bastard!" I feel wetness on my face as tears fall from my eyes.

"Look at you. Crying. Weak. This is why I need to take control, Garret. You're not strong enough to take the right path. To do what's best for you."

"You were trying to kill Jade." I say it out loud to myself as I remember what he just said about the robbery. This is all too much to take in and I'm trying to process it as fast as I can. "You sent a man who's been charged with rape and murder to my home to kill my wife? You really did that?"

He nods. "Yes."

Now I seriously might kill him. I don't have a weapon, but I'm so pissed I could do it with my bare hands.

"What the fuck is wrong with you?" I scream it at him.

"I was taking care of things. But it didn't work, so you have no reason to be upset."

"I have no reason to be upset? Are you fucking kidding me? You tried to kill my wife! And you just admitted to killing my mother!"

"They would've done that anyway, Garret. Once I'd convinced them it was the right choice, they saw the error of their ways. We can't allow people like her to marry one of our own. It's not right."

"They wouldn't have tried to kill Jade! I'm not a member. They have no reason to come after Jade. That was all you!"

"Getting rid of the obstacle is one of the conditions of your reinstatement into the organization. It has to be done."

"HAS to be? As in you're going to try this again?"

"Yes."

"I'll fucking kill you!" I lunge toward him just as he reaches into the side of the chair and pulls out a gun.

I step back. "You can't be serious."

"I'm obviously not going to kill you, Garret, but I knew this type of reaction was a possibility, so I had to be prepared."

I take a breath, trying to regain some composure. I need to know what he's planning, and he won't tell me unless I calm down.

"What are you going to do to her?"

"I haven't decided." He says it casually, like it's a decision about what to have for lunch.

I fist my hands and clench my jaw, doing everything possible to contain my rage. "When is it happening?"

"That's up to you."

"Just tell me what the fuck that means. I'm done guessing."

"The girl will not be harmed if you choose the path I've outlined for your future. You divorce her? You have no further contact with her? She'll be safe."

"And if I *don't* do those things?"

"You'll be left always wondering when and how. Just like your father did when he was awaiting his punishment for marrying your mother. But he didn't know his punishment would involve her. You have the advantage of knowing."

"You call that an advantage?"

"Let me explain. By doing this, I've given you the control. When I hired that burglar, I took control and didn't let you have a say in this. But now, I'm giving the control back to you. Let her go, she lives. Stay with her, and eventually she will be killed. It won't be right away. It could be months from now, or it could be years. But it WILL happen. And when it does, you'll know you had a part in it. That's not something you can live with, is it, Garret? Knowing you had a part in taking her life?"

He sits there, still so calm, his mouth turned up into a smug smile, his gun pointed at me.

This man, my grandfather, planned my mother's death. He orchestrated it and took pleasure in watching my father suffer. And a few months ago, he tried to kill Jade. Now he's promising to kill her if I don't do what he says. Get Jade out of my life or she dies.

I lock my eyes on his. "I'll kill you before I ever let you near her."

"You can't kill anyone. You don't have it in you. At least not yet. You need to suffer first. Feel real pain. Real anger. The kind that drives you to do things you never thought you could do. By the time you feel that, you'll understand why I did this. And if you still want to kill me, go ahead and do it."

I'm speechless. Without words. Stunned.

"I'll give you until the end of the year to make your decision. December 31st. The girl will be safe until then. After that, if you choose to remain with her, the clock starts ticking."

He stands up and walks to the door. "I said I would break you, Garret." He turns back and smiles. "Consider yourself broken."

Chapter 24

GARRET

*O*nce he's gone I lock the door and check all the windows to make sure they're locked. Then I search the house for listening devices and hidden cameras. I start in the living room, under the chair where he was sitting. Then I check the couch, under the cushions. As I'm searching the table in front of the couch, I notice my phone and turn it back on. I check it and see a text message.

It's from my grandfather. It reads, *You can stop searching. There aren't any. If you don't believe me, check your bedroom dresser.*

How the hell does he know I was searching? Is he watching me? Or does he just assume it's what I'd do, knowing I don't trust him?

I go in the bedroom and open the top drawer of the dresser. Sitting on top of Jade's socks is a device that checks for listening devices. My dad has one just like it. I don't know where he got it, but I've seen him use it. You wave it over stuff and if it beeps, you know it found something. They make hidden microphones so small now that it's nearly impossible to find them unless you have something like this.

I search the entire house with the device and find nothing. That doesn't mean there isn't something in here. The technology changes all the time. But I have to trust that there isn't, because right now I need to call my dad.

It's after five on the East Coast but I'm sure my dad's still at work. I hope he picks up. If he doesn't, I'll just keep calling and texting every minute until he does.

He answers on the fifth ring. "Garret, I was just about to go to a meeting. I'll have to call you later."

"Tell them you'll be late. This is important."

"The meeting is only an hour. I'll call you as soon as—"

"Grandfather was here."

"What did you say?"

"Grandfather was here. Just now. In my house."

"Did he tell you he was coming?"

"No. He broke in. He was here when I got home."

"What did he want?"

"To tell me things. Things you have to know, Dad."

"Like what?"

"I can't tell you over the phone."

"Why? What is this about?"

"Grandfather did something. Something bad. Something really bad."

"Garret, we all have. It's part of being a member. You know that."

"Yes, but he did this to his own family. To you. And to me. And he's about to do a hell of a lot more."

"You're overreacting. You misunderstood what he said. Your grandfather would never do anything to harm his family."

"He had a gun, Dad. He had a gun pointed right at me."

There's silence and then, "Where is he?" My dad tries not to show his anger, but when he does, he *really* does. And right now, his voice is filled with it. "Where did he go?"

"I don't know. He just left. You need to get out here. I need to talk to you."

"Just tell me what he said."

"I need to tell you in person."

"Dammit, Garret! Just tell me!"

"I can't tell you this over the phone!"

"Why the hell not?"

"Because it's...it's about Mom." I take a breath. "And Jade."

He's quiet, then says, "I'll leave tonight."

The phone goes silent. He hung up.

I collapse on the couch, tossing my phone aside.

He'll fix this. My dad will fix this. He always does.

I say the words over and over again in my head, but I'm not sure I believe them.

My dad is an expert at taking on enemies. He crushes them. Destroys them. Annihilates them.

But this time the enemy is family. His father. My grandfather.

So this time, I don't know if my dad can fix this.

I need to get out of here. I need air. I need to move. I grab my keys and go out the door to the beach. I walk quickly along the sand, hoping the sound of the waves will calm my thumping heart, which hasn't slowed down since I heard my grandfather's voice and saw him in that chair.

How did he even get here? There weren't any cars around when I got home. Somebody must've dropped him off and was waiting to pick him up.

I wonder how long he's been planning this. It had to be months. He said he changed his plan when the robber didn't finish the job. That was back in September, which means my grandfather could've given me this ultimatum a long time ago but he waited until now. Today. The 10 year anniversary of the plane crash. The day he chose to have my mom killed. The day he took her away from me. Away from my dad.

My grandfather purposely came here today, knowing exactly what day it is. To him, today is probably a celebration. The day he finally got rid of my mom. It's not enough for him to tell me he killed her. No, he has to do it today, the exact same day that she died. He knows how much I loved her. How much I miss her. How my life hasn't been the same since she left. Yet he looked almost happy when he told me what he did to her. And now he plans to do the same thing to Jade. He's fucking psychotic. Pure evil.

He said he wouldn't hurt Jade until after the New Year. And I think I believe him, which means I have just over a month until his deadline. Of course he made sure it was during the holidays, which is supposed to be the happiest time of the year.

It shows how much he wants me to suffer. I didn't obey his orders and now he wants me to pay. He wants me to agonize over the decision from now until the clock strikes midnight on the last day of the year. And if I don't do what he says, a whole new countdown begins. *You'll be left always wondering when and how.* It's like a game to him. An evil, twisted game that he has no intention of losing.

That's why I believe him when he says he won't hurt Jade until after his deadline. This is his game and he set the rules. If *I'd* set the deadline, he wouldn't honor it. But since *he* did, he will.

My grandfather likes to control the timing of things, like when my mother would die. The realization of that hits me again.

He did that. My grandfather really did that. He had her killed. And he determined the timing. He watched my mom live her life, thinking she had all this time. He let my dad think the woman he loved was safe.

My grandfather was never nice to my mom, but he tolerated her. He saw her at family dinners and holidays. She knew he didn't approve of her and she knew he didn't like her and yet she went out of her way to be nice to him. She even made him a cake every year on his birthday even though he wouldn't eat it.

And the entire time, all those years, he was planning her death. Waiting until the perfect moment. The moment when my dad, mom, and I were content, just living our lives, thinking nothing could go wrong. He saw how happy we were. And he destroyed it. He destroyed everything.

And now, 10 years later, he tried to kill Jade. He almost did. If my dad hadn't been visiting us Labor Day weekend, we wouldn't have put up those security cameras. I would've put cameras up eventually, but not that weekend. And if those cameras hadn't been there, that guy would've gone through with the plan. He would've broken in the house when I wasn't there. He would've shot Jade. He would've killed her. She'd be dead right now.

Fuck.

My job is to keep Jade safe. To protect her. And I didn't. I didn't do my job. The thing that saved her were those security cameras. Not me.

I saw that guy lurking around our house. I should've known he wasn't just some random burglar. I should've chased him down that day I saw him. And when Jade saw him get shot a few weeks ago, I should've put it together. I should've known that was the work of someone from the organization. They cleaned it up without leaving a trace of evidence. The average drug dealer couldn't do that.

My grandfather hired someone to kill that robber because the guy didn't finish the job and because he knew things he shouldn't. The grad student who got shot was just an innocent victim. A guy who was at the wrong place at the wrong time. I bet the fake cop is dead now, too. If he knew why he was hired and who hired him, he'd definitely be killed.

But how was I supposed to know my grandfather was behind all this? The fake robbery? The fake cop? How was I supposed to put the pieces together when I didn't know what the pieces were and how they connected?

Even my dad didn't know what was really going on. He had people investigating it. He asked the other members if there were plans to get me back and they told him no, probably because my grandfather threatened them if they told my dad the truth. Then my dad asked my grandfather about it and my grandfather dismissed his concerns. He told my dad he was being paranoid and my dad believed him. He kept telling me not to worry.

So how could I possibly know what my grandfather was up to?

It doesn't matter. I still blame myself. I'll always blame myself because I didn't do my job. I didn't protect Jade.

I don't know what I would've done if she'd been killed. I couldn't live with the fact that I hadn't done anything to stop it. I'd spend the rest of my life reliving the past, telling myself what I should've done differently. It would've destroyed me to know I'd done nothing to save her.

I reach down and pick up a rock in the sand. I run my fingers over it, focusing on the contours and the texture, trying to calm myself, but it doesn't work. I throw the rock in the ocean and scream as loud as I can, "I fucking hate you! You hear me, Grandfather? I fucking hate you!"

I drop to the ground and just sit there, letting my eyes follow the pattern of the waves. It lulls me into a place where my mind is numb, and I remain there until my phone rings, startling me. It's my dad.

"Garret, I'll be there first thing in the morning. I just talked to my pilot. He's getting the plane ready but I need to take care of some things before I leave, which means I probably won't arrive there until the middle of the night."

"Just come over when you get here. I don't care how late it is."

"But Jade will be home."

"Yeah? So?"

"She can't know about this."

"You don't even know what this is about."

"No, but if it involves your grandfather I'm guessing it also involves the organization. Is that true?"

"I don't know. Maybe. I'm not sure."

Although the organization knows about my grandfather's plan to reinstate my membership, I'm not really sure if they have anything to do with his plan to kill Jade. It sounded like that was all him. Like they weren't involved.

"Then we need to keep her out of this, Garret. I know you don't like lying to her, but telling her their secrets only puts her in danger. Just wait until we talk and then we'll decide what to tell Jade."

I hesitate because I have no freaking clue how I can possibly keep this from her. She'll be able to sense something's wrong and then she'll ask me about it.

"Okay," I finally say. "I won't tell her anything."

"I'll see you in the morning. What time does Jade head to campus?"

"Around nine. I have class at 10 but I can skip it."

"I'll be there at nine. See you soon."

I get up and walk back to the house and wait for Jade to get home.

Fuck. How the hell am I going to hide this from her?

Chapter 25

JADE

*O*nly one more day of classes and then we leave for Thanksgiving break. I can't wait to go back to Des Moines and see Frank and Ryan and have Thanksgiving in Frank's new house.

I wouldn't tell Frank this, but I never liked going out to eat on Thanksgiving. I always wanted to have a meal at home with the turkey cooking in the oven all day. But none of us knew how to cook so we always went out to eat. And then last year I had my first real Thanksgiving dinner at Garret's house and I loved it. I couldn't wait to have it again and now I will, thanks to Chloe. It's really nice of her to offer to make everyone dinner. Ryan better marry that girl and he better not keep waiting or she's going to find someone else.

My phone rings and I answer it as I'm leaving class. It's Frank. "Hey, I was just thinking about you. I can't wait to see you guys and check out your new house."

"We've got your room all ready. And Ryan stocked up on potato chips."

I laugh. "I might be too full from Chloe's dinner to eat them."

"You can have them with the leftover turkey sandwiches we'll be making. Ryan got a 22-pound turkey. We'll be eating that thing for weeks."

"I'm so excited about this dinner. It's like a real Thanksgiving. I mean, not that the other ones weren't but—"

"I know what you mean, honey. Eating at the casino every year didn't really seem like Thanksgiving. I'm looking forward to having everyone here at the house and a having home-cooked meal."

"Tell Chloe if she wants any help, I'm happy to do whatever she needs."

"I think she's already recruited Ryan to be her helper in the kitchen. But yes, I'll let her know you offered. Anyway, I called because I wanted to tell you I saw Garret last night on one of those Hollywood shows. I was flipping channels and saw his picture. I didn't catch the whole story but they were saying how he's living in California now."

Shit. Brook was supposed to stop those stories from going out.

Frank continues. "Why were they talking about Garret? Is this about that reality show? Are they getting him involved again?"

"No. Someone found out he was living here and the story just kind of spread. We're hoping it'll just go away."

"I don't want photographers following you around like last year. It's not safe."

"There aren't any photographers. Nobody's following me."

"Good. Well, I just wanted to ask you about that. I'll let you go. We'll see you soon."

"Okay, bye."

As I put my phone away I feel someone tap my shoulder. I turn to see Sara there.

"Hey. You didn't come in today."

"Yeah, I'm trying to avoid the coffee shop until that Justin guy goes away. Did he show up there again?"

"No. He hasn't been back. Why are you avoiding him?"

"Because I don't know who he is and it's kind of freaking me out that some strange guy is looking for me."

"But he went to school with Garret. And he seemed to know you."

"Did he say how he knew me?"

"No. We didn't talk long. Where's your car? I'm parked on the side street."

"I am, too. Are you heading home?"

"Yeah, I'm done with work. I have to get Caleb at day care. Come on." She motions me to follow her. "Walk with me. I can't be late to day care or they'll charge me for another hour."

I take a few steps to catch up with her. "So are you ready to meet the family?"

She rolls her eyes and smiles. "It's not like that, Jade. He's not taking me there to meet his family. We're just going for Thanksgiving dinner."

"He wouldn't take you there unless he wanted you to meet them. He really likes you, Sara. Stop acting like he doesn't."

"I just don't want to get my hopes up. I already like him more than I should, which means it's going to suck when he dumps me."

"Why do you think he's going to dump you?"

"Because he doesn't want an instant family."

"Did he tell you that?"

"No. But I'm sure he's thinking it. No guy his age wants that."

"Sara, if he felt that way he wouldn't be dating you. And he always tells you to bring Caleb when you guys go out."

"Because he knows I can't afford a sitter."

"Yeah, but he also knows Garret and I would watch Caleb for free, so that's not the reason. He likes Caleb. And he likes you. A lot."

She smiles. "Okay, maybe he does. But I'm still not getting my hopes up." She looks over at the street as a limo goes by. "What's a limo doing here?"

"I don't know."

The limo is going really slow and almost stops as it approaches us, but then drives off. The windows were so dark, I couldn't see inside.

We turn and go up the side street toward our cars.

Sara gets her keys out. "The only time I see limos here is during prom season, and even then, it's rare."

"Maybe a celebrity's passing through town. I bet it's one of the parents of someone who goes to Camsburg. A lot of them have celebrity parents."

"Yeah, it's probably some famous actress visiting her kid. Wouldn't that be weird to be related to someone who's in the movies or on TV all the time?"

"Yeah, it would."

Sara doesn't know Garret was on a reality show. Well, he wasn't really on it, but she doesn't know about his involvement with the show. She doesn't have cable and she never watches TV.

"Hey, there it is again." Sara points back to the street we were just on. The limo is driving by, the other direction this time. "They must be lost." We're at her car now and she stops to give me a hug. "Have a great Thanksgiving."

"You, too. Tell Alex I said hi and give Caleb a hug for me."

"I will. Call me when you get back." She gets in her car and drives off as I walk farther up the hill to my car.

I open the door, but before I get in I look back at the street. I'm getting a strange feeling about that limo. People in the organization often drive around in limos. And that limo slowed way down when it approached Sara and me. Why would it slow down?

Dammit. Why am I even thinking about this? I told myself I was not going to think about the organization, because if I do, it'll ruin my Thanksgiving. That whole thing with Brook trying to fix Garret's image got me thinking about last spring and what the organization did to us. I've been trying to get it out of my head but then I'm reminded of it again when I think about Sean and Harper.

I don't want to think about any of that this week. I just want to enjoy the holiday. I want to set aside all the bad things that are going on and focus only on the good. Because I have so many good things in my life right now.

My classes are going great. My counseling sessions are going well. Garret and I are closer than ever. And in a few days, I'm going to have an awesome Thanksgiving.

As I drive home, I think about what a difference a year makes. Last Thanksgiving, when I was at Garret's house, I told him it would never work between us. I loved him so much, even back then, and it scared me. I knew it would hurt really bad when things ended between us, so I just wanted to get it over with. I wanted to end things before I loved Garret even more. Because I was sure our relationship would end. I was convinced people would always be trying to tear us apart. And they tried, but they didn't succeed.

That's another reason why I need stop worrying so much and just be happy. And thankful. Thankful that Garret and I are finally together and married and no one can tear us apart.

When I pull in the driveway, I see Garret's car there. He's supposed to be at class now. Maybe he got out early.

I get that fluttery feeling inside because I can't wait to see him. I know I see him every day, but when I'm away from him all day I get excited when I'm about to see him. Maybe that's crazy but I can't help it. I love that man.

Chapter 26

GARRET

Jade bursts through the door. I'm standing there waiting for her because I heard her drive up.

"Hey." She gives me a kiss. "What are you doing home? Did you get out of class early?" She sets her backpack by the door.

"Class was canceled." I try to act normal, hoping she doesn't pick up on the fact that I'm a fucking mess right now.

"So no swimming today?" She loops her arms around my neck.

"I thought I'd take a day off."

"Good." She hugs me. "I want you home. I missed you."

"You see me all the time."

"I know. But sometimes I have these days where I miss you even though I just saw you. Like I don't want to be apart from you. It's weird. I can't explain it."

What the hell? Does she have psychic powers now? Could she feel that my grandfather was here, trying to take her away from me? The thought of that makes me hold her tighter.

She laughs. "I think you're cutting my circulation off."

"Sorry." I loosen my arms a little. "I guess I missed you, too."

"Do you want to show me how much?" She bites her lower lip and her eyes dart to the bedroom.

This may be the first time I've ever thought this in the entire time I've known her, but I'm not really in the mood for sex. Not after what happened earlier.

"Maybe later. Maybe after dinner."

"You're turning me down?" She slides her finger down my chest. "What if I do all the work? I'll be on top."

My wife wants to have sex and I'm telling her no? What the hell is wrong with me? Now I'm letting my asshole grandfather control my sex life?

I dip my head down to her neck and kiss just below her ear.

"I thought you said later," she whispers.

"I changed my mind."

We make our way to the bedroom and I slowly undress her, taking time to look at her. Memorize her.

As we're having sex, I pay attention to every detail. The way she feels, her scent, how we move together. I did this last spring, too, when I thought I'd never see her again.

But this time is different. This time, I'm savoring every detail, burning it in my brain—not so that I don't forget her, but to make myself stronger. To make sure I never even let myself think I can't fight this. Jade will never be taken from me. My grandfather will never win this battle. I don't know how I'm going to defeat him, but I will find a way. Because he is not taking Jade from me. Not now. Not ever.

We have dinner later but I'm not hungry and can only eat a few bites. Afterward, I lie on the couch but Jade remains in the kitchen.

I look over and see her taking stuff out of the fridge. "What are you doing?"

"I thought I'd clean the fridge before we go out of town. I need to toss stuff out and wipe the shelves down."

"Just leave it and come over here."

"I'll be done in a few minutes."

"Jade. Just come over here." I need her next to me, held safely in my arms.

She tosses whatever she took from the fridge in the trash and comes over to the couch. I put my arms out motioning her to get in her spot.

She smiles and lies down in front of me. "Are you trying to get me to be lazy with you?"

"I just want you here." I wrap my arms around her, tugging her into place.

She turns the TV on, then rotates her head back to kiss me. "I love you."

"I love you, too."

We remain there and Jade falls asleep. At midnight I take her to bed and watch her sleep until my eyes finally fall shut.

On Tuesday morning, as Jade's filling her travel mug with coffee, I say, "I forgot to tell you. My dad's coming by here today."

She sets the coffee pot back on the warmer. "Your dad is coming? Here? Today?"

"Yeah, he'll be here later this morning." I reach in the fridge and grab the milk and hand it to her.

"And you just forgot to tell me?" She pours some milk in her travel mug, making her coffee so light it almost doesn't look like coffee.

"I just found out last night. He called and said he's out here for a meeting and wanted to know if he could come by and see us."

"Where's his meeting? I mean, like where in California?" She screws the cap on her mug.

"I can't remember. We didn't talk long. Anyway, he'll probably be here when you get back from class."

"You have class at 10. Are you skipping it?"

"Yeah, but it's not like I'll miss anything. We weren't doing much in class since so many people have already left for Thanksgiving."

"Isn't your family going to St. Croix? I thought they were leaving tomorrow morning. Shouldn't your dad be getting back to Connecticut?"

"They're not going. Katherine canceled the trip so she could spend the weekend with her boyfriend."

"Oh. So they're having Thanksgiving at home?"

"Yeah. I guess Charles will have to make the big turkey dinner again like he did for us last year."

"Last year was so great. That dinner was so good. And remember when Charles made those homemade donuts? I wish I had one right now." She opens one of the cupboards. "Do we have any granola bars? I don't have time for cereal."

I open a drawer and pull one out. Even after living here for months, Jade still doesn't remember where we keep stuff. I hand it to her, but keep hold of it when she takes it. I pull on it, forcing her to walk toward me and then I grab her around the waist. "You know what else we did last Thanksgiving?"

She thinks about it, then smiles. "We had sex for the first time. Which means Wednesday night is our sexiversary."

I laugh. Leave it to Jade to make me laugh even when I'm completely stressed. "I don't think that's a word."

"It's a new holiday. Just for you and me. But we won't be able to celebrate our sexiversary because we'll be at Frank's house."

"How do you celebrate it? By having sex?"

"Well, yeah, I guess. I've never celebrated it before."

"We have sex all the time, Jade. It wouldn't be any different if we did it on Wednesday night, so I don't think it'll be much of a celebration."

"I still think we should celebrate it. Maybe when we get back on Sunday."

"If you really want to celebrate it Wednesday night, we could have sex at Frank's house. We'll have our own bedroom."

"We could, but it seems wrong."

"Jade, we're married."

"I'll think about it." She gives me a quick kiss. "I have to go. I'll see you in a couple hours. How long will your dad be here?"

"I'm not sure. Probably not very long."

"Tell him I want to see him before he leaves."

"I will." I catch her arm as she walks away. I go around her and hug her and don't let go. I'm working my ass off to act normal, but watching her leave really got to me. I don't want her out there alone. Out in the world where bad people are lurking, waiting to hurt her.

Maybe I should go with her. But then she'll know something's up.

She'll be okay. My grandfather won't do anything. Not yet. He gave me his deadline and he wants me to suffer. And waiting for something to happen? Wondering if it will? It's agonizing. Pure torture. He'll want to keep that going as long as possible. He wants me to be punished for not following orders, just like he punished my dad.

"It's too tight again." Jade laughs. "I think you need to go back to hug school. You're doing it all wrong."

"Sorry." I release her, but I don't want to.

"I'm just kidding. I love your hugs. Loose ones. Tight ones. All of them." She walks to the door. "See you soon."

Ten minutes later, my dad arrives. We skip any small talk and get right down to business.

I'm sitting on the couch and my dad is sitting in the same chair where my grandfather sat.

"Tell me exactly what he said." My dad turns his phone off and sets it on the coffee table.

I replay the conversation, almost word for word, stopping before I get to the part about my mom and Jade. Up until now, I've told him how my grandfather wants me to transfer to Yale, work at the company every summer, and take it over someday. I haven't told him the really bad stuff yet.

"Garret, go ahead."

"I don't know if I can tell you this." I lean forward, resting my forearms on my knees and staring at the floor.

"I'm your father. You can tell me anything."

I nod. "Okay. Here it is." I take a deep breath. "Grandfather killed Mom."

I squeeze my eyes shut. I don't want to see my dad's expression.

"He didn't kill her, Garret. The organization killed her. You saw the memo."

"Yes, they arranged for the plane to go down, but he... your father...it was his idea. They were going to punish you by doing something to the company. I don't know what. He didn't say. But he didn't want them touching the company so he offered them an alternative. A different punishment." I pause. "Mom."

The room is silent. I still can't look at him. I need to get this out first. It's hard enough just saying the words. Seeing his reaction would just make it harder.

"Once they agreed, he decided when it would be done. They were going to do it right after you married Mom, but he told them to wait." I finally look up at my dad. "He picked the timing. And he waited 12 years."

My dad's rubbing his chin, his face blank, expression-less. His eyes are on the floor, barely blinking.

"No. That's not true. He wouldn't do something like that. He may not have approved of Rachel, but he wasn't involved with her murder."

"Dad, I swear to you, he wasn't lying. He was dead serious. He said he purposely waited because he wanted you to suffer, always wondering if she would be harmed. He wanted you to suffer for years because he was so mad that you didn't do what he told you to do. He said that was your punishment for disobeying him."

I see my dad's chest rising and falling at a rapid pace. It's the only sign of any kind of emotion. He's angry. Extremely angry. But for some reason, he's holding it all inside.

His eyes return to me. "What else did he say?"

I tell him how my grandfather made it sound like he knows about Arlin and what he did for me last spring. Then I describe the plan my grandfather has for Jade, and how he said I have to make a decision by the end of the year.

"Dad, I'm not leaving Jade. I'm not divorcing her. There's no fucking way. Which is why I need your help. After Grandfather left yesterday, I tried to think of ways to stop this. And I was thinking that the only option is for Jade and me to go into hiding. Get out of the country. Change our identities. I haven't figured it all out yet. That's why I need your help."

"You and Jade aren't going anywhere. I'm not losing my son. Or my daughter-in-law."

"Then what are we going to do?"

"*You're* not doing anything. Let me handle it. This is between my father and me."

366

"But now it involves me."

"Yes, but it's not about you. This has nothing to do with you." He huffs. "It all goes back to him and me. That's what this is about, Garret."

"No, this is about *me*. He's trying to control me. He's angry I didn't go along with the plans he had for me. And now he's punishing me, just like he punished you."

"Did he say you needed to keep what he told you confidential? Did he say not to tell me?"

"No."

My dad shakes his head. "Then he wanted me to know. He was sending me a message. He's using you, Garret. He's using you and he's using Jade. And it's all to get back at me."

"Dad, that's not true. He wants me to run the company and be part of the organization. That's his goal here. That's what this is about."

"That's just part of it. You don't understand my history with him, Garret. He's tried to control me my entire life, and for the most part, he's succeeded. Until I married your mother, and had you, and started raising you differently than my father wanted me to. And ever since then, he's been trying to get back at me. This is his way of doing that, by taking away your choices, destroying your life, taking away the person you love. He wants to punish me twice. He's already ruined my life and now he wants me to watch as he ruins yours."

I sit there quietly, letting this sink in. So by doing this, my grandfather punishes both my dad and me. As if killing my mom wasn't enough.

My dad lets out a heavy sigh. "I think he knows."

"Knows what?"

"I think he knows I had a part in what happened last spring. You just said he knew Arlin was involved, and if that's true, then he knows about me and knows I was partially responsible for you being released of your obligation to become a member. Which is all the more reason why my father wants you back at the organization. He has to prove to me that he's the one in control. And that he will remain in control until the day he dies."

"So what are you going to do?"

He gets up from the chair. "I'll take care of it. And in the meantime, don't tell Jade about this."

I stand in front of him. "I can't keep hiding this from her. She'll know something's up with me. I'm a fucking mess right now."

"Then pull yourself together because you can't involve her in this."

"Why? Do you think the organization is in on it?"

"I can't say for sure, but as of now I don't think they are. They don't want you back, at least not the people I've talked to. I'm guessing your grandfather used his new position to force them into reinstating your membership. I think this plan is all his doing. But I still don't want Jade knowing about it. It's best if she doesn't."

"How do we stop this? How do we get him to end this? Just tell me. I'll do anything."

"Just stay out of it." He walks quickly to the door.

I race after him. "Stay out of it? I'm not staying out of it! Jade's life is at stake here!"

He turns back. "She'll be safe. I promise you."

"Safe until the end of the year. But then what?"

"She'll be safe."

"You mean after his deadline?"

"Yes."

"Then you're saying I have to leave her? No! I'm not—"

"Garret!" He grips my shoulders. "Listen to me. Ignore everything your grandfather told you. There's no decision to make. There's no deadline. You will go on living your life with Jade as if the conversation you had yesterday never occurred."

"I don't understand."

"I'll take care of this." He opens the door and hurries down the steps to the driveway.

I follow him. "You're leaving? Right now?"

"I have things that need to be done."

"Can't you just stay for a few hours? Jade wants to see you. She's going to ask me why you left so soon. What am I supposed to tell her?"

He gets in his rental car. "Tell her I'm sorry and that I'll see her another time. Goodbye, Garret." He goes to shut the car door but I grab it.

"Dad, just tell me what you're going to do."

"I'm going to settle the score with my father once and for all." He rips the door from my grasp and slams it shut, then starts the car and peels out of the driveway and speeds off.

He's angry, but not nearly as angry as I thought he'd be. I thought when I told him what happened, he'd yell and scream and maybe throw something or bang his fist into the wall. He has a bad temper and when he's really angry, he can't control it. After I told my dad about my grandfather, I was sure he'd go into a total rage. But he didn't. His reaction was almost robotic. Lacking emotion. And when he said goodbye, his eyes were cold and dark, and he wouldn't look at me.

I don't know what he's going to do. But I know what he's capable of.

My family is all about rules.

Rule number one? Never ask questions.

Rule number two? Protect your family above all else.

Protect your family

Above all else

But what do you do when your enemy is also your family?

My father knows the rules.

He lives by the rules.

So when he said he'll take care of it, he will. I know he will.

I'm just not sure what that means.

CPSIA information can be obtained
at www.ICGtesting.com
Printed in the USA
BVHW031303171221
624366BV00013B/46